PRAISE FOR
THE MYSTERY OF THE GREEN STAR

"There is only one thing better than a new book by David Bentley Hart, and that's a new book by David Bentley Hart and Patrick Robert Hart. *The Mystery of the Green Star* not only sees the return of Gorilla MacGorilla ('Gor-Gor') and his friends, but initiates the reader, through a splendid assortment of karate gis, koans, and anecdotes, into the most marvelous new philosophy, the Way of the Idjit (which makes one think and think), and introduces a splendid new cuisine: Chinese-Welsh fusion. While the ghost at the heart of the mystery represents, for the dramatis personae, 'sour cabbage' (as the delightful Porculina describes it), for the reader its arrival in the story is honey on a crumpet. This is a delicious work. A book for the ages, and for all ages."

　—**STEPHEN MCINERNEY**, author of *In Your Absence* and *The Wind Outside*

"The Harts have gifted us yet another charming whodunnit: two parts Arthur Conan Doyle, one part Lewis Carroll, and a dash of P.G. Wodehouse for good measure, a confection as strange and somehow congruous as Sino-Cymric cuisine. Don your teal *uwagi*. 'I feel a mood of whimsy coming on.'"

　—**STEVEN TOUSSAINT**, author of *The Bellfounder* and *Lay Studies*

"Set in a cursed château, this delightful and philosophically rich detective tale brings readers deep into the captivating world of the soft toys. Infused with the mystical arts and ancient wisdom, this beautifully illustrated book begins in doubt and ends in magic. This is one of those books you live inside of for a while, and then it lives inside you."

　—**JENNIFER BANKS**, author of *Natality: Toward a Philosophy of Birth*

"Together, David Bentley Hart and his son Patrick Robert Hart have written a supernatural mystery—the second of the MacGorilla series—that will be enjoyed as much by adults as by children. It pursues a distinctively Hartian project of bewitchment, with a world where magic is an organizing principle of the universe and of the 'renunciation of sterile rationalism.' These educated soft toys display too much heart and subversion to lapse into parody, and ask the reader to consider 'that we are all moral by nature' (and that it is neither complacent nor childish to think so)."

　—**TARIQ GODARD**, author of *High John the Conqueror*

The Mystery of the Green Star

The Mystery of the Green Star

By
DAVID BENTLEY HART
and
PATRICK ROBERT HART

Illustrations by
JEROME ATHERHOLT

Angelico Press

First published in the USA
by Angelico Press 2023
Copyright © David Bentley Hart & Patrick Robert Hart 2023
Illustrations copyright © Jerome Atherholt 2023

For information, address:
Angelico Press, Ltd.
169 Monitor St.
Brooklyn, NY 11222
www.angelicopress.com

ppr   978-1-62138-948-4
cloth   978-1-62138-949-1

Book and cover design
by Michael Schrauzer
Cover image: Jerome Atherholt

Humbly — if Presumptuously — Dedicated to the Memory of
THE COMPOSER JOHN WALTER BRATTON (1867–1947)
and
THE LYRICIST JAMES KENNEDY, OBE (1902–1984)
Two Universal Benefactors of Humankind,
Whose Mighty Ode "The Teddy Bears' Picnic"
Will Sound Down the Ages

CONTENTS

Sometime around the middle of the twentieth century,
and a little off the beaten path . . .

CHAPTER 1

Arrival by Train

OUTSIDE THE TRAIN COMPARTMENT'S WINDOW, the lush countryside of the Loire Valley had been flowing past for some time: rolling pasturage, sprawling vineyards basking in the late afternoon sun on low hillsides, dense woodland now near and now far away, small villages hugging the distant banks of the broad, flat, glassy blue river, all under a nearly cloudless late summer sky. Inside the compartment, three figures were seated: one reading a letter that looked as if it had been read a few times before, one staring avidly out through the glass, and one deeply immersed in a book lying open in his lap.

"Very curious," murmured the first, whose name was Theodore Bear (Teddy to his friends and, coincidentally, a teddy bear, small and tan and always quite dapper in his neat red bow tie, retired for slightly more than a year from his position as a detective with the New York City Police Department and now a writer by trade). "Very curious indeed." He refolded the letter and slipped it back into its envelope.

"What's curious?" asked the small pink plush pig sitting across from him without turning from the window. This was (the "c" pronounced like an "s") Porculina, an English toy sow from an old family line and the creator and co-owner of *Fluffed and Painted, Inc.*, the world's largest manufacturer of cosmetics for soft toys. "Porridge and pomegranates," she immediately added, "I never knew there was so much more to France than Paris!" She sat back with a small contented sigh, stretched out her short legs, wiggled her trotters excitedly, straightened her pale yellow sunbonnet, and exclaimed, "It's peaches and peas! Just absolutely cake with walnut filling!"

Teddy, however, was still too lost in thought to answer with more than a quiet, distracted "*Hmm*" of agreement.

"Teddykins," she said after a few seconds in an emphatic voice, "don't be dour! It's unbecoming for a teddy bear."

"Hmm?" Teddy said again, this time as a question. "Oh, I'm sorry, Pigsy." He raised his eyes to hers and smiled. "I'm just a bit perturbed by my cousin's letter. When I first read it, I thought he was joking, but now I don't know."

"Joking about what?" asked Porculina. "Not the cider festival? I mean" — a slight, suspicious scowl appeared on her face — "he's not the sort who would joke about *food*, is he?"

"Oh, not at all," Teddy assured her, waving a paw before him.

The letter had come the month before from his cousin Angus, a teddy bear of Franco-Scottish extraction who also happened to be le Comte de Petit-Ours (or "Count Little Bear," as he was styled on his estates in Britain). It was an invitation to Teddy to visit — along with

2

any friends he might care to bring with him — Angus's ancestral home, the Château de Petit-Ours on the banks of the River Cher outside of the city of Amboise, and to attend the annual "First Harvest" cider-tasting festival that the estate had hosted at the end of August for more than two centuries. Teddy was living these days in Scotland, at the castle of his dear friend Gorilla, Laird MacGorilla — who happened to be the third occupant of the train compartment — and had convinced both him and Porculina to come along for a holiday.

"Well, what then?" Porculina persisted.

"It's just that his letter ends with a somewhat . . . puzzling reference to . . . well . . ."

"*Yes?*" Porculina prompted after another few seconds.

Teddy swallowed somewhat shyly. "Well . . . 'a little trouble with a ghost.' I didn't mention it before because, as I say, I thought . . ." But here he fell silent, seeing the look of wide-eyed dismay that had banished the excited smile from Porculina's face.

"A . . . *ghost?*" she rasped, a hint of a squeal in her voice. "That's a bit of bitter butter on the crumpet, I have to say."

"Again," said Teddy, adopting his most reasonable tone, "it may be just a witticism. It's so hard to tell with the French. Their humor is very dry."

The little pig did not seem at all reassured. "But ghosts, after all — they can be very disagreeable I've heard. Crumblies!"

"Well, if he's being serious," said Teddy, "he doesn't seem worried. So, it wouldn't seem to be a particularly discourteous ghost . . . as ghosts go, that is . . . if ghosts *do* go . . . as such . . ." His voice dwindled away into an awkward silence.

Porculina furrowed her brow, smirked slightly, and turned to her left. "What do you think, Gor-Gor?"

There was no reply, however, from the round, compact, dark brown, amiably plumpish figure seated beside her. His handsome, nearly spherical little head was still bent over the book that lay open in his lap, spread across a stout pair of legs only half as long as his arms. His lips were

3

pursed, his brow deeply wrinkled, his eyes alight with an expression of profound thoughtfulness. He might have looked like any other ordinary soft toy gorilla deep in an interesting book on a long train journey had it not been for the additional detail that he was clad in a bright white karate *gi*, tied around his rather substantial midriff with a cloth belt of soft purple.

"I don't think he heard you," Teddy remarked after several moments.

Porculina sighed. "Really," she said, "he's scarcely set that book aside since we boarded." Peering at her reflection in the window, she adjusted her bonnet again. "You know," she said, turning back to Teddy, "you've never explained to me how an American soft toy like you comes to have a cousin who's a French count . . . with a real château and everything."

"A distant cousin," Teddy replied. "Remember, I may be an American, but I'm of Franco-Scottish teddy bear extraction. We became acquainted some years ago when I was researching family history, just from curiosity, and discovered that one of my fore-bears was the youngest he-cub from a branch of a French family that had been ennobled for many centuries, and that many of its members had received royal appointments as teddy bears to the crown of France or had been companions of some very notable Frenchmen. I became interested in one especially glamorous figure from my ancestral lore, a bear named Pierre Louis Jacques Saint-Clair Bouvard de Petit-Ours who was a famed explorer during the Napoleonic period and after."

"How romantic!" said Porculina. "Where did he explore?"

"Principally the Near East," said Teddy. "You've heard of the famous scholar Champollion . . . the fellow who deciphered Egyptian hieroglyphics?"

Porculina nodded vigorously. "Not at all," she said.

"Oh." Teddy coughed into his paw. "Anyway, Pierre de Petit-Ours was Champollion's beloved teddy bear, and accompanied him to Egypt in 1829, and helped him in his work. Pierre made several subsequent visits as well, and helped discover and restore many Egyptian antiquities, and brought some back—with permission—to France. He became the first curator of the *Musée des Antiquités des Peluches*."

"The . . . ?" said Porculina, tilting her head inquisitively.

"The *Peluches' Museum of Antiquities*," said Teddy.

"Umm . . ." She tilted her head a little more sharply. "*Peluches*?"

"Soft toys," said Teddy. "A *peluche* is a . . . well, one of us."

"Oh, of course!" she replied with a gasp of delighted recognition, clapping her fore-trotters to her cheeks. "That explains it! One of my governesses when I was a piglet was French — Mademoiselle Amelie, a poodle from Marseilles — and she *always* used to call me that. It was so very sweet. 'You are ze silliest little *peluche*,' she would say. Or 'You're eating too much, my little *peluche*.' Or 'You don't need a zird snack before bedtime, my darling little plush *peluche*.' Or '*Ça alors*! Put down ze spoon, you relentless, gobbling, omnivorous little *peluche*!' Well, I thought it just meant something sweet, like 'little sow.' Oh, she was such a dear. Strange, though — she stayed on for only four months before having to return to France. She explained that she had very, very urgent business and was so sorry to . . ."

"Ah, yes," interrupted Teddy, evidently feeling things were drifting in the wrong direction. "In any event, I was so fascinated by what I'd learned of family history, and Pierre's expeditions to Egypt especially, that I wrote le Comte de Petit-Ours, introduced myself, and asked for information; and to my surprise Angus — the Count, that is — replied in the warmest, most generous way. And, before I knew it, we were fastest friends. *Amis par correspondance* — 'friends by mail,' as it were."

"So, you've never met face-to-face?"

"We've exchanged photographs," said Teddy, "but until now we've never had a chance to shake paws."

"Oh, how delightful then!" she exclaimed shrilly, clapping her trotters together.

At this, Gorilla was at last roused from his reading, and looked at Porculina. "I say, Piggles," he said in his boomingly cheerful voice, "is everything all right, old girl?"

"Oh really, Gor-Gor," she replied with a small, impatient shake of her jowls, "you haven't heard a word we've said, have you?"

"I'm sorry," Gorilla answered with an effusive grin, "it's just that this is such an absorbing book . . . such a *deep* book. Once you start reading, well, it just grips you. Like an otter who wants to dance."

"Oh, is it a mystery novel?" asked Porculina. "I can never set them down."

"No," said Gorilla, "though it's full of mystery, if you take my meaning." He held up the handsome, soft-bound, scarlet-beribboned, cream-colored volume, opened to its title page, showing it first to Porculina and then to Teddy: *Idjitsu-Do: The Way of No Way*, by F. D. MacGorilla. "It's not just a technical manual, you know," he added after a moment, setting the book down beside him. "It's very, very philosophical. It's full of things that just make you think and think. Very subtle things."

Teddy arched a dubious eyebrow. "By your cousin, you've said?"

"Cousin Freddy," said Gorilla. "Frederick Duncan MacGorilla."

"It must be fascinating," remarked Porculina. "Teddy says you've been practicing day after day for . . . oh, it must be months now."

"Three months," said Teddy. "It's been hard to miss him out on the west lawn, going through his exercises. They're very . . . *energetic*."

"They are, aren't they?" said Gorilla with a wide, eager smile. "That's just the word. And *deep*, as I said. And also, again, very, very *mysterious*."

Teddy nodded. "They're certainly that."

"But how does your cousin know so much about a martial art?" asked Porculina.

"Oh, that's simple, silly old Piggles," said Gorilla with a fond shake of his head: "it's his own invention."

"Gosh!" she said, her eyes narrowing. "That's even more surprising. But your family — well, it's just so amazing, isn't it?"

"Is it?" asked Gorilla ingenuously.

"Much more than mine, certainly," she answered. "I expect your cousin went on a long quest — explored strange, exotic, remote lands, learned all sorts of secret teachings and techniques . . ."

6   "Indeed," said Gorilla. "He traveled all over the Mystic Orient."

"China?" asked Porculina in a tone of mounting excitement. "Japan? Tibet? India?"

"The East Midlands," said Gorilla.

There was a momentary pause.

"The . . . East Midlands?" Porculina repeated, her brows knitting.

"And even further into the Mystic Orient than that," added Gorilla, his voice dropping to a more secretive register. "He went as far as . . . *Ipswich!*"

Porculina drew in her breath sharply in astonishment and again clapped her trotters to her cheeks. Then, however, her brows knitted once more. She lowered her trotters and said, "But, Gor-Gor, even I've been to Ipswich."

"Ah," said Gorilla with an evocative glint in his eyes, "but have you been to *mystic* Ipswich?"

Porculina's eyes and mouth widened drastically. She shook her head slowly from side to side, as if struggling for words. Finally, in a hushed and awed voice, she said, "No. No, I haven't. I had no idea there *was* a mystic Ipswich."

"Ah," said Gorilla, knowingly tapping the side of his round, flat nose with his forefinger, "that makes all the difference, old girl."

Porculina slowly exhaled. "There're so many wonders in the world," she whispered.

At this, Teddy coughed, cleared his throat, and said, "Yes, well . . . *ahem* . . . that's very . . ."

"But what does it mean, though?" Porculina interrupted, clearly unable to contain herself. "Idjitsu-Do, I mean."

"Well," replied Gorilla, "*Do* means 'way,' according to Freddy's introduction, and so altogether it means 'the way of Idjitsu.'"

"But what does 'Idjitsu' mean? Why did he call it that?"

"Ah ha!" cried Gorilla. "That's a very deep story too. It's a grand piece of family lore. You see, Freddy didn't have a name for his new martial art at first. He'd come up with all sorts of techniques — the Dizzy Octopus method, for instance, or the Baffled Stoat method — but he didn't have

7

any name for the art itself. Then one day, back at Castle MacGorilla, he was practicing some of his especially clever and confusing tumbles — there are quite a lot of tumbles in Idjitsu, you see . . . and some very ingenious somersaults . . . and collisions too . . . and quite a few flailings of the arms and legs and such . . . and a bit of tripping over your own toes now and then — well, there he was, practicing away in a very . . . *energetic* way, as Teddy puts it, and along came Great Uncle Donal. You've never met him, but he's a wonderful old Gorilla . . . very traditional Highlander too. And he always has just the right turn of phrase for things. He stood there watching Freddy for a long time, and then — it must have been an inspiration — he said, 'Och whit're y' daein' thaer, y' wee witless ape? Y' keek juist lik' — that means 'you look just like' — 'Y' keek juist lik' an idjit!' Well, that was that! Right away, Freddy knew it was . . . well, a sign. He had what he calls 'instant enlightenment.' Like a lightning flash. He just knew." Gorilla stared into Porculina's eyes meaningfully. "He *knew*."

"Golly!" said Porculina with another gasp, this time punctuated with a tiny squeak. "Cream pastries and honey-butter! So . . . the Way of the Idjit . . . "

"Yes," said Teddy, once again attempting to steer the conversation back on course, "that certainly is a very . . . humbling story. But the reason for Pigsy's outcry a little while ago was this business about . . . well, about . . . "

"Oh, that's right," said Porculina, the anxious look returning to her face: "about a ghost."

At once, Gorilla's expression changed to an elated smile, and he bounced forward in his seat. "A ghost?" he exclaimed. "What ghost? Where?" He looked about hopefully.

"At the château, apparently," replied Teddy. "At least, if my cousin is being serious. His letter vaguely mentions 'a little trouble with a ghost' of late. And . . . "

"Oh, I say!" cried Gorilla, growing even more ecstatic. "Do you think it could . . . ?" He clenched his hands before him, trying to contain his jubilation. "Could it be Henry, do you think?"

Teddy groaned softly.

"Oh, Gor-Gor," said Porculina gently, "don't you remember? There isn't any Henry."

Gorilla turned to her with an indulgent expression. "Silly old Piggles," he said fondly, "of course there is. You remember — tall chap, with a longish beard and a largish nose and a pleasant smile."

"No, no," Porculina replied, just as fondly. "You just ... well, came up with him last year when you were trying to guess who'd broken into your treasure room and stolen the treasure ... back at the castle .... Remember?"

Gorilla pondered this for several moments. "Don't be silly, old girl," he finally said. "Henry wouldn't break into a boring old treasure room, and he certainly wouldn't steal anything. I thought he might have accidentally, you know, stumbled in, and then simply misplaced the treasure — as one tends to do. At least, I'm always misplacing it. At least, misplacing the room ..."

"Yes, yes," Teddy interrupted. "But no, I don't think it's, um, Henry."

"Probably not," said Gorilla after a moment's reflection. "Not if there's been actual trouble. He's not the sort ..."

"Oh, Gor-Gor," Porculina now practically cried out, a rising note of exasperation in her voice, "we've never met any ghost named Henry! He doesn't exist!"

Gorilla shook his head sagely and again looked at her affectionately. "Silly Piggles. Right there, you see, you're not thinking *philosophically* at all. How can you possibly know he doesn't exist if you've never met him?"

Porculina opened her mouth, but then said nothing. After a few seconds she turned to Teddy. "You know, Teddykins, I hadn't thought of that."

Teddy stared at her for several seconds, struggling for words. Then he stared at Gorilla, who was beaming back at him, for several seconds more. "Ah ..." he began at last, but that was as much as he could manage.

Just then, the door of the compartment slid open, and a rich, warm, dignified voice, with the faintest hint of a kindly growl behind its very refined Oxbridge accent, said, "Excuse me, m'laird, miss, sir — we're about fifteen minutes from our destination."

The three friends turned to the medium-sized, shorthaired dog standing in the corridor. His fur was a mottled white with gray speckles and large brown patches (including two that entirely covered his ears and eyes), his salt-and-pepper snout was capped by a handsome glossy coal-black nose, and he was attired in a valet's dark frock coat.

"Oh, Rolandus," said Teddy with a relieved release of breath, "it's so good to see you."

"What ho, Roly old fellow!" cried Gorilla ebulliently. "Where had you got to?"

Rolandus winced slightly at the name by which Gorilla always addressed him. "Just in the luggage car, m'laird, seeing to it that everything was packed away again for unloading."

"Rolandus," said Porculina, "I was just going to look for you. Do you think there's time for a little something to eat before we reach town? Just to tide us over?"

Rolandus raised a single eyebrow, "In addition to the six-course meal you finished just twenty minutes ago?" he asked.

"Precisely," said Porculina. "It's been hard waiting so long, and who knows when we'll reach the château."

"It's roughly a twenty-five minute drive from the station," said Rolandus.

"Well, there you go," said Porculina. "Ages and ages. We have to keep our strength up."

Rolandus stared at the little pig for a moment without any obvious expression on his face. Then he said, "I suppose I could just nip into the kitchen car and assemble a sandwich before we arrive."

"Just one?" asked Porculina with a slight pout.

"Oh, ah . . ." said Rolandus, hesitating and looking around the compartment. "Three, then?"

"Yes, please!" said Porculina. "And maybe Teddy and Gorilla would like something as well."

Amboise soon came into view, its lovely skyline dominated by the high roof and turrets of its castle, the handsome clock tower, the steeple of the Chapel of St. Hubert, and the elegantly tapering *Pagode de Chanteloup*. As the train pulled into the station the glittering blue of the River Loire came progressively into view, its currents enfolding the narrow *Île d'Or* (Isle of Gold) at the city's heart. The prospect elicited a gasp of delight from Porculina as she finished the last of her final sandwich. "Golly!" she piped. Clearly, the combination of her snack and the bracing sight of the city had chased any thought of ghosts from her mind.

Within moments of disembarking, the three companions were greeted by a hearty cry, with only the faintest of French accents: "My dear cousin! There you are!"

On turning, they saw the small, spruce, debonair figure of the Comte de Petit-Ours, a little gingerbread-colored toy bear, smoothly hastening toward them in a dapper ash-gray linen suit. His bowtie was of a red and black tartan design, one that matched the lining of his paw-pads and inner ears. He held a bouquet of white roses in one arm and what appeared to be a box of chocolates in the other. Close behind him and to either side came what appeared to be two very peculiarly shaped toy St. Bernard puppies, low of carriage and with very short legs.

"I'm so deliriously delighted!" he cried out as he reached them. "And I'm ecstatic to meet your friends."

"Oh . . ." Teddy began, extending a paw.

But, before he could say another word, the little bear handed Teddy the roses and turned at once to Porculina. "Mademoiselle Pig," he said, with a small bow of the head and tip of the hat, "it is my special pleasure to welcome such beauty to my humble home. Please accept these chocolates — a dozen silly little confections — as a token of my joy."

"Oh, my goodness," said Porculina, perhaps blushing slightly. "How sweet of you! It's just butter and . . ." She paused, puckered her lips, and then said — pronouncing the words very carefully — "It's just *crême anglaise* and *blancmange* of you." Then, with a demure smile, she snatched the box from his paws, ripped off its lid, and thrust her snout into it.

The little bear seemed momentarily taken aback, but a second later, still overflowing with cheer, he took one of her trotters in his paw and delicately kissed it. "My sincere pleasure, mademoiselle," he said. She, however, was too preoccupied to notice.

"Oh, I say," Gorilla exclaimed, "that's a jolly sort of handshake!" And immediately he took hold of the little bear's paw and bestowed a robust (and somewhat noisy) kiss on it. Then another for good measure.

"Ah . . ." said the count, momentarily at a loss for words. Then he smiled more broadly and, in a tone of utmost graciousness, said, "But of course! You are my cousin's famous friend, Laird MacGorilla. I've heard so much about you."

"Have you?" asked Gorilla with an expectant smile. "What, for instance?"

"Well, ah . . ." The count seemed to be struggling for precisely the right words. "My cousin says you are . . . unique . . . inimitable . . . *indescribable.*"

Gorilla continued to stare at him, now grinning radiantly. "And . . . ?"

But here Teddy intervened. "Cousin," he said, handing the bouquet of flowers to Gorilla and holding out both his paws, "Monsieur le Comte, it's so good to meet in person."

The count exhaled gratefully. "At last," he said, taking Teddy's paws in his, "our family's far-flung houses unite. Oh, but you must all call me by my name, my good Scottish name, Angus." (He pronounced it "Ahn-goose.") "We are all friends now." Then he embraced Teddy.

12

"Oh, I say!" Gorilla exclaimed again, impetuously wrapping the both of them in a mighty hug.

"Those were absolutely delicious," remarked Porculina, closing the empty box and tucking it under her arm.

Disengaging himself gently from Gorilla, Angus looked at her, his face expressionless for several seconds; then his cordial smile reappeared. "I'm delighted that my little gift pleased you." He gave his head a small shake, almost as if he were trying to dislodge a pebble. "Oh, yes," he said a moment later, "these" — he indicated the two strangely shaped toy dogs that had accompanied him — "are my footmen, Bow and Wow."

"I'm Bow," said one in a low, gruff voice.

"I'm Wow," said the other in an almost identical voice.

"They've only recently entered my employ," remarked Little Bear, "but they're the ablest footmen who've ever worked for me."

"We were designed as slippers for a child, you see," said Bow.

"Oh, yes, so you are," said Porculina. "I see that now."

"So it seemed like an ideal position for us," said Wow, "once we'd retired from our former line of work. Little Luc grew up, you see, and had no further need of our services." He sighed softly.

"One gets a little tired of being trod upon, of course," added Bow. "But we miss little Luc even so. An accountant now." Here he too gave vent to a small sigh. "Tragic," he whispered.

Just then, Rolandus appeared over Gorilla's shoulder. "M'laird," he said, "miss, sir, our luggage is ready to go." He indicated the porter (a tall slender man with a thin mustache and a bored look on his face) waiting some five yards or so farther along the platform beside a large trolley loaded with four moderately sized cases and five enormous bright pink steamer trunks.

"Oh, *alors*," said Angus, his smile somewhat diminished. "You . . . you are a . . . real dog . . . *de chair et de sang* . . . of flesh and blood, I mean?"

Rolandus gave a little bow of the head. "Just so, Monsieur le Comte," he said. "I have that honor."

"Ah," said Angus. He cleared his throat somewhat uneasily, leaned toward Teddy with a slightly strained smile, and very quietly asked, "He does not . . . um, how do you say? He does not . . . *chew*, does he?"

"Only my food, monsieur," remarked Rolandus blandly. "And then with considerable aplomb."

"But of course," replied Angus, a little abashed. Then, turning to look at the luggage, he said, "So many trunks. Are they all yours?"

Porculina, licking the last traces of chocolate from her snout, replied, "They're mine. One for my clothes, one for mystery novels, one for necessities — bibs and bobs and things — and the other two for snacks."

Angus again stared at her in silence for a few moments. Finally, he said, "As it should be. A lovely lady should never want for anything." Then, turning to Bow and Wow, he remarked, "How fortunate that we brought the large van."

CHAPTER 2
Le Château de Petit-Ours

B OW AND WOW TOGETHER WERE SOMEHOW ABLE
to drive the spacious, old-fashioned van with its polished oak
siding, though the three companions could not see how from
their seats on the other side of a darkened glass partition. "At least they
should have no trouble with the pedals," Teddy murmured to Porculina

at one point. The car traveled along a country road into ever deepening, ever more shadowy forest, the trees seeming to become more ancient and immense by the mile, the rays of sunlight slipping through their branches more golden. After about half an hour, they turned onto a white gravel lane that soon brought them to two enormous iron gates standing open between high pink brick walls. As the car entered the grounds, the Château de Petit-Ours blossomed into view at the far end of a wide emerald lawn shaded by towering elms and oaks.

"Tarts and treacle!" gasped Porculina as they turned onto the long circular drive leading to the door. "It's like something from a fairy tale. Or a cake shop."

It was indeed a splendid edifice: a great central manor house flanked by two enormous wings, all of its stones smoothed and whitewashed and gleaming in the sun. The steep roofs were covered with scalloped clay tiles of glossy gray, as were the still steeper roofs of the six slender turrets irregularly arranged along the length of the building. The eastern wing, supported on a series of white stone arches, stretched grandly over a broad reflecting pond, beyond which another large lawn sloped gradually downward to the gleaming River Cher. The western wing gave way to a gentle, steady rise of the land toward a low hill, thickly wooded with the château's famous orchards. Within a minute, the van arrived at the large, black, double front door, which stood only three marble steps above ground level.

"I say," exclaimed Gorilla enthusiastically as he bounded down from his seat, "I have one of these too."

Angus, also alighting from the van, turned a curious eye on him. "One of . . . ?"

"Castles," said Gorilla. "Yours is prettier than mine, though. I especially like the pointy bits on top."

As he stepped down onto the gravel, Teddy looked upwards. "It's lovely," he remarked.

Angus answered with a slight bow of the head. Then he turned to smile at Porculina, who was struggling down from her seat while the two footmen hastened floppily to her assistance. *"Voilà*, mademoiselle, my humble home."

"Golly," said Porculina when Bow and Wow had managed to help her to the ground, "I've seen postcards of old châteaux, but I never ever imagined they were so . . ." She opened her short arms as if trying to embrace the entire scene before her.

"Large?" asked Angus.

"Scrumptious," she replied.

At that moment, the front doors of the château opened and what appeared for a moment to be an extraordinarily dignified bowling pin wearing a peach-gold ascot emerged from inside and descended the steps in a slow, stately waddle. It soon became evident, however, that it was a rather large, stiffly upright, strikingly graceful toy emperor penguin. His back and wings were jet black, his breast and abdomen bright white, and what had appeared to be an ascot now proved to be a lovely fan of natural ochre coloring, glowing like an autumn sunset and matched by a bold circle of the same hue beside each of his ears. His eyes were like yellow topaz, while his beak—which at the moment was turned upward—bore streaks of gold along the length of its lips.

"Ah, Auguste," said Angus, "as timely as ever. These are our honored guests. And this," he said to Teddy, Gorilla, and Porculina, "is my indispensable butler, Auguste."

The penguin turned a haughty expression toward the party. *"En effet, mon seigneur,"* he replied in a dry, deep voice, with perhaps a slight hint of disdain in it.

"Oh, in English, please," said Angus. "Our guests must feel at home."

For a few silent moments, the penguin gazed at the three visitors appraisingly. Then, sighing and arching an eyebrow, he said, "At your service, mademoiselle . . . messieurs."

"Hey-ho!" Gorilla replied heartily, striding forward, seizing one of the penguin's short wings, and bestowing two loud kisses on its tip.

A look of pure horror came over Auguste's face, and he staggered backward awkwardly. With a somewhat strangled squawk, he said, "Really, monsieur, I ... I am ..." He turned a pair of wide eyes to Angus.

Angus cleared his throat. "Well, yes," he said. "Auguste will conduct you to your rooms. It's not long till we dine and you may wish to rest after your journey. Tomorrow it would be my great pleasure to give you a small tour of the grounds."

"Oh, that would be lovely," said Porculina. "Is the kitchen very nice?"

Auguste had by now regained his composure. Smoothing the white "plumage" of his chest, clearing his throat, and resuming his splendidly pompous expression, he said, "I'll have your luggage seen to directly, mademoiselle ... messieurs ..." He paused and stared for several seconds at Gorilla's karate *gi*. Then he sighed again. "Will you need any clothes laid out, my lord? For dinner, I mean?"

"Oh, I never eat clothes," replied Gorilla cheerfully. "But it's jolly nice of you to ask." He winked at Porculina. "I told you the French have an unusual cuisine."

"I can see to his lairdship's attire," said Rolandus, now arriving from the other side of the van. "And I'll help direct the luggage to the right rooms."

The penguin's eyes widened again. He took a single uneven waddle backwards. "*Un vrai chien!*" he gasped.

"*Oui, monsieur,*" said Rolandus in a calm but weary voice, "*vrai, mais aussi doux.* Quite gentle, in fact. I don't bite ... very often."

For a few tense moments, dog and penguin stared at one another in icy silence. Then the latter sniffed loudly, raised his beak again, and said, "If you will all follow me ..."

As the party ascended the steps to the door, Angus whispered to Teddy, "You must excuse Auguste. He is, after all, an emperor penguin. He can't help being somewhat ... imperious."

"I understand," said Teddy. "We're all what our stuffing makes us."

They entered a great foyer, all of white and rose marble and brightly lit by the high, wide windows of the landing at the top of the main staircase, which was also of marble. Oil portraits lined the walls — elegant

French teddy bears in the various attires of bygone epochs — the grandest of which was of a handsome walnut-brown bear wearing a white powdered wig, a long frock-coat, and silken breaches and holding a scroll of papyrus against his chest. This, it seemed clear, was Pierre de Petit-Ours.

Auguste led the three visitors up to their rooms, each of which was lavishly appointed: a large canopied bed, an immense parlor, a private bath, ornate mirrors and furnishings, oil paintings in elaborately scrolled frames and depicting classical scenes — gamboling frogs, hedgehog orchestras, monkfish tiptoeing through flowered meadows, and so forth — and enormous windows through which the golden sunlight of rural France positively poured.

When the dinner hour arrived, Teddy, Porculina, and Gorilla together descended the stairs to the foyer, where Auguste awaited them, his posture rigid, his face expressionless, and — when he noticed Gorilla advancing upon him a little too eagerly with outstretched paw — his wings protectively folded behind his back. "Mademoiselle," he said stiffly, "sirs, may I . . . ?" But he paused as his gaze came to rest fully on Gorilla.

Whereas Teddy had donned his best crimson bowtie and Porculina had wrapped a lovely sky-blue silk scarf around her shoulders, Gorilla had changed into another karate *gi*, this one of vivid green and red tartan, though he still wore his purple belt.

Auguste seemed frozen for several seconds.

At last, Gorilla asked, "Are you all right, old fellow? Would you like me to kiss your flipper now?" He advanced another step.

"Oh, dear, no!" replied the penguin, perhaps a little too loudly. "It's not at all . . . necessary . . . monsieur . . . my lord . . ." Then he cleared his throat. "Did you . . ." He cleared his throat again. "Did you intend to wear that . . . very interesting attire into dinner, or was it perhaps . . . an accident? Perhaps your lordship stumbled and simply . . . *fell* into it by mistake?"

"No, no," replied Gorilla with a pleased smile, looking down and running his paws appreciatively over his garment, "though I often do get

19

dressed that way, like everyone." Then an expression of earnest concern came over his features. "Do you think it's too splendid, though? You don't think it'll put the other guests to shame, do you, or make anyone else feel, you know, a little dull and un-stylish?"

Auguste took a deep breath. "I assure you, my lord, there's no danger of any, ah . . . any feelings of envy."

"Jolly good!" said Gorilla, resuming his smile. "Are you sure you wouldn't like that kiss now?"

"This way, if you please," said Auguste hastily, a faint quaver of dread in his voice, as he turned on his feet and began hurriedly wobbling toward the west wing.

The banquet hall was a grand affair, obviously little changed by the centuries. Apart from some electric lighting discreetly placed along the walls and in the great crystal chandelier, everything spoke of the late Renaissance: the domed ceiling was a dark midnight blue thronged with golden stars; slender columns of white and gold rose to the vault like graceful French cypresses; the floor was tiled in rose and milky white marble; ruby red and tawny gold tapestries hung along the walls, covered with all sorts of fanciful scenes from the age of chivalry, like valiant teddy-bear knights on rocking-horse chargers, or teddy-bears engaged in contests with dragons over checkers-boards, or teddy-bear minstrels strumming lutes beneath balconies from which lovely teddy-bear dam-sels in flowing samite gowns gazed down adoringly, and so forth. At the center of the room, covered with a white tablecloth, glowing cande-labra, gleaming plates and silverware, and glasses filled with frothing fresh brown cider, stood an ornate dining table of dark polished wood. The other dinner guests, who varied greatly in size and shape, stood for the most part about the room, amiably chatting. Only one was already seated, at the table's far end: an elderly lady toy rabbit with mist-gray fur, an elegantly quivering little pink nose, and long floppy ears draped over her shoulders; her sumptuous gown was of blue satin and billowing lace, a delicate diamond tiara glittered on her brow, and a dainty silver

20

lorgnette lay on the table before her. She was watching the other guests with an expression of courtly benevolence.

"My, look at her," whispered Porculina to Teddy and Gorilla. "She's so majestic . . . just like a wonderful bunny queen!"

"My dear friends," Angus nearly cried out as he came positively gliding toward them, "cousin, how splendid! Please, let me introduce you to someone I cherish."

He led them to the lady rabbit, who looked up as they approached with a faint, kindly, aristocratic smile on her delicate face.

"It is my great honor," said Angus, "to present you to Madame la Comtesse Lapin de Gris, one of my family's closest friends, and like an aunt to me." He named each of the three companions to her in turn.

The elderly rabbit smiled a little more warmly and extended a languid paw toward Teddy. Before the little bear could take it, however, Gorilla called out, "What ho!" and seized it impetuously. "Charmed!" he said with obvious sincerity as he leaned forward, twice kissed her paw with considerable vigor, and then — after a moment's thought — kissed it once more.

"It's so jolly to make your acquaintance!" he said, grinning broadly and stepping back again.

"Ahh," replied Madame Lapin de Gris, a little above a whisper. "So gallant a gentle-ape. So chivalrous and . . . *bold* in social graces. So . . . *énergétique.*" Her exquisite smile shimmered with gentility.

"Golly," murmured Porculina. Then, with a gulp, she curtseyed, at least as best she could on her stout little legs. "You're . . . glorious . . . your majesty."

"I'm not a queen, my dear," the rabbit replied, "or even a duchess. A plain 'your ladyship' is sufficient."

"Oh," replied Porculina in a slightly embarrassed tone. "But chestnuts, you really are splendid!"

Madame Lapin de Gris nodded graciously, as if generously deigning to accept Porculina's praise.

Teddy, clearing his throat, at last gently took her paw in his and, far more lightly than Gorilla had done, bestowed a kiss upon it. "I'm very pleased to make your acquaintance, your ladyship," he said as he released her paw and took a single step back. "Or, rather, *je suis très heureux de faire votre connaissance.*"

"A gallant bear *aussi*," she replied with a small arch of an eyebrow. "Scarcely any trace of a barbarous American accent at all. I feel we are already friends."

"I'm honored," Teddy replied

"I wish I could rise, so as to look at your faces properly," she said, "but I fear my condition prevents me."

"Oh dear," said Porculina, "you're not ill, are you?"

The lady rabbit waved her paw limply in the air. "Nothing out of the ordinary. Mine is a chronic condition."

"Oh dear," said Porculina again, obviously dismayed.

"May I inquire as to the nature of the complaint?" asked Teddy.

"*Mais bien sûr,*" Madame Lapin de Gris replied. "My physicians have diagnosed me with incurable cases of 'acute elegance' and 'morbid sophistication'—afflictions tragically common among toy rabbits of my social

22

station. I'm burdened with a nature so refined that I'm condemned to permanent weakness, since robust good health would be very vulgar."

"Oh, that's very sad," said Gorilla with genuine feeling. "Very sad indeed. I'd best kiss your paw again."

"Ah, no, dear Laird MacGorilla," said the rabbit, drawing her paws to herself with practiced frailty, "I fear my general delicacy forbids it."

"Well," said Angus briskly, breaking in on the exchange, "perhaps we'd all better take our seats, and continue the introductions over soup. I'm to be seated at the other end of the table, with dear Mademoiselle Porculina on my right, and Laird MacGorilla beside her, and you, my dear cousin, on my left hand, so that we may all become better acquainted." He turned to the rabbit with a bow. "My good and beloved lady, if you will excuse us."

Madame Lapin de Gris consented with a restrained smile, a slight tilt of her head, and a gracious twitch of her nose.

"In fact," Angus whispered to the three friends as they accompanied him to the other end of the table, "she's as strong as a bull — physically the most powerful toy rabbit I've ever known. Especially her hind legs. She could kick down these walls, and she can cover yards with a single leap. But she would be mortified if she thought anyone suspected her of anything as uncouth as good health."

"Marshmallows," said Porculina, obviously even more impressed than before. "Shortbread," she sighed admiringly. "Absolutely ladyfingers."

Once everyone was seated and the soup had been served by two toy tigers in dark blue footmen's liveries, Angus welcomed all his guests. To the table at large he first presented the visitors from Britain and asked Teddy briefly to relate how the three of them had come to know one another. Teddy explained that they had been fast friends since childhood, as they had attended school together at the prestigious Advanced Academy for Soft Toys in New York City. Then Angus began the rest of the introductions.

"To your right, Laird Gorilla," he said, indicating two small, sleek horses, jet black but with chalk-white hooves, manes, and diamond-shaped blazes below their forelocks, "are my indispensable orchard-keepers and treasured friends. The lovely mare next to you is Mademoiselle Onyx, and the brawny stallion to her right is her twin brother Monsieur Obsidian."

"Hello there!" said Gorilla eagerly. "I've always wanted to be a horse myself!"

With a sound somewhere between a whinny and a giggle, Onyx looked at the three friends in turn, her gaze coming finally to rest on Gorilla. She smiled sweetly, batted her long lashes, and said, "My, what a lovely dinner-jacket. What a sense of color you have."

Gorilla smiled, took her hoof in his hand, and bestowed the now predictable loud kiss upon it. "I'm glad you like it," he said. "I'm fond of colors. I think they're quite the nicest things. You should see some of my finger-paintings."

The other horse emitted a low, somehow morose neigh and then a soft snort. "Pleased to make your acquaintances," he mumbled. "Excuse us for not dressing for dinner," he added in a somewhat depressed voice. "We're not accustomed to grand occasions."

Angus shook his head fondly. "And yet you eat here every night, my friend."

"Well . . . your chef is excellent," replied Obsidian, a tad grudgingly. "And the hay is always fresh."

Onyx giggled again, then snuffled. "You must pardon my brother," she said. "He's gruff in manner but pure in heart."

"As for this handsome young aquatic specimen," continued Angus, indicating the figure seated to Obsidian's right, near Madame Lapin de Gris's end of the table—a rather enormous dolphin, pale blue with a white underbody, deep dark eyes, and a kindly smile on his face—"he keeps the grounds . . . or, rather, grounds and waters. This is Monsieur Kippernicus—or Kipper, as we all call him. He was away when you arrived this afternoon, or he would surely have greeted you."

The dolphin, however, was staring off into space with a dreamily distracted look in his eyes, obviously unaware that anyone was talking about him.

"Oh, Kipper, my lad," called Angus in a sing-song voice, "are you with us?"

Kipper turned his smile toward Angus and then looked about the table in a gently baffled way. "My apologies," he said in a lovely, dulcet, clicking, clacking, and whistling voice, "what was the question?"

"None," replied Angus with a small laugh. "I was just telling our guests that you were unable to greet them when they arrived, *because* ..." And here Angus cocked his head questioningly toward the dolphin.

"Oh yes," said Kipper. "I'd quite forgotten the time. I do often, especially when I'm ... Well, today I was upstream. Jacques and I" — he nodded toward the guest seated directly across from him — "were having tea together and playing draughts and discussing his latest book on the family-structures of starfish."

"Monsieur Jacques Tout-en-Dents, he means," said Angus, "the esteemed marine biologist and nature writer." This guest, a toy shark just as large as the dolphin, cut an especially striking figure: pale gray with a cold white underbody, eyes like black pearls, a wide maw filled with rows of pointed teeth.

"*Mon plaisir*," he said in a voice that sounded like the rumble of a distant avalanche, if more genial.

"Oh, I know your work," Teddy remarked. "Didn't you write that wonderful book on rubber-duck folksong traditions?"

The shark's smile widened in a way that was somehow simultaneously shy and unnerving. "I'm flattered you know it."

"Jacques has been my guest this past year," said Madame Lapin de Gris. "He's cataloguing the vegetation and fishes of the Cher."

"Your generosity," said the shark, turning to the rabbit, "has made my research an absolute delight."

Just then, however, Porculina was unable to suppress the strained, timid,

25

gurgling noise that had been rising in her throat. Every eye turned to her. She looked around nervously and then back at the shark. "Excuse me," she said after a moment. "It's just that you're quite . . . quite an overwhelming sight to take in . . . all at once . . ." Her voice sank away in a feeble tremolo.

The shark's smile became a touch rueful. "I'm afraid I do have that effect sometimes," he said in a meltingly gentle growl. "It's my general toothiness. If it's any comfort, my teeth are all made of felt. And I eat mostly salad and alfalfa sprouts . . . though I can't resist buttered toast."

"Oh, neither can I!" cried Porculina, obviously all at once feeling less anxious. "Especially with marmalade."

"*Oh yes,*" replied Jacques in a wistful purr. "*Marmalade . . .*" He drew the word out lovingly and closed his gleaming eyes. "Strawberry . . . gooseberry too . . . blackberry . . . oh, and black currant jam!"

Now Porculina's expression was of someone who had found a kindred soul. "I'm ashamed of having made a personal remark," she said.

"Not at all," said Jacques kindly, opening his eyes again. "Candor is the shortest path to true friendship."

"I too sometimes excite an initial dread," remarked the figure to the shark's right in a warm, deeply resonant voice.

"This," said Angus with a note of pride, "is the very esteemed poet Rex Homerosaurus — whose name I have no doubt is known to you."

The toy tyrannosaur did in fact have features of a somewhat fearsome cast — especially the long rows of pointy teeth and the fiery yellow eyes — but he was on a smaller scale than the shark, the expression on his face was disarmingly sweet, and his colorations were as dazzlingly lovely as any butterfly's: his jaws, limbs, and underbelly were a deep plumb purple stippled with jet, streaks of pale cherry ran down his sides, and the rich forest green of his back, from his head to the tip of his tail, was bordered by wavy lines of limpid turquoise. Even the row of small black dorsal plates on his neck and between his shoulders looked more dashing than dangerous.

26   "You don't seem at all scary to me," exclaimed Porculina.

A slightly crestfallen expression appeared on the dinosaur's face. "Oh," he said.

"I mean," Porculina hastily added, "you *are* scary . . . I mean, *brrr*" — she shivered dramatically and briefly threw her trotters up as if in terror — "*Help, help!* and all that. But you're also so very . . . well, beautiful."

"I'll say!" Gorilla interjected. "Like a carousel — one with all its lights flashing." He looked about at the other guests with a broad smile, as if inviting them to agree. A murmur of assent ran around the table.

"Oh," said Rex, looking about him, and his expression grew somewhat more cheerful. "Well . . . well, yes, I suppose my conspicuous beauty does rather distract from my terrific dreadfulness."

"I say, what sort of poet are you?' asked Gorilla eagerly. "I like poems. Especially ones about bunnies or rubber balls or things like that."

A look of quiet dignity came over Rex's face. "Those aren't my preferred subjects, except in passing. I'm what is called an epic poet. Mine is narrative verse to be read aloud, celebrating great contests of will, cunning, and strength."

"*Ohh*," intoned Porculina. "You mean knights and jousts? Or heroes rescuing dragons from ferocious damsels? Or . . . "

"Not exactly," replied Rex, raising his eyes to gaze off dramatically into the distance. "Principally my works concern those mighty struggles known as . . . *flower competitions.*"

"I like flowers," remarked Gorilla.

"Ah," said Teddy, "you're the author of . . . um . . . *War of the Roses*, aren't you?"

The dinosaur turned to the teddy bear with an expression of delighted surprise. "You know my work too? What a bear of letters you are! You've read it then?"

"Well" — Teddy cleared his throat — "some of it, yes. I haven't finished it . . . it's very long, after all, but . . . "

Rex, however, was too pleased to contain himself. "It's so good to speak to an educated toy. I'm writing its sequel now, which I have entitled

27

Antheiomachiad. That means 'Song of the Flower-Battle' in Greek."

"What does it mean in English?" Gorilla asked.

"In . . . ?" Rex frowned thoughtfully. "I don't think . . ."

"Well, it's a jolly pretty name, whatever it means," said Gorilla. "I like it." Then he squinted thoughtfully and pursed his lips. "Of course, I also like the name Enid. I'm not sure which I like better."

Angus coughed into his paw. "We must not forget our final guest," he said. "May I introduce — and with a tingle of awe, I assure you — Mademoiselle Ellie Phant, the magnificent English ballerina."

All eyes turned to the next soft toy, who until now had not said a word, and had perhaps not even been noticed by everyone at the table. She was a dainty, teacup-sized gray toy elephant with small dark eyes and lovely bright white tusks, seated not at the table but rather on it, upon a minuscule upholstered stool, dipping her trunk in her soup (in which she could have easily gone for a swim), bringing it to her lips, and then sipping delicately. She paused. "Oh, my," she said in a high, musical, enchanting voice, "have we come round to me?" She smiled at everyone modestly.

"Ah, there you are," Madame Lapin de Gris remarked.

Teddy looked to see the elderly rabbit staring at the tiny elephant through her lorgnette, which he now realized was a pair of opera glasses. He turned to Ellie. "I saw you dance *Giselle* in London," he said in a tone of admiration. "I bought a telescope for the occasion."

"Oh, my!" chimed Ellie. "Do you follow the ballet, then?"

"When I can," replied Teddy. "Especially when it's danced by artists as gifted as yourself."

The little elephant smiled, blushed, and lowered her eyes. "What a charmer you are," she said.

"Mademoiselle Phant and Monsieur Homerosaurus are also guests of the château," Angus remarked. "They are this year's ambassadors to our cider festival from the Soft Toys' Arts Council. There's always a little performance, you see, before the tasting."

"How wonderful," said Teddy.

"This soup is delicious," Porculina suddenly remarked, clearly unable to suppress the urge. "What is it?"

"Sweet and sour leek and potato stew," answered Angus. "My chef specializes in Sino-Cymric food."

"I'm sorry, Sign-of-...?" Porculina's voice trailed away inquisitively.

"*Sino*-Cymric," repeated Angus: "Chinese-Welsh fusion cuisine."

"I've never tasted anything like it," she said.

"It's his special invention."

Each dish, in fact, was more delicious than its predecessor. Gorilla at one point remarked in bafflement that none seemed to contain any banana, but admitted that the flavors were so "jolly nice" that it almost — *almost* — did not matter. The meal progressed delightfully and the conversation flowed like a sparkling stream, the evening floating by on its placid surface. Just, however, as the remains of the entrée — a creamy Szechuan Rarebit over potato pot sticker dumplings — were being removed by the footmen, Madame Lapin de Gris cleared her throat with such volume and force that everyone else all at once fell silent.

"Excuse me," she said, looking about at the other guests gravely. "This has been a joy, but the time I believe has come to acknowledge the crisis threatening this château, which I feel must be addressed before the cider festival commences."

"Crisis?" said Ellie in a small peep. "Is there a crisis?"

"Surely, my dear," replied the elderly rabbit, "you've heard of the strange events that have shattered the peace of this noble house this last month? I refer to the matter of the ghost... the haunting." Her eyes narrowed. "Which I believe to be connected with the château's notorious..." — her voice dropped ominously in pitch — "... *curse*."

A chorus of small gasps and alarmed whispers rippled through the air.

"What a coincidence!" exclaimed Gorilla merrily. "My castle has one of those too!"

29

CHAPTER 3
A Curse and a Ghost

"I SPEAK," SAID MADAME LAPIN DE GRIS, TAKING NO note of Gorilla's remark, "of the curse of the Green Star, which lies like a mantle of abysmal darkness upon this noble house."

A flurry of alarmed whispers gusted around the table.

"Dear lady," said Angus in a strained voice, "please let's not . . ."

But she would not be dissuaded. "Please everyone understand that Monsieur le Comte — Angus, who is to me as a son — is what we in France call a 'rationalist,' *hélas*, which means that he refuses to believe in anything beyond what he can touch and see."

"Dear lady," Angus again interjected, "I protest. I'm not a small-minded bear. I've no doubt that there are more things in heaven and earth than we know, but I trust first in solid and rational things — things that make perfect sense by themselves and require no 'magical' explanations — such as earth and sky, good cider, the natural life-force that animates beasts and humans and soft toys . . . magnetism, gravity, mathematics . . ."

"La Maison de Petit-Ours and la Maison de Lapin de Gris," continued the rabbit, "have enjoyed an alliance of many centuries. Each has supported the other in times of crisis, each has been the other's second archives — keeping copies of one another's records and documents, that is — and each has been privy to the other's affairs. Most may not know the long, terrible chronicle of the curse, but I do." She drew herself up grandly in her chair and cast a solemn glance around the table. "Most of you know that Angus's illustrious ancestor Pierre de Petit-Ours helped Champollion translate the Rosetta Stone — he did most of the work, I suspect — and that in later years he brought many antiquities back from Egypt to France. But what you are unlikely to know is that, on one of his last journeys to the land of the Nile, he became fast friends with the Khedive of Egypt's beloved teddy bear Aldubu Aljabbar — or Jab-Jab, as he was fondly known — who gave Pierre a splendid gift on the day of the latter's departure for home: a glorious, flawless, exquisitely cut emerald, the size of a walnut in its shell. Its worth was incalculable. Pierre was overwhelmed but out of courtesy could not refuse. That emerald was called the Green Star of the Nile, and it became the greatest glory of the Château de Petit-Ours's already fabled treasures."

"I've never heard this before," said Teddy, clearly fascinated, "for all my research into family lore."

"*Sans aucun doute*," said Madame Lapin de Gris. "For unbeknownst to Jab-Jab, he had given his friend an emerald that bore an ancient curse, one going back to the days of the pharaohs . . . something having to do with a crocodile magician . . . I forget. In any event, the terrible truth was learned only by chance, from an ancient papyrus that Pierre had acquired on an earlier expedition but that had not yet been deciphered. Even when the story was learned, however, Pierre was not dismayed. He too was a rationalist — it was the spirit of the age, and every soft toy in the land believed a new age of enlightenment had dawned — and he discounted the legends altogether. Yet, from the moment the Green Star came to the château, catastrophe followed upon catastrophe."

"Like what?" asked Porculina, her eyes wide, her snout tensely quivering.

"Well, the very day of Pierre's arrival home from his journey, the château, on account of an unexplained fire in the kitchen, lost its most prized and irreplaceable . . ." — the rabbit lowered her eyes sorrowfully — "*cookbook*."

Several minutes later, when Porculina had at last been revived with the help of smelling salts brought by a footman and with the encouragement of Gorilla — who kept gently tugging at her ear and cooing, "Yoo-hoo, Piggles, wakey-wakey!" — Teddy turned to Angus and asked, "Is the emerald still here?"

"My dear cousin," replied Angus with a laugh, "I do not believe it ever was. This is all a family fable for entertaining children — ancient Egypt, a curse, a missing emerald — that came to be mistaken for a true story."

"*Alors!,*" the rabbit practically snapped, "were my ancestors fools then? It's firmly attested in the chronicles of my house that the Green Star was real, that it was brought to this château, and that it began to exercise its baleful influence at once."

"May I ask," interjected Rex at this point, "if it's not too impertinent of me, where's the emerald now?"

"It was lost," she replied. "Rather, it was concealed, by another of Angus's ancestors, the finger-and-oil painter Octave de Petit-Ours. It was a time of civil unrest, which was something of a seasonal occurrence in France in former days, and so he arranged to have a secret chamber built on the grounds here where the Green Star could be kept safe until order was restored."

After a moment of suspenseful silence, Ellie raised her trunk and meekly asked, "What happened then?"

Madame Lapin de Gris sighed deeply, stared at the tiny elephant through her opera glasses once again, and said, in a mordant voice, "The silly *peluche* forgot where it was. Octave was not very . . . *vif* . . . the English term eludes me."

"Bright," said Teddy.

"He was forgetful," she said. "He was always forgetting things: books, pens, hats . . . boathouses . . . "

"I say," exclaimed Gorilla delightedly, "I do that myself. We've a lovely little boathouse I regularly forget about, right on the loch's eastern . . . no, western . . . no, wait, now that I think of it, I believe it's in the garden . . . and it's a cucumber frame."

"Well," interrupted the rabbit with an indulgent smile, "so it was with Octave. He put the emerald somewhere, in a chamber he'd hired someone to build, but when the time came to retrieve it he'd completely forgotten where it was, and whom he hired to do the work, and even what an emerald looks like, and . . . "

33

"I say," Gorilla began, in an even more excited voice, "I've done that . . ."

"Which was the most disastrous thing that could have happened!" the rabbit suddenly cried out, in a voice somehow enormously loud and yet melodramatically frail. "For now the cursed stone is still here upon the estate, casting its malign influence over everything and everyone, but we cannot find it, let alone expel its evil."

"Have you never thought to look for it?" Teddy asked Angus.

"Again, cousin, I do not believe it exists. My grandfather made a thorough search of the château's environs, and if he couldn't find it there is almost certainly nothing to find."

"It wouldn't matter anyway," Madame Lapin de Gris told Teddy. "If Angus were to discover the emerald, he would simply put it on display, like any ordinary gemstone, as an item of family lore."

"But of course," said Angus. "Curses don't exist. Why would I part with an heirloom so splendid and mysterious out of superstition?"

Here the elderly rabbit laid down her lorgnette with just enough force to suggest her patience was wearing thin. "How can you remain so obtuse?" she asked, her nose twitching furiously, her ears and whiskers vibrating. "Don't you see it's the curse that has summoned the ghost who's been terrorizing these premises these past months?"

"Sour cabbage!" exclaimed Porculina. "Terrorizing?" She turned to Teddy. "I thought you said it was all just a little bother."

"It is," said Angus. "Some credulous workmen late at night — you know how silly humans can be when they haven't had their naps — helping to build a marquee for the cider festival, thought they caught a glimpse of something large and misty and glowing, and then a young maid thought she saw something similar in a darkened corridor a week later. Tricks of moonlight, nothing more. And there've been sounds, and a few things that appeared to have been moved about in the night — some books in the library, some old bits of armor on display in the back hallways of the château's central keep . . . oh, and a somewhat insipid vase that was broken in a room where no one had been. But . . ."

34

"Well," Gorilla said softly to Porculina, "not Henry, then. He'd have cleaned up the broken vase. And left a note with an apology, probably."

"Oh, you infuriate me sometimes," said Madame Lapin de Gris to Angus. "I told you of my dream. And you know my dreams have a way of coming true."

"A dream, you say?" asked Kipper, in a tone more curious than anxious.

"Yes," she replied. "A very vivid dream, of some disaster to come on the day of the cider festival." She closed her eyes and shivered once, violently. "I saw a two-headed beast of some kind, astride which came a great dark rider, clad all in midnight blue . . . with a bit of pink, I think . . . thundering across the sward. I saw . . ."

"Please, madame," implored Angus, "in your condition, you mustn't work yourself into so fretful a state. Look, the dessert has arrived. Let us talk of happier things."

For a moment, Madame Lapin de Gris stared forlornly at her host. Then her expression softened into one of gentle resignation. "Very well. But this conversation isn't finished."

The Red Bean Monmouth Pudding was delectable, and slowly the conversation resumed a lighter tone, and began to ring with occasional laughter. Porculina, however, obviously still shaken by the tragedy of the lost cookbook and talk of a ghost, was more subdued than normal, and was not even distracted from her worries when Gorilla made several futile attempts to balance a spoon on his nose.

Later that night, after the three friends had parted from Rex and Ellie in the corridor leading to their various rooms, and just before they themselves retired for the night, Porculina confided to Teddy and Gorilla that she planned to sleep with all the lights on.

"Too bad Roly couldn't find room to pack my bagpipes," said Gorilla, shaking his head regretfully. "That would have put the bloom back in your cheeks."

At this, a tremor of something worse than mere terror seemed to pass through Porculina. But then, with a dawning smile of relief, she said, "Thank-you, Gor-Gor. I . . . I feel so much better now."

Two hours later, all was quiet throughout the château. Every light had been extinguished or dimmed. The rooms occupied by the various guests were arranged along a western gallery that overlooked the grand foyer through a series of high pointed arches resting atop an elegant parapet. All the room's doors were shut — all but one, that is, which stood wide open and through which a mild golden glow spilled out into the hallway. At regular intervals a soft sound issued from the room within — a quiet, carpeted *thwip* sound — followed by a small rubber ball arcing through the air, striking the top of the parapet with a muted but distinct *thonk*, and then bouncing back the way it had come. Every now and again, the sequence was punctuated by a hushed but delighted exclamation of "I say, fine catch that!" or "Hello again, my bouncy friend!" or "Oh, dash it!" This eventually came to an end when, after a *thwip* somewhat louder than the others, the ball sailed over the parapet and plunged into the inky darkness below. A moment later, a series of noises, diminishing in volume but increasing in rapidity — *toonk-toonk-toonk-toon-toon-t-t-t-ttttt . . .* — rose up from the foyer. "Bother!" whispered the voice in the room. A few moments after that, Gorilla thrust his night-capped head out into the corridor, looked right and then left and, satisfied that no one else was about, emerged from his room, clad in silk pajamas cut like a pale yellow *gi* with a belt of red and blue polka-dots, and carrying a lit candle in its brass holder. He made his way to the stairs as stealthily as he could — which was not very stealthy at all, truth be told, given his irrepressible need to hum bagpipe melodies to himself as he went — and descended.

It took him only a moment to find the bright red rubber ball resting at the center of the foyer's marble floor, and he would have taken it directly back to his room had he not noticed a wide, inviting passageway just to the right of the stairs, through which he could see a long, broad corridor, softly illuminated by candles in little lanterns ensconced high on the walls. Again, he looked about to make sure he was unobserved; then he said to the rubber ball, "What a splendid place for a race, ay?" Blowing out his candle and setting it on a small table near the corridor's entrance, he crouched down in a rough approximation of the posture of a sprinter in the blocks and eagerly whispered, "First one to bounce off the far wall wins. Ready, Steady, Go!" He tossed the ball underhand down the passage.

It was not an especially close race. The ball reached the corridor's end before Gorilla had crossed half the distance. But, rather than bouncing back toward him, it glanced off an ornamental pilaster and bounded away to the left, apparently down an adjoining corridor. "Hey-ho," Gorilla called out quietly, "don't do that!" But, on reaching the mouth of this new corridor for himself, he could not contain his delight. "I say," he muttered, "there's a jolly sight!"

Another series of small ensconced lanterns cast a gentle glow over everything. This corridor was far broader than the other. Really, it was more of a large, open exhibition hall with a high vaulted ceiling, and at its far end stood an imposing wall of what looked like great granite stones of considerable age. Arranged along both sides of the hall, moreover, were suits of armor in styles spanning centuries of teddy bear chivalric design, each posed atop a dark marble base with its visor down and ear-caps pertly upright. Two of them sat astride rocking-horses. Another held an enormous lollipop in its gauntlet. Yet another held a wand for blowing bubbles. And two, both directly to Gorilla's right, were flying kites — or brightly dyed pennons shaped like kites — from strings that crossed one another above the lintel of a doorway in the wall. It was there that the rubber ball had come to rest, against the dark oak door, which was several inches ajar. "I see you, you little scamp," said Gorilla as he retrieved his toy. He slipped it into his pocket, then stared for several seconds at the door, then glanced about, again assuring himself that he was unobserved. "I'd better just have a look," he whispered — though there seemed to be no particular reason why this might be so — and gently pushed the door further open. Apparently its hinges were well-oiled, as they made no sound at all. The scene that met Gorilla's eyes, illuminated by the blue moonlight shining in through two enormous, elaborately ornamental windows, was a splendid old library. There were four long rows of shelves filled with glossily bound tomes in the middle of the room, several other bookcases lining the walls, three or four busts of teddy bears in stiff collars and spectacles sitting on small plinths, an antique desk near one of the windows, and — somewhat out of the ordinary, it seemed to Gorilla — the tall, shimmering form of a ghost, slowly rocking from side to side, with its back turned.

At least, so it appeared. It was somewhat difficult to tell back from front, given the figure's general featurelessness and luminosity — rather like an upside-down candleflame unsteadily balanced on its tip. But it betrayed no sign of having noticed Gorilla, and at the moment it seemed to be entirely preoccupied with the books shelved along the left-hand wall. Gorilla lifted a hand and was about to call out a friendly greeting, but then recalled his manners. He was not sure of the proper etiquette for addressing ghosts, he realized, especially not in France, so he decided that moderation was the best strategy. Not wanting to alarm the poor creature, he chose to creep up on it from behind, in a very friendly way. When he was a few feet from the large luminous shape, he quietly cleared his throat and casually remarked, "I say, what an unexpected pleasure to meet you here."

The ghost screamed. The sound was outlandishly loud — more of a shriek than anything else, of the sort one makes when a cube of ice is dropped down one's back. It whirled about — not that this revealed anything. If it had a face, no features were visible through the gauzy glow that shrouded them. For several seconds, the ghost did nothing, except perhaps tremble ever so slightly.

"Look here, old fellow," said Gorilla after a while, displaying his best reassuring smile, "I didn't mean to startle you." He eyed the glowing figure up and down. "I'm, um, not sure where you keep your hands, but I'd gladly kiss one of them if you like. Or both."

For a few moments more, the ghost did nothing. Then, almost timidly, it raised two amorphous appendages and held them out to either side. But, just as Gorilla was reaching out to take hold of one of them and bending forward with lips puckering, the ghost shook them violently, seemed to rear up another inch or two in height, and rattled out a long, high, hollow "*OooooooOooooooOooooo* . . ." It did not seem to have put much conviction in the remark. It paused, shook its "head" in apparent consternation, uttered what sounded like two soft, dry coughs, and repeated itself, though this time with far more brio and volume: "*OooooooOooooooOooooo* . . . !"

"I say, well done!" replied Gorilla, genuinely impressed. "I wish I could do that . . ." He paused, knitted his brows, drew in his breath, and then gave voice to a long, high, desolate "*OooooooOooooo* . . ." But, before he could reach the end of the phrase, it dissolved into something between a gasp and a wheeze. "You see," he said shaking his head, "I just don't have the wind for it, or the right resonance." He licked his lips twice. "Never give up, though. That's how I mastered the bagpipes, after all. Here, let me give it another . . ."

Just then, however, the ghost threw up its arms — or the ill-defined protuberances that served as arms — spun about, and dashed toward the door in a swaying, almost ethereal manner, although with considerable speed.

"Oh, don't go yet!" called Gorilla. "I'll get it right!"

But the glowing figure had already passed through the library doorway and into the hall, turned to its right, and was now wavering away out of sight.

Gorilla pursed his lips, shook his head, and murmured, "I must have embarrassed the poor chap." Then he followed, calling out, "I say, there's only a wall that way . . . " But, as he emerged from the library and looked in the direction the ghost had taken, he saw that the hall was now quite deserted. For several seconds he stood in silence, a forefinger pressed thoughtfully to his lips. "*Hmm,*" he said once or twice, "that's curious." After several seconds more, he remarked, "Well, I suppose that's

39

what ghosts do. Still ..." He began to stroll toward the end of the hall, pausing once or twice to admire the suits of armor, but otherwise carefully looking for some sign of an opening. He could find none. Then he decided to check behind each of the suits of armor in turn, just in case, repeatedly burbling, "Hey-ho, Mr. Ghost, are you there?" as he went. When he had reached the mouth of the hallway again, he sighed in a rather forsaken way. "Gone," he said softly. He decided, however, that before returning to bed he should peek one last time into the library, in case the ghost had doubled back, as a bit of a prank perhaps. Sadly, it had not. Gorilla shrugged in disappointment, stroked his chin pensively, and leaned distractedly against one of the two kite-flying suits of armor. At once, it gave way, tipped over, and crashed to the floor, Gorilla tumbling backwards with it. The noise was enormous. The clatter of heavy steel plating on the stone tiles of the floor echoed through the hall like thunder, rebounded from the walls and ceilings, and coursed away along the corridor beyond like a great, sleek weasel.

Some moments later, when Auguste and Rolandus arrived in the hallway, and Auguste switched on the electric lights interspersed among the glowing lanterns on the wall, Gorilla was still resting on his back, his finger still pressed against his lips, as if deep in thought.

Rolandus, clad in a long white nightshirt, gave voice to a small groan and approached the recumbent figure. "M'laird," he said evenly, "are you quite ... all right?"

Gorilla turned his eyes up toward the dog. "Oh, hullo, Roly," he said. "What brings you here?"

Auguste — also in a nightshirt, though one with gold epaulets and masses of gold braid — waddled over to the disordered heap of armor on the floor. He was clearly in a state of some agitation, and rasped, "*Comment cela* ...?" Then he paused, swallowed deeply, and asked, somewhat more calmly, "How could this have happened?"

Rolandus gave the penguin a weary look. "The real question is how could it *not* have happened?" He turned back to Gorilla, who was still

40

serenely supine on the floor and now softly humming to himself. "Shall I assist you, m'laird?" he asked.

"If you like," said Gorilla, with what for him was a rather dour smile.

Rolandus helped Gorilla to his feet, brushed off as much of the dust shed by the collapsing armor from his pajamas as possible, straightened his nightcap for him, and said, "Did you become lost?"

"Not a bit of it," said Gorilla carelessly. "I was just out for a stroll, thinking about some very, um..." — he discreetly felt for his pocket to make sure the rubber ball was still there — "...very important matters... things, you know...."

Rolandus arched a single eyebrow. "I have no doubt," he murmured dryly.

"I say, you two," said Gorilla with a furrowed brow, "did either of you happen to pass someone on your way here? A sort of tall, pale chap? Rather luminous? You know, in a glowy sort of way?"

The dog and the penguin exchanged baffled looks.

"I can't say that we did, m'laird," replied Rolandus.

"We tend to discourage luminosity in our guests," said Auguste haughtily.

Rolandus stared at the penguin for a moment. "That's an established policy of the château, is it?" he asked in a dry voice.

"Well..." Auguste drew himself up straight and momentarily wrinkled his brow. "Perhaps it's not — how do you say? — writ in stone, but it's implied... by our devotion to good taste. Glowing after all — it sounds very vulgar... even American."

Just then, a babble of anxious voices came drifting in from the corridor. A moment later, Teddy, Porculina, Angus, Rex, and Ellie arrived, all in a single party.

"My goodness," exclaimed Angus on taking in the scene, "what has happened? Is everyone all right?" He hastened toward Gorilla, followed closely by Teddy and Porculina. "Are you harmed, my dear friend?" he asked, in a tone of genuine concern.

"What magnificent carnage," remarked Rex. "Like the grand aftermath of some great ... snowball fight."

"Oh, Gor-Gor!" Porculina cried out. "I just knew ..." But then she fell silent and looked about somewhat guiltily. "I mean, I just *worried* so that something might have happened to you!"

"Nothing to fret about, Piggles," said Gorilla, patting himself down gingerly to make sure everything was in place. "Just a bit of an unexpected encounter."

"What happened?" asked Teddy, looking his friend over. "How did you ...?" He glanced about, saw the scattered armor, met Rolandus's gaze and saw the expression of calm resignation there, then looked back at Gorilla. "Never mind. But" — he narrowed his eyes quizzically — "what do you mean an encounter?"

"I know what you're thinking," answered Gorilla ruefully, "but it wasn't Henry."

"Who's Henry?" peeped Ellie.

"*What* wasn't Henry?" asked Porculina, a look of dismay spreading over her features.

"Oh, didn't I say?" asked Gorilla. "There was a ghost here, just a little while ago — shiny fellow, seemed rather nice, but then ..." Here, however, a long, gurgling gasp from Porculina curtailed his words. "Steady on, old girl," he said. "I don't think I said anything terribly offensive to him. I can't imagine why he dashed off."

"Wait, wait," Teddy interrupted. "Tell us the whole story, please, starting from ... well, from whatever brought you here."

As briefly as he could — which, to tell the truth, was not very briefly at all — Gorilla recounted the events of the night, omitting mention of the rubber ball but otherwise filling in the details with considerable relish. Only when he had reached the end of his narrative and several seconds of tense silence ensued did he become somewhat despondent again.

Angus was the first to speak. "My apologies, dear friends," he said, his eyes averted toward his own feet. "I have discounted the reports of a haunting too hastily it seems. Now, however, I have the indubitable testimony of Laird MacGorilla to confirm them."

"Well," said Teddy, wincing slightly, "I'm not sure 'indubitable' is exactly . . ." But here he paused, noting the pallor in Porculina's cheeks. "Are you all right, Pigsy?"

"All right?" she replied in a high tremolo. "Peaches and pumpkins! I'm ecstatic!"

Teddy was somewhat taken aback. "Really? I assumed you were terrified."

"Oh, well, yes . . ." She shrugged. "I suppose I am. Help, help, and alack, and all that too. But don't you see? It's another mystery! We're in a mystery story again! And here you are, the brilliant investigator soon to be on the trail of . . . well, something . . . and here I am, ready again to play your slow-witted sidekick, proposing absurd solutions and asking foolish questions — and this time hobbled by her irrational fear of ghosts and goblins and things of that sort. Think of the possible complications."

"I see . . ." said Teddy.

"Oh, Teddy really is fabulously clever, you know," she said, turning to Angus. "You should see him in action. A mind like a steel breadbox! I've seen him solve the most bewildering mystery imaginable in a little more than a day — we all have." She waved excited trotters in the directions of Gorilla and Rolandus.

"Should I not summon the police, mon seigneur?" asked Auguste, plainly unimpressed by Porculina's praise. "I'm sure that . . . your American guest has his talents, but in France . . ."

"Oh, my goodness, no!" said Angus almost vehemently. "Ask the police to investigate a ghost? If word were to get out — and it would — the château would become an object of general ridicule, and just as the cider festival is commencing." He raised his eyes, looked first at Porculina, and then at Teddy. "Perhaps, cousin, I might avail myself of your skills. I confess, I'm quite at a loss to know what to do. I mean, ghosts indeed! I've never considered such a thing."

43

"Are you really a detective?" asked Ellie curiously. "I thought you were a travel-writer."

Teddy smiled bashfully. "Well, I do have some experience. My former profession was, as it happens, police detective."

"He's brilliant!" said Porculina.

"There's nothing so admirable as a soft toy who has mastered his craft," remarked Rex. "I confess, I find this whole situation alarming, but also very . . . *dramatic*. In an epic way, I mean. Not in a coarse theatrical way."

Teddy looked about at the others. Then, with a slight tilt of his head and shrug of his shoulders, he said, "I'll see what I can do. But I think we could all use some rest first."

Angus smiled. "I am grateful, cousin." He turned to Auguste. "Don't worry about clearing things up in here tonight," he said. "You must rest as well."

"In fact," said Teddy, "we should leave everything as it is till I've had some time to inspect the area in the light of day."

The penguin looked about with disdainfully hooded eyes, shot Gorilla an aloof glance, but only said, "Of course."

As everyone at last — after exchanging a few more remarks — began to make their way toward the corridor, Porculina took Gorilla by the arm and began to lead him along with her. "What's the matter, Gor-Gor?" she asked. "I can always tell when you're feeling sad."

"Oh, I don't know, Piggles," replied Gorilla, wagging his head glumly. "It's just the way that ghosty fellow dashed off, as if he didn't want to have anything to do with me. I really didn't think I'd said anything offensive, but . . . "

"Oh, Gor-Gor," replied Porculina gently, "no one could take offense at you, what with your darling little round apey head and your kindly smile."

"I'm not so sure," said Gorilla. "I can be very thoughtless . . . something of a brute, sometimes."

"He was probably just a very shy ghost," said Porculina soothingly. "Not everyone has your gift for friendship."

44

CHAPTER 4
Meetings and Investigations

THE NEXT MORNING, IN THE COMPANY OF THEIR host and the other two guests, Teddy, Porculina, and Gorilla enjoyed a bracing country breakfast laid out as a buffet in a small, elegantly furnished pavilion room whose walls were French windows and whose domed ceiling was mostly clear glass panels. The food was plentiful and diverse: congee (Chinese rice porridge) with toasted

45

almonds and honey, onion soup, waffles, black truffle savory custard, fresh strawberries, steamed won tons filled with leek and potato, batter pudding with blackberries, Oolong tea, pommes frites, and breads and jams. Everyone tried to taste some of everything, and Porculina succeeded; then she did it again.

Almost everyone was anxious to discuss the events of the night before, but Angus prevailed on the others to speak of other things over the table. Clearly he was still somewhat uncomfortable with any talk of mysterious forces, and perhaps somewhat embarrassed as a host who had supplied his guests with every material comfort only to find he had neglected to provide them the psychological comfort of not having to worry about being wakened in the dead of night by roving phantoms. Even when the meal was over and Teddy suggested that it was time to inspect the scene of the previous night's events, Angus still seemed reluctant, and implored the three friends to allow him first to give them the tour he had promised them.

Thus, while Rex and Ellie went off to rehearse their performances for the cider festival, le Comte de Petit-Ours, clad now in a light, stylishly casual pearl-gray morning suit and crimson cravat, conducted Teddy, Gorilla, and Porculina through the grounds of his estate. The gardens behind the château were in full and glorious flower, the river sparkled like millions of liquid diamonds, the spreading lawns and great shady trees were lush and perfectly tended, and cool breezes constantly wafted down from the murmuring orchards on the western slopes. There was also something of an exotic and mysterious quality to the grounds, as they were adorned throughout with decorative statuary in the style of Egypt in the times of the pharaohs.

"Golly gosh!" exclaimed Porculina as the party stood on the banks of the Cher staring at a small island amid the currents, separated from the embankment by about twenty yards of shallows, at the center of which a modestly tall Egyptian obelisk of pale marble — albeit with a crown of what looked like clear quartz — rose above leafy verdure and blossoming

46

vines and white rocks. "Plum pudding and custard tarts! It's like a dream!"

Angus breathed a deep and satisfied smile. "My illustrious ancestor loved everything from the mysterious land of the sphinx and the pyramids," he said.

"I have some of those too," remarked Gorilla cheerfully. "Illustrated ancestors, I mean."

"But of course," replied Angus. "Even I have heard of the legendary Grand Gorilla of Mickle Fame. Recall, I have Scottish estates. In fact, it's strange our paths have never crossed before."

"Maybe they do," said Gorilla thoughtfully. "I mean, a good many of the paths around my way cross with other paths, and who knows where they go?"

"I meant..." Angus began. Then, thinking better of it, he said, "What marvelous attire you've donned today."

"It's very jolly, isn't it?" replied Gorilla with a gratified smile. He was wearing yet another *gi*, this one a deep peach color with borders of sky-blue, tied with the same purple belt as he had been wearing the day before.

"Indeed," said Angus. "I know very little of this noble art you practice — this Idjitsu — but it seems so much more colorful than other martial arts I know of."

"That's absolutely right," replied Gorilla eagerly, his smile widening. "That's one of its chief strategies. Being colorful, I mean." He reached into a hip-pocket on his *uwagi* (his *gi* jacket) and withdrew the small volume he had been reading on the train the day before. "It's all right here. It's a way of distracting an opponent, so he'll forget whatever discourteous thing he was contemplating doing. Say he wants to grab a rubber ball from you without first saying 'please' — well, he might want to but, *oh ho!*, just as he reaches for it he can't help noticing your dashing green and violet *gi*, the one with blue stars and bunnies embroidered on its cuffs and lapels, and all at once he quite forgets to be rude and instead says, 'I say, what an absolutely cracking *gi* you've got on there!' And

47

then, just as the rubber ball has entirely slipped his mind, you politely ask him if he'd like to play with it, and he's so overwhelmed by gratitude that from that day forward he mends his unmannerly ways. This is called 'the honorable art of disarming your foe with great prettiness.'"

"Ingenious," said Angus in a tone of genuine admiration.

"It's also called the 'Flashing Cuttlefish method.'" Then, however, Gorilla scowled uncertainly and began to flip through the book. "Or maybe it's the 'Cuddly Flashing Fish method.'"

"And that belt?" asked Angus. "That... I'm sorry, what exactly would you call that color?"

"Mauve," said Gorilla, smiling and closing the book again.

"And what does it signify?"

"Cheerfulness," said Gorilla.

"I mean," said Angus, "what level of attainment does it signify? How far advanced must you be to earn a, um, mauve belt? Novice? Adept?"

"Oh, it doesn't mean anything like that," said Gorilla earnestly. "That would be showing off, which is always in very bad taste and very rude, as it might make other toys feel you look down on them. No, in Idjitsu they're called 'mood belts,' and you wear them according to how you're feeling, so your friends will know, oh, whether you need bucking up, or might like a chocolate-dipped banana, or might be up for a good game of conkers, or..."

"Oh," remarked Teddy. "Now it makes sense to me." Then he too scowled. "I mean, a sort of sense."

"I'll be changing to teal later," said Gorilla. "I feel a mood of whimsy coming on."

"It's all very deep," interjected Porculina: "full of Eastern mysteries and ancient wisdom and the like."

"Are you too a student of the art, lovely lady?" asked Angus.

"Oh, no," answered Porculina with a gigglish snort. "I don't know anything about mystical arts and ancient wisdoms. I find philosophy very confusing, especially when it's about cuttlefish and deep things like that. But Gorilla's told me how mysterious and wise it is." Now it was her turn to scowl. "Though you haven't actually told me any of the mysteriously wise things *in* the book," she said, turning to Gorilla.

"Oh, I say, there are ever so many!" said Gorilla, laying a fond and reverent hand on its cover. "For instance, there are loads of these clever things called *koans*. Freddy learned about those in Ipswich, I think. A *koan* is a short, very puzzling sort of little tale or question or such-like that just makes you think *very, very hard* about things. Just about *things*, you see. Sometimes it just leaves you hanging there, thinking and thinking."

"Oh, tell us one, please!" Porculina implored with a small, zealous snuffle.

"Well," said Gorilla, biting his lower lip. "Let me think… Oh, I know. There's one that goes like this: 'What is the nature of the hippopotamus who isn't there?' You see what I mean? You can just think and think about it all day — or at least till teatime."

Porculina gazed at him for a moment. Then she narrowed her eyes, pursed her lips tightly, knitted her brows, pressed her trotters together before her, and seemed to be exerting herself to think *very hard*. She even seemed to be holding her breath. This went on for several seconds. Occasionally, she emitted a small groan or grunt, as if she were lifting something heavy. Finally, she released her breath in a dramatic sigh of frustration and shook her head dolefully. "*Oh*, I just can't do it. It's just too deep for me."

"I understand, Piggles," said Gorilla almost tenderly. "It's not easy for beginners. It had me dazzled, I can tell you, for the longest time. But I finally came up with an answer. You don't have to, but I did any-way. Mine was… well, a very *thoughtful* answer." He fell silent here, his expression all at once enigmatic.

"Oh, Gor-Gor," said Porculina after several seconds, "don't leave us in suspense. What was it?"

With a serene look of profound wisdom, Gorilla said, "The nature of the hippopotamus who isn't there is… " — he leaned toward her, one eyebrow raised — " … *somewhere else.*"

49

Porculina's mouth fell open. Her eyes grew very wide. It was obvious that she could think of nothing to say.

"Don't strain yourself, Pigsy," Teddy cautioned. "Some things take patience."

Just then the conversation was interrupted by a dragon descending from the sky.

"Golden syrup!" squealed Porculina.

"Why, hullo!" said Gorilla amiably.

He was not, in fact, an especially dreadful dragon, given that he was a soft toy and had such plush, small, satiny wings that his flight was more like a hummingbird's than a great swooping monster's. His long serpentine body was lime-green, the fins running down his back and the triangular tip of his tail were a soft golden green with dark green speckles, and his "scales" were only scallops of moss-green dye. True, his facial features *could* have been fearsome — the crocodilian eyes, jutting ears, long snout, pointy teeth, and crimson maw — but they were arranged into so extremely pleasant an expression just now that it was obvious he intended no harm. "Excuse me," he said in a deep, melodiously Welsh accent as he came to hover a few inches above the ground, "Forgive my intrusion..."

"Ah, Draco!" said Angus, turning about. "Wonderful! This" — he said, turning back to the three friends — "is my superb chef. He's very..."

But Porculina had already pounced past Angus and, with trotters clasped before her face in irrepressible enthusiasm, was saying, "How I've *longed* to meet you!"

"Really, miss?" asked Draco, with a pleasant smile of surprise. "Bless you, but I can't imagine why."

"Why, why... you're a *genius!*" the little pig all at once blurted out.

Draco's eyes grew wide and for a moment he desisted from fluttering his wings. Before he could sink to the ground, however, he resumed his flapping and said, "Goodness, miss... I mean, well... look you, that's the kindest thing. But I don't deserve..."

"Oh, but you *do*," she insisted all the more earnestly.

"She's quite sincere," interjected Teddy. "She's something of a connoisseur... or, um, *connaisseur*... or, rather, *connaisseuse*, I mean..." He smiled. "In any event, she knows how to appreciate fine food when she's served it — like that meal last night, and breakfast this morning..."

"I'll say!" added Gorilla exuberantly. "I mean, a few banana dishes would have livened things up a bit, but otherwise it was absolutely splendid."

Draco blushed, which turned his cheeks an extremely odd murky purple. "Ah, sirs, miss, it's too kind of you. It's a humble dragon I am, and as a chef I know I've still so much to learn..."

"But how on earth did you come up with such wonderful ideas?" asked Porculina.

"Well, miss, the long and short of it is that I wanted to honor both sides of my heritage. You see, my father was a Chinese dragon and my mother a Welsh. They met when my mother was in China studying the principles of *Feng Shui*."

"*Ooo*," said Porculina, "is that another of the mystic oriental martial arts of the mystic martial oriental East?"

"Very like, miss," replied Draco. "It's a sort of... well, very mystical art of interior decorating."

"Golly!"

"You see, its general principle is that, when designing an interior space for, say, a house, you should imagine it's being built for a dragon. That way, the design of the rooms and open areas will have a flow, you see, that makes room for any inhabitant, dragon or otherwise."

"Well, that would be handy," said Gorilla. "I mean, if a dragon should come to visit, the house will be just right for him."

"And that's how a Chinese and a Welsh dragon came to fall in love and get married," continued Draco. "But those are two very different kinds of draconian culture, and both are very ancient, and much is expected from anyone who belongs to either. So, you see, it was important to me to do right by both my parents, and when I entered the Soft Toy Academy for the Culinary Arts in Aberystwyth, I said to myself, 'Look you, boy-o, you're going to become the first Sino-Cymric chef in history or count yourself a failure, and that's a fact.' And that's why I went to study in Hong Kong too."

"It's miraculous," interrupted Porculina with a deep sigh of admiration. "I don't know how you could do better."

"I think you've honored both your cultures remarkably," added Teddy.

"Ah, thank-you, sir," said Draco, lowering his eyes bashfully. "Mind you, it's always a tightrope where my families are concerned. Different things are expected from dragons in the East and in the West. In the East, it's all warm vitality and life and mystery and wisdom and flying freely among the clouds of heaven, as a portent on the wind as it were; in the West it's all greedy hoarding of treasure and an obsession with things cold and heavy, like gold, and things that shine and glitter and gleam, and lurking deep in the dark cold places of the earth; and... well, naturally, you can't please everybody all at once. Not that I don't try. To do right by my Eastern side, I try to be joyful and mysterious and warm and wise, with a quick wit and penetrating mind, while I honor my Western side by trying to be gloomy and sullen, suspicious and greedy, and even a little belligerent. But, look you, all that happens is that the two sides more or less cancel one another out, and I come across as just politely restrained... repressed, even... almost English."

"Poor chap," said Gorilla, sympathetically shaking his head.

"I strive on, though. And in the realm of cooking — there I can be true to both my heritages without contradiction. It's amazing how well Welsh and Chinese food can merge when you ask it of them."

"I've found that asking usually works," said Gorilla, sagely raising a forefinger, "at least if you ask very *nicely*. That's the important thing. I mean, it wouldn't do to point rudely at Welsh and Chinese food and just order them to get together. But if you show a little..."

Angus, who now wore the expression of someone who had not so much lost the train of the conversation as found it dashing about his feet yapping and playfully nipping at his ankles, cleared his throat and coughed into his paw. "My goodness, it must be getting near to lunch soon. Is that what you came to talk to us about, Draco?"

"Indeed it is, m'lord," replied the dragon, assuming a somewhat more officious tone. "The footmen were all engaged so I thought I'd let you know myself that lunch will be served in half an hour in the patios of the western rose garden. Mademoiselle Phant and Monsieur Homerosaurus have a lunch engagement in town, but Monsieur Longmuzzle has phoned to confirm that he will be joining you."

"Excellent," replied Angus.

The day was ideal for eating in the open. The garden's glistening green grass was enclosed by arbors and lattices, upon which the magnificent roses — red, yellow, white, and peach-pink — profusely intertwined and hung in full and fragrant blossom. A light lunch — salads, sandwiches, berries, fresh lemonade — had been laid on an iron trellis table under a large blue parasol, and at the sight of this Porculina clapped her trotters together and exclaimed, "What a pretty first course!"

At this, Angus shot a glance at the tiger footman who had just finished laying the fifth place-setting, beckoned him over, and whispered, "Please ask Draco to send along some torte or something later... and maybe some cheese and nuts..." He looked over his shoulder at the little pig. "And perhaps... six or seven other somethings..."

"I say," said Gorilla, thrusting his snout into a cluster of red roses and breathing in their perfume deeply, "I do like flowers. They're so very...*flowery*."

"Yes," said Teddy, "one can't disagree with you there."

Further conversation was momentarily curtailed, however, by a sudden sniffing and snuffling noise, coming from just beyond a low arch in an arbor thronged with yellow blossoms. Everyone turned to look just as a very large nose entered the garden. A moment later, it was followed by the rather small soft toy monkey to whom it was attached.

"Ah, my dear Muzzles!" cried out Angus elatedly, "just in time."

"Oh, ah, um," said a somewhat diffident and quavery voice, emanating with a distinctly English accent from beneath the enormous snout, "I've found you. I wasn't certain I was right, but then I caught the scent of lettuce...and of bread...and of soft toys...and of a silly remark..."

Muzzles was a rather wonderful sight, both in his extravagantly odd proportions and in his immediately obvious air of bashfulness. His snout had rather the shape of a great eggplant, though with an uncommonly broad base, and constituted perhaps two-thirds of his head. It, along with the remainder of his face, his somewhat protuberant rounded ears, and his very small hands and feet (which looked almost like mittens and ankle socks) were all of a buttery cream color. The rest of him — crown, legs, arms, a pear-shaped body that in its totality was at most two-thirds the size of his head, and a long tail — was covered in a lovely reddish-brown and cream-white fur that suggested nothing so much as the hue of sprouted bulgur wheat. And he had two oval, glossy black eyes that seemed to radiate gentleness.

"You can catch the scent of a silly remark?" asked Teddy.

"Oh, yes, indeed, dear me, yes," answered Muzzles, "if you've the nose for it."

Teddy smiled. Then he cleared his throat. "I'm sorry, I'm forgetting my manners. We haven't all been introduced..."

"That falls to me, of course," said Angus. In short order, he made the three companions known to the little monkey, who rather shyly acknowledged each by extending a hand and making a rather hesitant remark along the lines of "Oh, goodness, what a delight," or "Gracious, how nice," or "I say, what an absolutely cracking *gi* you've got on there!" This last observation was met with his hand being not politely shaken but rather heartily gripped and firmly kissed, which seemed to startle him slightly but to which he responded with a courteous "Oh, dear, thank-you kindly."

"And this," said Angus, laying a fond paw on the monkey's head, "is the very talented, very young Egyptologist William Wadsworth Longmuzzle."

"Egyptologist?" said Porculina. "How romantic."

Muzzles smiled meekly.

"He's a meteorologist also," added Angus.

"Really?" asked Gorilla. "Are there many meteors in this part of France?"

"No, um, you see..." Muzzles glanced at Angus for encouragement. "A meteorologist studies the weather. Or, well, in my case I don't really study it. I simply smell it — about four to five days in advance."

"It was his vast knowledge of ancient Egypt, however, that brought us together," said Angus. "He's the curator and chief scholar of the antiquities brought back from Egypt by my ancestor Pierre, as well as the château's librarian."

"Are you?" Teddy asked Muzzles. "That's actually very fortunate. You see, we've had something of a mystery arise, and it seems to have something to do with the library. You're the very toy I need to speak to, I think."

"A mystery?" asked Muzzles, raising his eyes in a way that suggested immediate interest. "In our library? Oh, goodness, how exciting."

Angus sighed. "I suppose we can't delay talk of this any longer," he said. "But please, dear friends, let us be civilized and continue our conversation over this splendid meal."

The meal passed very pleasantly, and the food (of which Porculina had seven helpings) was delightful — even the hastily provided torte, cheeses, nuts, and other somethings. But the principal topic of conversation was the extraordinary events of the previous night. At the description of the ghost, Angus became predictably embarrassed and made several remarks to the effect that the whole thing was no doubt rationally explicable.

55

Muzzles, however, seemed sincerely fascinated. "My goodness," he remarked at one point, just as the lunch was nearing its end, "you know, there are ever so many ghost-stories in Egyptian lore. And the curse of the Green Star supposedly has something to do with a haunting."

"Well, there you see!" exclaimed Porculina. "That marvelous Madame Lapin de Gris was right! Oh, are you going to finish that slice of cheddar, Gor-Gor?"

Angus winced. "Ghosts..." he murmured.

"Well," said Teddy, "whether she was right or not, I don't think we can delay investigating the scene any longer." He looked at Angus. "Cousin, whether the explanation is rational or... irrational, if that's possible, the fact remains that there have now been several sightings of this phantom, or whatever or whoever it is. I ..."

"Alphonse," Gorilla interjected.

Teddy paused and gazed at Gorilla blankly. After four or five seconds, and with an expression that suggested he was not especially eager to ask, he said, "I'm sorry, what? Who?"

"Alphonse," repeated Gorilla with firm confidence. "I mean, we know it's not Henry. And Alphonse seems a very likely name for a French ghost. If you think about it ..."

Teddy cleared his throat, perhaps a little too loudly. "Yes, well, indeed... who knows?" Then he looked at Angus again. "In any case, we can't keep delaying our investigation. Evidence and time are both probably slipping away."

Angus sighed deeply and, with a resigned smile, nodded his head in silent assent.

"And I believe," Teddy added, "that our friend Muzzles here should join us — if that's agreeable to him." He looked at the small monkey.

"Oh, yes," said Muzzles, "I can't imagine anything keeping me away. I'm frankly obsessed with the legend of the Green Star, for one thing. And, being English, I have to believe in ghosts."

For a time Teddy lingered amid the disorder in the old exhibition hall while the rest of the company stood apart, at the mouth of the adjoining corridor. Rolandus had joined them but was standing still further apart, keeping a watchful but discreet eye on Gorilla. Auguste had supplied Teddy with a magnifying glass and a flashlight, and the little bear was just now inspecting portions of the floor at the threshold of the open library door. Then, gradually and diligently, he began to move away from the doors in the direction of the hall's far end. There he stopped, placed his paws on the wall, and began inspecting the stones. This went on for several minutes. Then he turned back and disappeared into the library itself for several minutes more. When at last he emerged again he returned to his companions, his jaw set, his brow furrowed, and an expression of deep thoughtfulness on his face. "I almost wish your staff weren't so good at keeping things neat and clean here," he remarked to Angus. "A little more dust on the floor might have helped me form an impression of whether or not our ghost was a genuine apparition or something more solid."

Angus shrugged. "Auguste is fanatical in his devotion to cleanliness and order."

Teddy nodded. "I notice that there are Egyptian hieroglyphics engraved in all the stones of the wall at the hall's end."

"Indeed," said Angus. "As you will have noticed, Egyptian images and motifs are to be found everywhere in the château, on anything installed after the period of Pierre's expeditions."

At this, Teddy raised an eyebrow inquisitively. "So that wall isn't part of the original building?"

"No," said Angus. "Muzzles could tell you more, as he's more familiar with the records than I, but I believe it was built as a supporting wall because..." He turned to the small monkey. "That's right, isn't it?"

"Oh, yes, quite," said Muzzles. "This great hall used to extend all along this side of the central keep, and it opened out into both wings. But apparently the roof was in danger of falling in at one point, so the

57

wall was erected, dividing the hall into two equal parts. You can see the other side by going around to the other end of the keep and taking the corridor from that side."

"And do the hieroglyphs say anything?" asked Teddy. "I mean, I know they all have meanings, but as they appear in the wall here do they form coherent sentences?"

"No," said Muzzles. "I'm afraid that they're just decorative, and in purely random order."

"Ah," said Teddy softly, momentarily lost in thought.

"What is it, Teddykins?" asked Porculina. But then, as if suddenly remembering herself, she adopted her hearty slow-witted sidekick voice, cleared her throat gruffly, and said, "I say, old bear, that's significant of something!"

"Is it?" asked Teddy, emerging from his thoughts. "What?"

Porculina froze, staring at him vacantly. "No, no," she said after a moment. "You're supposed to say something like 'It very well could be, my good pig.' Something like that."

"Oh, yes," said Teddy, "of course. Well, as it happens, you're right. It could be. But now we should all go into the library. Gorilla, if you'll just show me where everything happened..." Here he paused with a small doubtful frown. "I mean, do your best to..."

"Right-o!" exclaimed Gorilla effusively, at once striding forward. "This way, you lot."

CHAPTER 5

Library Riddles and Penguin Laments

I N THE WARM GLOW OF THE EARLY AFTERNOON, the interior of the library had an almost mysterious peacefulness to it: the rich dark hues of antique wooden bookcases and old bound volumes, the soft golden light of the sun, the slightly green tint of the glass in the high windows all combined to create an atmosphere like that of a shadowy forest. As soon as the party entered, Gorilla at once went to the shelves where he had encountered the ghostly figure on the previous night. "Here we are," he said, indicating the spot with a some-what theatrical sweep of his hand. "This is where Alphonse and I had our little misunderstanding..." — and here his expression became slightly more somber — "and where I seem to have scared the poor fellow off...or offended him." He lowered his head in apparent contrition.

"Oh, twaddle!" said Porculina impatiently. "Sour milk and stale bis-cuits, what nonsense! You couldn't give offense if you tried."

Teddy, however, at first said nothing. Instead, he was slowly looking back and forth between Gorilla and the opposite side of the library, with an obvious expression of perplexity on his face. "This is unexpected," he said.

"What?" asked Porculina in a hushed and excited voice. "Some clue? Some...?"

"It's just that all the evidence I was able to find from displaced dust on the floor and such seems to indicate that Gorilla just now went to the right place on the first try." He stared at Porculina in wonder. "He got it... *right*."

An expression of pure delight appeared on the little pig's face. "Gor-Gor," she cried, dashing over to him and placing a fond trotter on his arm, "I knew you could do it!"

"Silly old Piggles," replied Gorilla, patting her trotter with equal fondness, "one never forgets where one meets one's first ghost."

"I suppose that's true," said Porculina. "After all..."

"Or one's first tricycle," Gorilla added.

Angus and Muzzles exchanged somewhat baffled glances. Then Muzzles coughed politely into the end of his tail (the only appendage on his body capable of reaching the end of his snout), and remarked, "My goodness, well, that's the set of shelves where the archives of the château used to be kept, along with copies of those of the château of House Lapin de Gris, before they were all sent to Paris for preservation — they were old and falling apart, you see, and needed repair and professional curation. Now it's simply where we put bound yearly issues of scholarly journals — on Egyptology and history and cider-making and so forth."

"Archives?" asked Teddy.

"Genealogies," said Muzzles, "and architectural logs, records of the château's constructions and renovations, and work on the grounds... and records of apple harvests... catalogues of Egyptian antiquities..."

Now, however, the shelves — which were set directly into a recessed portion of the wall — were mostly bare. The bound periodicals were stacked on the floor to either side, except for a few that had evidently been knocked over when the ghost had fled from Gorilla. Teddy approached and stared for several seconds into the vacated spaces. "Obviously our intruder wasn't looking for anything in the books that were here," he said. "He was looking for something *behind* them."

"Probably a rubber ball," remarked Gorilla with an air of certainty. "Very easy things to lose behind other things."

Teddy cleared his throat. "Well, yes, ordinarily that might be the case, but I have a feeling..." He leaned forward, switched on his flashlight, shined its beam into the wall's recess, and peered more intently. "There are hieroglyphics impressed in the bricks here too."

"I say, are there?" asked Muzzles with a sudden note of eagerness in his voice. He approached and joined Teddy, staring into the empty shelves. "Why yes, there are. I had no idea. I should have smelled them... well, except for those musty journals..." His voice dwindled away into a fascinated silence. "My, my," he murmured after several seconds.

"Do they seem to say anything?" asked the little bear.

"Well," replied the small monkey, "not as such. But..." He paused and pressed his small hands together. "I'll be dashed. May I use your torch?"

Teddy handed him the flashlight.

Muzzles took it in his mouth and turned it toward one brick on the far left of the wall behind the fourth shelf down. "Dw yu zee tht hywogwyf?" he asked. The beam of light fell upon an engraving that looked like this: ⌐⌐★.

"Yes..." said Teddy, an inquisitive note rising in his voice.

"Wlpf, id meenz..." began Muzzles. Then he parted his lips and set the flashlight down upon the shelf. "That's better," he said. "I mean to say, it indicates a single star — or perhaps a *singular* star, if you take my meaning."

"Does it now?" asked Teddy, tapping his lips thoughtfully.

"And do you see the hieroglyph on the brick next to it?"

Teddy took up the flashlight and pointed it at the next brick. The engraving looked like this: ⌐⌐°°°. "What does that mean?"

"I believe," said Muzzles, stepping back from the shelves, "that it means a green stone. Perhaps malachite, but also perhaps an emerald."

Now everyone in the room pressed forward. After a moment, however, Angus invited Porculina to precede him.

"Gosh," said the small pig, staring at the figures in the bricks. "Crumpets and blackberries and cream!"

"If I ever knew there were hieroglyphics here," said Angus when he had had his turn, "I had quite forgotten."

"Jolly pictures," remarked Gorilla. "Splendid little birdy, isn't it?" He turned. "Would you like a look, Roly?"

Rolandus, who had been quietly standing near the library door, merely observing everyone else, replied, "Not just at the moment, m'laird."

"It's really very fasc-..." said Muzzles with a distracted air, drawing near to the shelves again and then thrusting his enormous snout up against the two bricks to which he had called attention. "I say, everyone," he suddenly announced in an excited voice, "I smell something out of the ordinary here!"

"What?" asked Porculina.

"Nothing," said Muzzles.

"Oh, that's not so remarkable," said Gorilla. "I often smell nothing out of the ordinary. There's quite a lot of it about."

"I mean, rather..." Muzzles drew the air in through his nose especially vigorously. "I mean I can detect an absence...a space, I mean. Everywhere else the wall has a solid bricky sort of fragrance. But here it's more like there's a cavity. Old air and... something... parchmenty."

At this, Rolandus did at last approach. "May I?" he asked as he came to stop next to Muzzles.

"Please," replied the monkey.

"With your leave," said Rolandus, looking at each of the others in turn. "It's a talent I rarely have occasion to call upon." Turning back to the shelves, he smiled wryly and then thrust his snout into the corner of the empty shelf as Muzzles had done. For several seconds he sniffed with considerable vigor. Then he withdrew his snout again, adjusting his tie and smoothing his lapels. "I can confirm Mr. Longmuzzle's discovery," he remarked with dry dignity. "There's definitely something behind those bricks."

"Oh, oh," squealed Porculina, dancing from side to side excitedly on one pair of trotters while she clasped the other pair before her face, "a secret compartment! I just knew it! And there'll be an... ancient clue or... or... or a letter from a king to his minister of finance revealing the location of a secret cavern where there's a chest in which there's... oh... a book that has a secret code that can only be deciphered by a wise pigeon who lives in..."

"*Ahem*," said Teddy, clearing his throat, "yes, well, very... simpleminded sidekick of you..." He paused and looked at her doubtfully. "That's what you're doing... yes?" He raised a single eyebrow and smiled feebly.

Porculina stared at him vacantly for a moment, and then returned a smile even feebler than his. "Why, naturally, Teddykins... my dear old bear, ho ho." She looked to Gorilla for support. "Ho?"

But the small ape was absorbed in thoughts of his own. "Now why would Alphonse be looking for a rubber ball in a secret compartment?" he said thoughtfully, tapping his lips with his forefinger. "It's an unlikely place for it. There are some very deep mysteries here."

"No, I don't think..." Teddy began, but then thought better of it.

"Well," interjected Angus, "surely we need to get behind those bricks." He turned to Muzzles and Rolandus, who were now quietly conferring with one another a few feet away. "You say there was a... parchmenty scent?" he asked. "Not, perhaps, the scent of... well, a very large and valuable gemstone?"

Muzzles shook his head. "No," he said. "There's no emerald behind the bricks. There's no fragrance of green, for one thing, or of facets, or of extreme monetary value."

Rolandus looked at the small monkey. "I confess that even my olfactory organs are not that magically precise," he said, and there seemed to be a note of earnest admiration in his words. "It may be possible to open the compartment without force," he added, turning to Angus, "assuming that whoever built it into the wall intended to be able to get to it without tearing out the bricks."

"Maybe," said Angus, "but I'm happy to use force if necessary."

"Quite right," said Gorilla sagely. "You can't make an omelet without breaking plates."

"Eggs," corrected Porculina. "You can't make an omelet without breaking eggs."

Gorilla smiled indulgently. "Silly Piggles. Just you try to make an omelet without breaking at least one plate, and maybe as many as four. It can't be done."

Rolandus sighed deeply. "He speaks from experience, miss."

In turn, Angus, Muzzles, Rolandus, and Teddy all examined the two bricks, employing a great deal of probing, poking, pushing, and sniffing. After several minutes, when each had assured himself that the bricks seemed to be securely and seamlessly mortared in place, Angus suggested that he should have Auguste bring them a chisel and hammer.

Just then, however, Muzzles — who was crouching down and examining the lowest of the empty shelves — thrust a tiny hand in the air and called out, "Aha!"

All eyes turned to him.

"Down here," he said in a state of happy agitation. "My word, I distinctly smell a spring." And, with an almost triumphant thrust of his snout, he pressed up against another brick, only inches above the floor. There was a slight rasp and a click from the level of the lower shelf; less than a second later, a sharp pop and then a sharper crack emanated from the other, higher shelf and, as the rest of the party watched, the two bricks bearing the suggestive hieroglyphs simply tipped forward. They were very narrow front to back, as it turned out, mere slices of brick, and they fell to the bare wood of the shelf with a high mineral clink.

"You've done it, *mon ami!*" Angus almost shouted, reaching down

to clap Muzzles on the shoulder. "What a clever device," he added, leaning forward and reaching into the now exposed cavity in the wall.

"Oh, I can't wait!" cried Porculina, shaking her clasped trotters almost uncontrollably. "Oh... *cake!*"

Teddy looked at her in surprise. "That's the best you could...?"

"Oh, hush, Teddykins," she cried, watching Angus withdraw his paw again from the compartment. "Look!"

Angus was delicately blowing the dust from the folded sheet of old yellow parchment he now held in his paw. He said nothing, but merely looked at each of the others in turn, silently inviting them to share his amazement.

"See," said Gorilla, "that's not a rubber ball. Alphonse was obviously confused." He shook his head. "Poor silly old ghost."

Teddy smiled wryly at his friend. "You know," he said, "I don't think Alphonse was really a ghost." Then he frowned and swallowed loudly. "Or named Alphonse," he added, looking about in embarrassment.

"Nonsense," said Gorilla with a grin. "He was about as ghostly a ghost as you could imagine. If you'd seen him... all glowing and wavering and shimmery..."

"I think it was a disguise," said Teddy. "I think he was a... well, I suppose a burglar, and he was after whatever that is." He pointed at the parchment, which Angus was now very gently unfolding.

"May I ask," Rolandus suddenly said, "precisely what we have discovered?"

"A map," said Angus quietly, staring at it intently.

"Of what?" asked Porculina.

For a moment Angus said nothing, turning the piece of parchment around in his paws, looking it over side to side and up and down. "I'm not entirely sure. It's very abstract, but it seems to be a map of the estate here, but... an incomplete one. It's only half a map, in fact. The bottom of it is missing. Here, all of you, have a look." He took the parchment to a small round reading table standing near one of the windows and spread it out so that the whole party could look at it. The image on the paper was indeed very spare of detail. It was mostly green with a coil of blue in one corner, as well as a few patches of deeper green clearly meant to represent trees, and in one corner there was a bright red X. There was writing as well in one corner, just above what was clearly the rough edge where the rest of the parchment had been carefully torn away. "See, here," Angus continued, "one of the bends of the Cher, and here what I assume is part of the eastern lawn of the château. But this part of the map doesn't show the position of the château itself, or give any indication which bend in the river this is, or what the scale is..."

"That red X, however," remarked Teddy, "seems to be marking a spot." He looked a little further down the page. "And I think we can be certain what's hidden there." He pointed to the writing on the parchment. It was in a florid antique hand, but quite legible. The first line read: *Ces huit vers devraient suffire à conduire le sage vers une pierre maudite...* "These eight lines of verse should... suffice to guide the wise to a curséd stone," he translated.

Porculina gasped.

This was followed by only four lines more, however, the remainder having been taken away with the missing other half of the parchment.

"Oh, oh, *please*, what does it say?" asked Porculina in an almost agonized tone of curiosity.

Angus read the lines aloud:

> *Les eaux sombres coulent, dans cavernes profondes;*
> *Le soleil ne les voit, ni ne touche leurs ondes.*
> *Notre nuit cède au jour, puis retombe la nuit;*
> *Où les ombres règnent, aucune aube ne suit.*

When he had finished, he nodded, almost as if in approval. "Classical Alexandrines," he remarked. "Quite elegant."

"Those sound jolly," said Gorilla. "What did you call them again...?"

"Alexandrines," offered Teddy.

"It's a kind of biscuit, I think," said Porculina, "soft and tasty, and you dip them in lime blossom tea, and then that summons up all sorts of interesting memories and such. That's what the poem must be about."

Angus turned to the little pig and, with a small but gallant nod of the head, said, "Nearly correct, lovely lady. An Alexandrine is a traditional poetic form consisting in couplets written in a strict meter, hexameters in fact, and governed by some very rigid rules. It was used in a great deal of classical French verse, and especially in the verse of France's golden age of drama."

Porculina scowled. "Then you can't dip it in lime blossom tea at all?"

"I think you could," remarked Gorilla, looking closely at the map, "but it would likely get it very wet."

"I think you are confusing them with madeleines, dear lady, which are, I quite agree, delicious when dipped in lime blossom tea. I have many fond memories associated with them."

Porculina smiled. "I remember, yes..." For a moment a dreamy expression began to spread across her features. But then she started, as if being shaken awake again. "Oh, but what does it mean? The poem, that is?"

"Well, if I had to render it extempore," said Teddy, looking the lines over again, "I would say it means..." He paused, spent a few moments in thought, and then with a slight smile of his own said:

> The dark waters flow, down in the deep caves;
> The sun neither sees them, nor touches their waves.
> Our night yields to day, then night falls again;
> Where reign the shadows, there follows no dawn.

"Excellent!" said Angus. "A very fine rendering indeed!"

"Well," said Teddy with a touch of a bashful smile still on his lips, "one tries to be..."

"That may be what it *says*," interjected Porculina, "but I still don't know what it *means*. Is it some sort of clue or not?"

"Yes," said Teddy. "At least, it *was* a clue—a clue in eight lines, according to what's written here, but we have only the first four. The rest of 67 the poem is with the other half of the map. And apparently that's also the part of the map that makes it clear what our half represents."

"So very curious," murmured Angus.

"What?" asked Porculina.

"Well, a map was made, with a clue written directly on it, and an X marking a spot that I assume is the place where the alleged Green Star of the Nile is supposed to be found. But then the map and the poem are neatly divided in two. Presumably that was done by my ancestor Octave de Petit-Ours, or someone of his time who had a hand in concealing the Green Star."

"So as, I would guess," said Teddy, "to make it all the more difficult for the gem to be found if the château were to be occupied or burgled by ... villains or ... oh, whoever might be looking for it."

"Alligators," said Gorilla with an air of authority. "Or buffaloes."

"*Bien sûr*, my dear cousin," replied Angus, looking toward Gorilla with an arched eyebrow but otherwise failing to react to him. "Again, I suspect this is all some sort of game, for the entertainment of children. But, whatever the case, to whom then would the other half of the map have been confided? And who might have it now?"

"Might that have been recorded in the château's archives?" asked Teddy.

"Perhaps. But, as Muzzles told you, those are now in Paris."

For a moment, Teddy was lost in thought, his head bowed. Then he looked up, toward the door of the library, and slowly turned his gaze rightward, almost as if following the corridor outside through the wall. "The same archives that include the architectural logs," he said softly. All at once he clapped his paws together and announced, "Right, then, one of us needs to make a trip to Paris."

"Oh, oh, oh ..." Porculina cried out, bobbing up and down eagerly.

"Not to go shopping, however," Teddy added. "To visit a library."

Porculina fell silent and instantly ceased moving — so instantly, in fact, that she remained momentarily poised on the tips of her trotters.

"Before we decide who's to go," said Teddy, smiling kindly at the little pig, "we'd better conduct a few investigations here." He turned to Angus. "With your permission, cousin," he said, "we had best talk to the staff first. How many of them keep quarters here at the château?"

"Like servants of old?" asked Angus with a small laugh. "Only Auguste. The rest live in town or thereabouts."

Teddy sighed quietly.

"Is there anything wrong, cousin?" asked Angus.

"No," replied Teddy. "But that means, I suppose, we should talk to Auguste first. And ... he strikes me as the sort who might take offense."

"Oh, not at all," replied Angus. "I assure you. He is mild of manner and takes umbrage at nothing."

"How dare you!" spluttered Auguste a quarter of an hour later, drawing himself up magnificently and raising his eyes to the ceiling. "I have never been so offended!"

It was still early afternoon and the sumptuous summer daylight, streaming in through the grand widows above the great staircase, filled the foyer where the penguin, Angus, Muzzles, Teddy, Porculina, and Gorilla were standing in the rough approximation of a circle in the middle of the floor. Rolandus stood several paces away, apparently lost in thought.

"But I only asked if we might have a moment of your time," replied Teddy.

"Which is to say you think my time usually wasted," said Auguste, "since I'm only a waddling, lazy, flightless bird."

"Oh, come, come, Auguste," protested Angus, "surely you can't think ..."

"With respect, *mon seigneur*," said the penguin, slightly lowering his beak so that his eyes could just meet his employer's, "what I think is that, after last night's lamentable events, this ... this ... *policeman*" — he pronounced this last word with an audible note of distaste, bordering on

69

revulsion — "naturally chooses to attach suspicion to me... to interrogate me, as though I were a common footpad... a... a *walrus*... no doubt to persecute me, for political reasons."

"Auguste," said Angus, his voice beginning to betray his impatience, "you are speaking of one of my guests. I implore you to regain your composure."

"Honestly," said Teddy, "I'm not accusing you of anything. I'm merely asking for your assistance in reconstructing the events of last night. And, besides" — he scowled in mild perplexity and looked to Angus for help — "I don't have any idea what your politics might be."

Slowly, the penguin lowered his beak entirely. His expression remained stern, but now more cautiously reserved than angry. "You mean to say you are unaware that I am — and proudly so — one of those loyal toy penguins who still cherish the delectable fragrance of the secret violet?"

"The secret...?" Teddy again looked at Angus, this time with brows inquisitively knitted.

Angus sighed. "Oh, yes," he said quietly. "That's a way of saying that he looks back fondly to the days of the Emperor. The first one, of course."

"Napoléon," pronounced Auguste firmly, thrusting out his chest and again raising the angle of his beak.

"Oh!" squealed Porculina. "That's my favorite pastry of all! Or at least one of the top fifty or so!"

"I say," chimed in Gorilla, "you mean those flaky cakey things with the cream filling and the lovely icings that go so well with bananas and..."

"*Quelle atroce!*" the penguin fumed, lowering his eyes and looking about at the three guests incredulously. "I mean the Emperor Napoléon Bonaparte. The greatest leader that France or Europe ever knew. Surely you have heard of him!"

"Yes, I knew who you meant," said Teddy. "I'm a little surprised..."

"I didn't," remarked Gorilla cheerfully, "but, whoever he is, his pastries are wonderful. Especially when topped with banana slices and..."

"I'm a little surprised," continued Teddy, "that you think that would be a concern of mine just now... or something of which I was even aware."

Now Auguste's expression became positively icy. "You're unaware of my family's distinguished past?" he asked. "Did you never think to inquire, once you'd seen the unmistakable air of... of imperial resplendence I carry about with me, like a crushing burden of... glory?"

"*Ummm*," Teddy replied after a pause of two or three seconds, "to be perfectly frank, no."

The penguin simply continued to stare at him, now in impassive silence.

Angus cleared his throat. "I should, of course, have told you," he said. "My apologies, Auguste. Yesterday was so hectic, and last night so dreadful, that it quite slipped my mind. Needless to say, I usually boast of my butler's extraordinary, ah, pedigree to guests, but..."

Auguste now lowered his head lugubriously, and in a somber voice said, "No, *mon seigneur*, I quite understand. I delude myself that anyone cares about such things any more. The glory of the past, *hélas*, is like the forlorn, dying echo of a bugle above an abandoned battlefield... the fading fragrance of that now forgotten violet, withered in the winds of winter."

"Now, now," said Angus, laying a gentle paw on the penguin's shoulder.

"But once," Auguste continued, raising his eyes and staring earnestly into Teddy's, "my family name positively shone with the luster of France's age of imperial greatness. My ancestor Valentin was a trusted member of the Emperor's staff. He was the imperial map-holder." The penguin pronounced this last with a flourish of pride.

"*Ooooo!*" said Porculina. "That sounds so splendid."

Auguste's expression at last softened and he turned a faint and melancholy smile on the little pig. "It was, mademoiselle, I assure you."

"What did he do?" asked Porculina, her eyes now widening in sincere fascination. "Valentin, I mean."

"He" — Auguste paused here for dramatic effect — "*held maps.*"

"No!" gasped Porculina in astonishment.

"Yes!" answered the penguin, no less emphatically. "When the Emperor gathered with his ministers to plan his campaigns, such as, say, invading

Russia...which, incidentally, wasn't really the best idea he ever had, but no matter...well, there was only one soft toy the Emperor felt he could invest with the high dignity and precious honor and demanding duty of holding the map, perfectly still so that everyone could see it, and even of rotating it when necessary. And that was my...my illustrious ancestor Valentin."

"I say," cried out Gorilla, "I have some..."

"But now," Auguste continued, taking no notice of the interruption, "see to what estate I, his descendant, have...well, descended. Been reduced, that is. Just a butler. A cringing servant to the vile, degenerate aristocracy of the old regime." Here he raised his eyes and looked at Angus. "If you don't mind me putting it that way, *mon seigneur*," he added.

Angus briefly raised his eyebrows. "Not at all, my good fellow, not at all." Then he shrugged. "But I do not recall ever having seen you cringe."

"There, there, old chap," said Gorilla in a deeply sympathetic voice, taking a step toward Auguste. "You mustn't go on so. Why, we've all had regrets. I wanted a blue tricycle for my birthday once, when I was just a little fellow, and got a green one instead. Or maybe that was last year. Mind you, as soon as I saw it, I thought, 'I say, that's a jolly shade of green!' and I was happy it wasn't the blue one after all. But you see what I mean."

The penguin looked at Gorilla with a slightly mystified expression. "I'm not entirely sure..." he began.

"I know just the thing to buck you up," Gorilla added, his kindly smile becoming a genial grin. He reached into the pocket of his *uwagi* and withdrew his small handsome copy of *Idjitsu-Do*. "There are some very deep things in here about being at peace with your life." He flipped through the book, backwards and forwards a few times till he came on what he was looking for. "Ah, here we go. Just listen to this: 'No goose ever prospered by wishing he were a duck. No duck ever became enlightened by seeking to be a goose. The duck grows great in his duckiness, the goose in his goosiness.'" Gorilla closed the book with an expression of satisfaction on his face. "See what I mean, old fellow?"

Auguste stared at Gorilla with a look of pure incomprehension. Then he narrowed his eyes and turned away, heaving a morose sigh. "*Hélas,* monsieur," he said, "I am neither duck nor goose. I am a penguin, and of a proud lineage, and for my kind there is no longer any place of honor. I cannot, as you say, be at peace. I can simply become resigned to my station, and conduct myself with poetically listless dignity."

"Oh, don't say that," replied Gorilla in a voice warm with affability. "There's a place for everyone *somewhere*. Why, that whole chapter is called 'Having a Place in the Universe.' Mostly it's about seating arrangements for meals, of course. I think Freddy often uses the word 'universe' to mean dinner-table. But you see my point. The universe is a very largish place, actually. You'd be surprised."

Auguste continued to stare away at nothing in particular. "I am not overly fond of the universe," he remarked in an even more doleful voice. "I find it frequently ... *impertinent.*"

The penguin was still vibrating with emotion, even after twenty seconds had passed, when Muzzles loudly cleared his throat and remarked, "I say, everyone, not to be a scold or anything — goodness, nobody likes a scold — but perhaps we should, you know — not to be pushy, mind you — we should get back to the, um, questions that Mr. Bear was going to ask. If it's not presumptuous of me to say so."

"Yes," said Teddy, "thank-you. You're right. It's not at all presumptuous of you." He turned back to the penguin, who had now directed his eyes dramatically toward the high windows above the landing. "Monsieur Auguste," he said, "how far away from the library were you at the time of last night's disturbance?"

Auguste slowly turned a frigid gaze on the bear. "So you do suspect me."

"To the contrary," said Teddy with a small, courteous bow of his head, "I rely on you."

Auguste continued to stare for a moment or two, but then sniffed haughtily and said, "Very well. I was asleep, as any civilized toy would be at that hour." Here he cast a scornful glance at Gorilla, who grinned back at him cheerfully. "I was dreaming," he continued. "Dreaming, in fact, of the Emperor's court. It is only in my dreams, you see, that I may imagine myself immersed in that imperial splendor. Only in my dreams that I may visit that vanished glory. Only..."

"Yes, quite," interrupted Teddy with a cough. "And it was the sound of the armor being knocked over that roused you?"

"Yes," said Auguste, "and from a particularly glorious dream, if I may..."

"And you saw and heard nothing out of the ordinary before retiring for the night?"

Again the penguin stared at Gorilla. "Well, there was that rather extraordinary...attire that his lairdship wore to dinner."

"Oh, I say," exclaimed Gorilla, clearly flattered and delighted, "it really is a wonderful bit of tailoring, isn't it?"

"As I say," replied Auguste, "extraordinary."

"What I meant..." Teddy began.

"I know what you meant," said Auguste. "The answer is no. Everything appeared to be in order when I lay down to dream my sad and beautiful dreams."

"I see. And were there any other members of staff on the premises at the time?"

"Sadly," said Auguste, "the days when domestics were boarded on the estate, and were willing to be called upon at any hour, are long gone."

"As they should be," Angus interjected. "France is a truly democratic republic now."

Auguste winced at this but then continued: "They departed all together an hour before I went to bed. They all have apartments in town. They went by van, driven by the two new footmen... their names elude me."

"Bow and Wow," said Angus with a tolerant smile.

"Yes, I recalled that it was something suitably...mundane. Anyway, I myself saw them out at the gate and locked it behind them. We are at present without a gatekeeper. We used to have one, a tortoise named Monsieur Teste."

"Oh, I have oodles of toy tortoise friends," remarked Porculina.

"Not a toy, mademoiselle," said Auguste. "A tortoise of flesh, blood, and carapace — and refined sentiment. I miss his cultured conversation. But one day he said to me, 'I'm a mere 89 years old, Auguste my dearest friend, and still in the full vigor of youth. I must see something of the world before I grow old and retire to some rock on a beach.' And so he went. I just received a postcard from him the other day. He was in the Caribbean, preparing to sail a catamaran in a race..."

"Yes," Teddy once again interrupted. "So, then, who else was here who might have heard or seen something? On the grounds I mean? Gardeners?"

"Our gardening is done by a service that comes thrice weekly in season... sadly," replied Auguste. "Only the orchard-keepers, Onyx and Obsidian, and of course Monsieur Kippernicus, who likes to sleep out by the shore of the island in the Cher, are here after dark."

Teddy turned to Angus. "Then we had best speak to them next."

"As for myself, however," Auguste continued, "I was, as I have said, fast asleep... rocked gently in the arms of Morpheus... enjoying the company of the Emperor..."

"Ah ha!" Porculina suddenly cried out, her voice slipping into the slightly lower register of her slow-witted sidekick persona, "and can either of them corroborate your alibi?"

The penguin drew himself up in alarm. "What?" he asked indignantly. "*Alibi? Corroborate?* Either of *whom*?"

"Well, Morpheus, of course," replied Porculina with relish, raising one trotter for emphasis, "or the Emperor!"

Teddy sighed and lowered his head. "Well done, old girl," he said. "You're discharging your role admirably."

CHAPTER 6

Inconclusive Interviews

"I PROBABLY SHOULD HAVE KISSED HIM ON HIS FLIP-per again," remarked Gorilla to Porculina. "It really does cheer a chap up."

"Really, Gor-Gor," replied Porculina, "you mustn't go about doing that all the time. It's not meant for all occasions, you know."

The party had just crossed the broad expanse of gleaming green lawn on the western side of the château, passing in and out of the shade of giant elms and oaks, and was now reaching the low open gate into the orchard on the rising slope of the hill — except, that is, for Rolandus, who was still hanging back somewhat, evidently absorbed in his own thoughts. Along the way, Angus (obviously still reluctant directly to address the matter of the ghost) had been talking about the various specimens of Egyptian statuary liberally scattered about the grounds — a little obelisk, a miniature reproduction of the temple of Karnak, a small sculpture of the Sphinx with the face of a teddy bear — and on this year's splendid apple harvest. As soon as the advance party had passed the gate, with Rolandus pausing just outside, Onyx and Obsidian appeared from under the branches of some trees farther along the central pathway and immediately approached them, the former at something of an eager canter, the latter at a more plodding pace. There was an air of peace here — almost magical — under the fruit-laden boughs. A soft but constant breeze was whispering and sighing through the leaves and causing the pale golden sunlight dappling the path and the grass below the trees to undulate and flicker.

"Cream and toffee," said Porculina, "it's just like a dream."

"Why, hello," Onyx whinnied delightedly as she reached the visitors, two or three long strides before her brother, "what a delightful surprise!"

"Hello," murmured Obsidian quietly, ambling slowly behind her as if carrying a heavy load. "What's wrong?"

Onyx laughed a musical, neighing laugh and fluttered her long eyelashes whimsically. "That's my brother at his most gracious," she said. "For him, a visit must be the result of a tragedy."

"Oh, nothing wrong at all, my dear friends," Angus hastily replied.

Obsidian snorted and lowered his head morosely.

"At least, nothing is wrong with the orchard... which you keep magnificently."

Onyx smiled widely. Obsidian did not.

"But, as you may have heard by now, there was a rather... well, a rather absurd incident last night, near the château library, where... well, where my very esteemed guest, Laird MacGorilla, encountered... someone who may or may not have been... someone whom he takes to have been... well, someone who no doubt gave every evidence of being..." Here Angus winced, momentarily pursed his lips as if in pain, glanced down at his own feet in what looked like mortified bashfulness, and said, "Someone who appeared to be... *un fantôme*... *un spectre*." He coughed uncomfortably.

"My, how exciting!" cried Onyx, lashing her tail joyously in the air.

"Isn't it just?" enthused Porculina. "It's just absolutely... *marmalade*."

Obsidian, however, merely heaved a sigh so deep that it terminated in a kind of groan. "I knew it," he said. "The harvest had been going so well, something monstrous was bound to happen. Well, we'd better cancel the festival. Tear down the bunting. Bring down the marquee. No point in hoping for better days..."

"Now, now," protested Angus, all at once animated, "none of that, surely! From what our good Laird MacGorilla tells us, he was evidently a rather timid ghost. Why, he dashed away screaming, as best I can tell..."

"I didn't mean to scare him," remarked Gorilla glumly. "I was even careful to creep up behind him tippy-toe so as not to startle him before I had a chance to introduce myself."

"You see?" said Angus. "Manifestly a craven sort of ghost. If, um, he is a ghost... which is very unlikely."

"Yes," interjected Teddy in an exceedingly calm and sober voice, "that's what we're trying to establish."

Obsidian, however, did not seem to be comforted. "Things had been looking up," he said in a dreary voice. "This promised to be the best harvest festival in many a year. Now it will live on only in infamy. *Quelle dommage!*"

Onyx rolled her eyes. "Oh, pay him no mind," she said. "He'd be devastated if the festival were canceled. He's so proud of this year's harvest. He simply loves prophesying doom. A drop of rain falls, and he foretells a great flood. A gentle breeze passes by, and he begins muttering about tornadoes." She turned to her brother with a smirk. "We don't get tornadoes here, you know."

"There's always a first time," replied Obsidian mordantly.

"Yes," said Teddy, "well, I agree with my cousin that there's no need to panic. Really, I'm sure everything will be all right."

"Then why have you come," asked Obsidian bleakly, "if not to deliver crushing news?"

"Just to ask a few questions," said Teddy, "in the hope that one or both of you might have seen or heard something. You see, I'm not yet convinced of the, um, immateriality of our visitor last night. But apparently he was definitely on the luminescent side, as it were, and so if he made his retreat anywhere across the grounds he might have been visible."

"Luminescent?" asked Obsidian, raising one eyebrow.

"Very glowy," said Gorilla. "I noticed it right off. Like that... oh, what's it called? Bosphorus?"

"Phosphorus?" asked Porculina.

"That's the ticket," said Gorilla. "You couldn't miss it. The very first thing that I thought when I saw him was, 'My, he seems to be glowing quite a lot!' And also, 'I say, I'll wager he's a ghost.' Not to mention, 'I wonder if he likes rubber balls as much as I do.' And..."

"Right," said Teddy. "And I understand that the two of you live right here? In the orchard?"

"Yes," replied Onyx. "It's lovely. We've stables, of course, but I prefer to sleep out under the stars."

"Good way to catch a terrible cold," said Obsidian. "I sleep under cover."

"Oh, goodness," said Onyx in a tone of fond exasperation, "it's summer. In France."

"No reason to court danger," muttered her brother.

"I like stars," observed Gorilla. "Especially at night."

Teddy opened his mouth to say something to Gorilla, then paused, shook his head, and turned back to the horses. "So, then, did either of you chance to see or hear anything out of the ordinary late last night?"

"Not I," replied Onyx.

"Nor I," said Obsidian. "I wasn't out risking pneumonia, you see."

"Did either of you perhaps merely momentarily *think* you might have seen something? And then perhaps forget?"

The two horses exchanged glances and then shook their heads in unison.

"On any other occasion recently, then?" asked Teddy. "Have there been any disturbances or inexplicable phenomena?"

"Not here," said Onyx. "Nothing I could see from the orchard."

"Nor I," said Obsidian again. Then, for good measure: "Not that I would be out in the bitter chill."

For a few moments, no one said anything. Then, with an amiable smile, Teddy asked, "You're happy here, I take it? I mean, in general, not just at this moment — happy working in the château's orchards?"

"Oh, I'm happy anywhere," replied Onyx with a whickering giggle.

Obsidian stared at Teddy in silence for a few moments, and then croaked, "Ecstatic."

Onyx sighed. "Excuse my brother. He loves the orchard, and he loves apples. And he's very fond of Monsieur le Comte. It's just that... well, this is our second career, and he's never really lost his taste for the..." — she batted her eyelashes shyly — "... his taste for the stage."

"The *stage*?" cried Porculina in delight. "You were performers?"

"Dancers," said Onyx.

"*Hmmph*," said Obsidian.

Here Gorilla interrupted, his brow slightly furrowed. "I can't say I know what a stage tastes like." Then the furrows deepened. "No, hang on. Now that I think of it, I've fallen on my face a few times on the local community theatre stage, when playing a part in the yearly Hogmanay pantomime." He grimaced faintly at the memory. "I don't recall it tasting very pleasant at all." He looked at Porculina and said, "It really is an odd cuisine they have here."

"I mean, he misses our days on stage together," said Onyx sweetly. "Oh, you're so witty!"

"Am I?" asked Gorilla, his expression instantly brightening. "That's jolly nice to know."

"Really," moaned Obsidian, "must we rehearse old regrets?" He breathed deeply. "I'm resigned to my fate."

Onyx smirked gently. "As I say, we were dancers. It's called dressage, of course, when horses do it. We were especially famous for our soft-hoof routines."

"Well, then," said Porculina, "why ever did you give it up?"

"It wasn't our choice," said Onyx, slowly shaking her head. "We had a business partner. A *human* business partner."

"Oh dear," said Porculina, "caramel and marshmallows, I think I know what comes next. You must never do business with humans. They're... well, they're not as morally competent as soft toys. It's not their fault, but many of them... especially the ones who didn't grow up with, say, a teddy bear to guide them, are capable of some very dastardly dishonesty."

"Then you understand," said Onyx. "But he was more reckless than dishonest. He invested all our money in a new venture — an invention for automatically slicing and serving pies — and it all fell through. We went into debt. We had to disband the whole dance troupe — there were seven of us, you see — and then sell the little theatre we owned in Amboise to a local dramatic society. If it weren't for our expertise in apples, we would have had nowhere to go. We love it here, of course, but my brother, he hasn't smiled since we sold off the last of our tap-horseshoes."

"My, that's so sad," said Muzzles, "if you don't, um, mind my saying. Not to presume, of course..."

Gorilla thrust out his lower lip mournfully for a moment. Then his smile returned. "I say, I'm very rich, I believe..."

"And so am I," interjected Angus. "My dear friends, I knew of your former life on the stage, of course. You were the most celebrated dressage duo in the whole of France. But I thought you had retired of your own free will." He turned to Teddy. "I am mortified to learn only now that I have been availing myself of their services without knowing that in their hearts..."

Obsidian moaned quite loudly now. "Really, Monsieur le Comte, you've nothing to reproach yourself for. As it happens, when I came here I was more than ready for retirement. I was defeated. These past three years have been a welcome refuge from..." — he momentarily glanced sideways, in the direction of the estate's faraway front gate, as if casting a cold eye on the whole world beyond — "... *out there.*"

Onyx smiled gently. "We love the orchard," she said.

Angus was now deep in thought, however, and it was some moments before he spoke. "I should like to discuss this with you again," he said at last, "perhaps after the festival has passed."

Onyx very prettily flashed a smile at him. "Of course."

Obsidian shrugged. "To dance well, one must have the will to dance," he said. "But we can always... talk."

"Well," said Teddy, clapping his paws together, "I'm so grateful for your time. We really must be going. The investigation has only just begun."

"Oh, but you can't go yet!" cried Onyx. "You haven't seen the orchard properly at all. And you really need to taste some of our apples."

"Oh, yes!" said Porculina with peculiar emphasis. "It's been ages since lunch!"

"It's been only..." Angus began, but then paused, smiled gallantly, and with a small bow of the head said, "Indeed, how thoughtless of me, dear lady. You must be famished."

Twenty minutes later, the small company departed the orchard, leaving behind a number of apple cores — one each for Teddy, Gorilla, Muzzles, and Angus, a dozen for Porculina. Their destination was now the nearer bank of the Cher, on the far side of the estate, but the day was so lovely that no one objected to the long, leisurely stroll that would take them there. They made their way along the southern verge of the gardens, enjoying again the late summer flowers, the cool glistening grass, the shade of the ancient trees, the delectable breezes from the west. They even paused for a time before the reflecting pond over which the eastern wing of the château stretched, its white stones and gleaming windows and stately arches perfectly mirrored in the still water, like a second, parallel, upside-down château existing in some fairyland below.

"Nougat and icing!" exclaimed Porculina, albeit in a subdued and breathy voice. "Butter and cream!"

"I concur," said Teddy.

"You know," said Gorilla thoughtfully, "if one were in the mood for a bracing game of pirates, this would be just the spot. I mean, if one had a pirate ship, and some treasure, and a few cutlasses…" He cast a hopeful glance in Angus's direction, one eyebrow raised inquisitively.

"Well," said Angus after a few moments, "we do have a few cutlasses lying about, I imagine, in our collection, though I believe they're made from *papier-maché* …. As for a ship…we have a rowboat or two of course." He smiled graciously. "I'm afraid we lack many of the refinements to which you are clearly accustomed."

Gorilla looked momentarily downcast, but then turned a kind smile on his host. "There, there," he said, reaching out to lay a hand gently on Angus's shoulder, "not every castle has *all* the marks of elegance about it. We do what we can."

"Most gracious of you," replied Angus.

Soon the party resumed its journey to the river, arriving at the western bank across from the pleasant little island amid its currents just as the afternoon sun had begun to turn the water's surface a burning gold. For a few moments, everyone except Rolandus — who yet again assumed a station some distance away, his head bent in thought — stood in silence taking in the scene. The elegant white marble Egyptian obelisk at the island's center shone out amid the verdure and blossoming vines, its apex glittering like a diamond. But then Porculina stretched out a trotter and said, "Oh, look, there he is… there they are, in fact. *Yoo-hoo!*"

Her companions all turned to look, and indeed two gleaming forms — one pale blue, the other soft gray — were coursing toward them just below the surface of the waves, sending out smooth glassy billows from their flanks. The faces of Kipper and Jacques Tout-en-Dents emerged from the water at their feet. Then, in a sparkling and agile arc, the dolphin positively vaulted out of the river, soared high above the grassy bank, 83 landed lightly upright on his tail flukes, and at once executed a courtly bow from his waist. "What a delight!" he said with a high, cheerful series of clicks.

A moment later, the shark had somewhat more laboriously made his way out of the river as well, dragging himself up by his fore-fins and then also standing upright, if a little unsteadily, on his tail-fins. "My goodness," he said in his deep, velvety avalanche of a voice, his rows of sharp white teeth terrifically bared, "what a splendid denouement to my visit. We were just at the end of our tea, and I was about to leave. It would have been such a pity to miss you."

"Tea and... buttered toast?" asked Porculina with obviously genuine interest.

"Unfortunately, no," replied Jacques. "I share your passion, as you know, for buttered toast, and for buttered toast with marmalade, but it's rather hard when one is having one's tea in a river. Toast tends to get soggy, you see, which quite ruins its... toastiness."

"Oh, yes," said the little pig. "I hadn't thought of that. So what do you eat with your teas?"

"Riverweed," said Kipper. "Biscuits made from riverweed. And riverweed salad. And riverweed marmalade. And, of course, apples."

Porculina pursed her lips thoughtfully for a moment. "Is it nice?"

"Dreadful," replied Jacques.

"Revolting," agreed Kipper.

"Oh," said Porculina.

"Except for the apples," added Kipper.

"Oh, yes, they're lovely," agreed Jacques.

For a few seconds, no one seemed to know quite what to say. Then, however, Gorilla remarked, "Well, it's always jolly to have friends visit. That's the important thing."

Kipper smiled, in that kindly and distracted way he had, and replied, "Yes, indeed, it is. So, to what do we owe the happy circumstance of your visit?"

"Not entirely happy," replied Angus. "Actually, the circumstances are mildly distressing... or, at any rate, perplexing." Here, however, he fell silent, again obviously a little embarrassed.

After a moment, Muzzles spoke up. "If I may... I mean, excuse me, everyone, if it's not impertinent, perhaps I can explain. You see..."

In as few words as he could manage — in the spaces between the *excuse-mes* and *if-you-don't-minds* and *I-mean-to-says* — the soft-spoken monkey related the events of the night before. At all the most startling details, the dolphin and the shark exchanged amazed gazes, but neither said anything until the story reached its end.

"Goodness gracious," clacked Kipper, and then emitted a faint whistle.

"It's incredible," said Jacques.

"I'd have said so myself," replied Muzzles, stretching out a hand to his right, "but Laird MacGorilla can confirm what he saw if you ask..."

Here, however, words failed him. Everyone had turned to look at Gorilla only to find that he had retreated several yards away and was now deeply engaged in what looked like a vigorous attempt to imitate a hopping frog, albeit one heavily burdened by the woes of the world (that or a sack of potatoes). It was not exactly a graceful performance. It consisted mostly in his propelling himself forward from a crouching position only to tip over his own arms and land on his snout in the grass. But he was clearly enjoying himself, as one could tell from his intermittent but cheerful exclamations of "*Sproing!*"

"Oh, Gor-Gor!" cried out Porculina in an exasperated voice, "what on earth are you doing?"

"Hey-ho, everyone!" called back Gorilla, rising to his feet and brushing off his *gi*.

"Is this the best time for your Idjitsu exercises?" asked Teddy.

"Oh, it's not that," replied Gorilla merrily, strolling back to his friends. "I was trying out that marvelous leap of Kipper's. That was really something, now, wasn't it?"

"Oh, but you're not a dolphin," said Porculina.

Gorilla, reaching the party and coming to a halt, stared at the little pig quizzically. Then, in his most indulgent voice, he said, "Silly, silly old Piggles... I thought you already knew that."

"Of course I knew it!" squealed Porculina, a hint of frustration in her voice. "Withered cabbage! What I meant was..."

"I think," interjected Teddy, "we shouldn't keep these two good toys from their tea much longer."

"Actually, I was just leaving," remarked Jacques. "We've finished."

"Even so," said Teddy, "we mustn't keep you. We just came to ask whether either of you might have been here last night at the time of the, uh, apparent haunting, and whether then either of you might have seen or heard anything out of the ordinary."

"For myself," Jacques rumbled, "there is not much to tell. At that hour, I was warm in bed in my room at Château Lapin de Gris, fast asleep. And indeed, my friends" — he smiled amiably (and horrifyingly), nodded his head ceremoniously at Angus and then at Porculina — "if you would excuse me, I am even now somewhat late in returning there. I have an appointment." And, waiting only for the polite farewells of the other toys, he more or less flopped backward over the edge of the riverbank, slipped into the water, and began rapidly swimming away upstream, all at once rendered graceful and lithe by immersion in his proper element.

"I say," Gorilla began, "I wonder if I could swim like that!" He took two steps toward the river.

The other toys immediately lurched toward him, forming something of a cordon between him and the river.

"That might be imprudent," said Angus.

"Yes, um, indeed..." said Muzzles, "...if you don't mind me saying."

"You haven't the tail for it, you see," said Teddy gently.

At this, Gorilla cast a quick glance backward over his own shoulder, thrust out his lower lip in disappointment, and then nodded his head slowly. "I suppose I haven't."

"And you're not waterproof like him," added Porculina. "Do you want to have to be laundered and hung up on a clothesline to dry this close to dinner?"

Gorilla sighed deeply. "Right you are, old girl," he said. "And, besides, we're forgetting why we're here."

"We...?" Teddy began with an incredulous expression.

"Now, then," said Gorilla, turning to Kipper and all at once assuming an officious manner, "did you happen to see Alphonse late last night?"

For a moment, the dolphin stared at Gorilla in silence, an utterly vacant look on his face. "Who?" he finally asked.

"Alphonse," Gorilla repeated. "You know, the ghosty chap...glows... sort of floaty and wavery."

"He's... he's called *Alphonse?*" Kipper looked from Teddy to Porculina to Muzzles to Angus in mystification.

"I doubt it," answered Teddy after a few seconds. Then, smiling kindly at Gorilla, he added, "But it is the right question... more or less. Did you see any sign of, well, a spectre... a phantom. Or anyone at all. Were you here at the time? Were you awake?"

"I was both," said Kipper, beginning to stare off into the distance and to smile to himself. "It was a lovely night. A full moon, cool breezes, the flowing of the babbling, sparkling river..."

"Well, then," said Teddy, "again, did you see or hear anything worth noting."

"I can't be sure," replied Kipper after a few more seconds had passed. He was still gazing away, almost dreamily now. "The moon was out, as I say, and the scene was so enchanting... and enchanted... well, I fell into something of a reverie. But, now that I think of it" — he lowered his eyes and met Teddy's gaze — "it's just possible I did glimpse something... out of the corner of my eye. I seem to remember a kind of flash or glimmer... soft and like... like starlit gossamer. But I think I assumed it was just a patch of moonlight quivering in the shadows of the trees as the breeze blew through them... or perhaps a small troupe of fairies or sprites dancing across the lawn."

"Of...*fairies?*" said Angus. "You are, of course, being whimsical?"

The dolphin looked at him. "It was the sort of night one might expect them to be out," he said simply.

Angus arched his eyebrows. "Very well," he murmured. "Ghosts and now fairies. The Enlightenment apparently never happened in this part of the country."

"I like fairies," said Gorilla. "Good chaps all."

"And where did you see this flash or glimmer... or these fairies?" asked Teddy.

"It would have been more or less in that direction," said Kipper, waving a flipper vaguely toward the long stretch of shady lawn extending from the eastern end of the château to the Cher. "But I may have imagined it... or may be imagining it now. I'm something of a dreamer, you know."

"So I gather," said Teddy with a genuinely gentle smile. "Is there anything, though, you can add to the description?"

Kipper shook his head. "I'm afraid not. I was too absorbed in gazing at the scene... and the sky... the moon in particular. It was nearly full, and was shining like... like a pure opal..."

"That's all you were doing?" asked Teddy.

"Well" — here Kipper's expression became mildly abashed and he lowered his eyes as if somewhat embarrassed — "that and... composing."

"Composing?" asked Porculina. "Music?"

"Verse," said Kipper. "Poetry. I write poetry... after a fashion."

"I had no idea," said Angus.

"I say," said Gorilla, "can we hear some? Have you written any poems about bunnies?"

"It's not very good, you see. It's really just for my amusement... absurd little ditties. I don't like to mention it. And when a famous and celebrated poet like Monsieur Homerosaurus is visiting, I'd be ashamed to recite any of it."

"Come, come," said Angus, "I have no doubt it's better than you think."

Kipper said nothing.

"Well, then," said Teddy when several seconds had passed, "I'm very grateful for your time and your help. We'll leave you now."

Making their farewells, the party left Kipper there and began their return to the château.

For several minutes, the dolphin watched their forms retreating, lost in thoughts of his own. And, when his visitors were a good distance away, far out of earshot, he began speaking to himself, in his most distracted voice:

> Cold wanderer upon the oceans of the stars,
> Bright lantern in the highest tower of the mind,
> Whose timeless beauty nothing earthly ever mars,
> We look to you when straying in the dark, to find
> A fire to fill the mirrors of our souls. We take,
> Like you, our radiance from a font of living light,
> To purge our glassy essence — too long opaque,
> And hidden from all eyes, and captive to the night.

Then, turning about, he dived gracefully back into the river.

A few minutes later, as the party was making its way back to the château, Rolandus drew near to Teddy and, with a faint, polite cough, said, "Excuse me, sir, if I may make a suggestion..."

Teddy paused. "Please," he said. "I'm always eager for your opinion."

"Not an opinion on this occasion," replied the dog. "It simply occurs to me that, since someone must go to Paris to visit the château's archives at *la Bibliothèque Nationale du Patrimoine des Peluches*, I might be deputed for the task. I'm familiar with that *arrondissement* and..."

"Oh yes," Teddy interrupted, with a ringing note of relief in his voice. "I can't think of anyone I'd trust more to examine the archives thoroughly and notice anything relevant. But I feared to ask you, in case you were unwilling to leave Gorilla... well, unattended, let's say, for an entire day."

Rolandus sighed, casting a glance at the slowly withdrawing, merrily bobbing figure of his employer. "Yes, I acknowledge that it is something of a grave risk, with potentially ... *catastrophic* consequences. But I believe I can trust you and Miss Porculina to keep an eye — and perhaps a restraining paw and trotter — on him till I return. I'm due for a day off, in any event, and Paris ... well, let's say I have connections there. I shall depart before dawn. All I shall need for access to the archives is Monsieur le Comte's *carte blanche*, of course."

"I'll ask him to write it up for you directly," said Teddy. "Again, I'm grateful."

Rolandus turned another glance toward Gorilla — now picking himself up after apparently having attempted a particularly energetic hand-stand — and remarked, "I hope you can say that tomorrow also."

CHAPTER 7

A Canine in Paris

T HE LATE MORNING SUN SHED A MILD, BUTTERY
golden brilliancy on Paris's 18th *arrondissement*, the historic dis-
trict of the largest Parisian *peluche* community. Le Boulevard
des Amis Moelleux, which rose gradually up the slope of Montmartre
all the way to the summit where the Basilica of Sacré-Coeur stood
(shining in the clear daylight like a towering fairytale palace of white

jade), was full of the bustling forms of soft toys — and occasional human beings, cats, or dogs — going about their daily business. A clamor of cheerful voices filled the avenue and rang from the lovely old stone façades of the shops lining it on either side. Open stalls of flowers and fruit overflowed with vibrant colors and delicious aromas. Even the dust raised from the street by hurrying feet cast a faint, sparkling haze over the scene, giving it something of the enchanted quality of an Impressionist painting. It was, in short, like any ordinary summer day in the city, until...

"*C'est Monsieur Rolandus!*" an excited, positively bell-like feminine voice cried out, followed by a tiny ecstatic yap. The words had been uttered by a small, daintily fetching black poodle (of the flesh-and-blood variety) in a bright yellow silk scarf who had just emerged in an obvious state of eager happiness from one of the streetside establishments, over the glass front doors of which a sign reading "*Café et Pâtisseries de Fifi*" was affixed to the lintel. "*Regardez!*" she called out again, pointing with a paw that she also could not refrain from waving up and down in elation. "*C'est vraiment lui!*"

And indeed, strolling at a brisk but easy pace along the pavement, stylishly swinging his walking stick with its cut-crystal handle back and forth, was the unmistakable figure of Rolandus, not now attired as a valet but wearing instead a dove-gray, long-tailed morning suit of the most elegant cut, a winged collar, a light blue cravat fastened in place with a silver pin, and a small crimson carnation pinned to one lapel; he wore a monocle in one eye, and on his head sat a tall, glossy top hat with a silk band. No sooner, moreover, had the little poodle called attention to him than a dozen or so of the soft toys in his vicinity immediately ceased what they were doing and, with a loud babble of delighted exclamations, gathered around him to shake his paw and clap him affectionately on the shoulders and even (in good French fashion) to kiss him lightly on both cheeks. Several happy, hearty cries of "*Mon ami!*" and "*Mon bon chien!*" rose out of the happy din.

A few moments later, having politely extricated himself from the excited crowd, Rolandus reached the small poodle; they embraced in the manner of old friends, and then stood apart to look at one another.

"It is so good to see you again, Fifi," Rolandus remarked with evident sincerity. And then, looking about at the sidewalk tables filled with patrons, he added, "And how nice to see your little establishment thriving so wonderfully."

"Oh, Rolandus," replied the little poodle, a note of impatience audible despite her effusive tone, "why did you not let me know you were coming?"

"I did not know myself," said Rolandus, "until the opportunity presented itself. But I would have visited sooner or later in any event."

"O, *la!*" said Fifi. "That's no excuse." Then, before Rolandus could say another word, she took him by the paw and led him to the sole unoccupied table in front of the café. "Sit here — no, I won't hear any nonsense about what a hurry you're in. You must tell me why you're here, and how long you'll be staying. I'll have hot milk and biscuits brought directly."

Rolandus opened his mouth to protest, but the little poodle had already hurried away to place the order. So, glancing about, exchanging a few courteous greetings with some nearby customers, he removed his hat, set it on the table, and took a seat under its open parasol. Some moments later, Fifi returned, bearing a tray with a steaming cup of boiled milk and a small dish of almond wafers, madeleines, and a miniature croissant.

"There," she said, setting her burden down and seating herself across from Rolandus. Then, with arched eyebrows and a hopeful smile, she asked, "Is it possible you've at last decided to move to Paris, after all? Are you here for good?"

"Alas, no," replied Rolandus, lifting a biscuit to his lips and taking a small bite. "Ah, delicious," he murmured. "No, my dear Fifi, I fear I'm here for the day only, at least for now. I have come to take care of some business."

The poodle's smile resolved into a small frown and she sighed. "I assumed as much," she said, "but hope springs eternal in the canine heart. But surely — surely — you're not still working for that... that ridiculous monkey in Scotland... the banana-grower."

"Ape," Rolandus corrected, "not monkey. And yes, I am still in the employ of Laird MacGorilla, and very happily so. I'm very fond of the old toy, in fact."

"But, Rolandus..." Fifi heaved another sigh, pursed her lips, and shook her head in perplexity. "But you — *you* — such a *bon vivant*... a *boulevardier*... *un chien du monde* — a dog of the world... well, it's absurd. You should be here, the heart of civilization, the homeland of all gallant souls..."

"I'm not sure I'd go quite so far as that..." Rolandus began.

But Fifi, her expression now becoming at once tender and regretful, continued without pause. "Scarcely a day goes by that someone sitting at one of these tables fails to mention your name to me and to wonder aloud when we'll see you again. There are many here who... who care very much for you, and should be very... very happy to see you every day." She momentarily dropped her gaze.

Rolandus smiled gently, raised his cup to his lips to take a sip of the milk, set it again in its saucer, and then said, "Fifi, would you be so kind as to accompany me to the ballet tonight?"

Fifi raised her eyes and with a small, fond smirk said, "You're trying to get around me, you... you hound, you."

"Nonsense," replied Rolandus. "I'm trying to make my brief stay in Paris as delightful as it possibly can be, and there's no one whose company delights me more than yours."

At this, the little poodle's expression softened. An involuntary but sweet smile appeared on her face and her eyes positively sparkled behind a flutter of eyelashes. "Charmer," she said quietly. "Always gallant, as I said. Oh well. Yes, of course I'll go to the ballet..."

"Why Monsieur Rolandus!" a thin, crackly voice exclaimed. "What a joy!"

Rolandus raised his eyes to see a small teddy bear standing beside the table in a red waiter's jacket, his beige fur worn smooth, his head almost perfectly spherical, an ancient pince-nez perched on his snout.

"Why, Gaston, you old pin-cushion, are you still working here...?"

An hour later, having at last disentangled himself with some difficulty — and some reluctance — from his friends and acquaintances, Rolandus approached the immense, imposing marble structure of *la Bibliothèque Nationale du Patrimoine des Peluches*, one of the two or three largest edifices in the city (in keeping with the central importance of soft toys in French history). A long flight of broad steps rose from the pavement to its front portico, which was sumptuously adorned with soaring columns, elaborate bas-reliefs, and colossal specimens of elegant statuary (a teddy bear holding a pinwheel, a bunny doing a headstand, a snail dancing in a tutu, a frog in an aviator's hat and goggles, an octopus holding a flower in one tentacle and sniffing it delicately, a very fluffy billy-goat doing nothing in particular, and so forth). Rolandus for his part was now carrying a bouquet of white lilies, acquired on the advice of Fifi, who had told him that the chief librarian was of a romantic cast of mind and would be all the more helpful if presented with flowers.

When he reached the top of the stairs, Rolandus entered the grand foyer of the library and removed his top hat. It was a gorgeous sight: all peach and pearl marble and gleaming brass and polished rosewood furnishings under a high vaulted ceiling at whose center was a dome of softly rose-hued glass. And there, in the very center of the floor, standing on a compass-rose of green, red, and blue marble mosaics and gazing up distractedly into the glowing dome, was a lovely lady toy dog. She was a large toy, relatively speaking. Her face was round and symmetrical, her ears elegantly floppy. Her fur was a combination of warm ginger brown (at her limbs, jowls, throat, and eyebrows) and glossy raven black (everywhere else). Her nose was a large triangle of black felt, as dark as coal, and her eyes — when she lowered them to greet Rolandus — proved to be a deep liquid brown. For a moment she stared at her visitor with a mild, dreamy expression, as if lost in thought. Then, in a sleek, satiny voice, she said, "Why, hello there."

Rolandus was slightly surprised. "Greetings, mademoiselle," he replied. "But how did you know that I speak English?"

"From the way you wear your cravat," she replied simply, "and of course the polish on your shoes."

Rolandus's eyes widened. He looked down at his cravat in bafflement, and then at his shoes. "I had no idea one could..." he began.

But then the toy dog laughed and said, "Don't try to understand. One has an eye for such things or one doesn't. May I help you, though? I'm the chief librarian here. My name is Guinevere. And... oh, are those for me?" She was now staring covetously at the lilies.

"Why, yes, indeed," replied Rolandus, regathering his wits. "How discourteous of me. Yes, I brought these for you." And he approached Guinevere and extended the bouquet toward her with a courtly nod of his head.

At first tentatively, but then robustly, Guinevere placed her nose in the bouquet and sniffed. And sniffed. Then finally, with a sweet smile, she took the flowers in her arms, cradled them for a moment, and said, "How very considerate of you. I adore flowers, and lilies especially, and white lilies especially especially. Come, let's put them in water. My desk is this way." She turned to her right and began walking toward the large rosewood counter that stood to one side of the foyer, near a large staircase leading to open galleries above. "I assume you're here for some reason other than bringing me flowers," she called over her shoulder.

"Well, yes, as it happens," replied Rolandus when they had reached the counter and Guinevere had taken her place behind it. "I'm here to do some research into one of the special collections here."

"Let me guess," said Guinevere, producing a pretty crystal vase from below the level of the counter, evidently kept there for just such occasions

96

as these. "Like me, I imagine you're devoted to the literary heritage of the great age of soft-toy chivalry, aren't you?" Before Rolandus could answer, she had slipped into a small alcove behind her desk, from which she returned a moment later having filled the vase halfway with water. "The truly great age of French toys," she resumed as she unwrapped the lilies, placed them in the vase, and arranged them to her satisfaction. "The last truly romantic period of toy culture, when our valiant and gracious forebears and fore-bears laid the foundations of French civilization as we now know it." She sighed. "An age of knights and damsels, great ladies and scheming kings, of small pink rabbits with great hearts and daring octopods..."

"Well I do indeed enjoy the chronicles of those days," Rolandus interrupted, "but just at present..."

"I spend the better part of every day in that section of the stacks," she continued. "We've the loveliest reading room in the mediaeval section, with stained glass windows and a roof with an octagonal spire supported on the loveliest little mediaeval squinches and..."

"Squinches?" said Rolandus, furrowing his brow.

Guinevere laughed yet again. "Yes, of course. Perhaps you're not perfectly familiar with the architecture of the period."

"Apparently not."

"But one can sit there daylong under those squinches reading those marvelous tales of daring velveteen squirrels and taffeta toads, chewing on a stick of cinnamon — cinnamon's wonderful for aiding one in contemplation, you know — and never have to think of the... *dull* modern world at all."

Rolandus cleared his throat. "It sounds like paradise, mademoiselle," he remarked, "but just now..."

"Oh, call me Guinevere please," the toy dog interjected. "And what's your name?"

"Rolandus, mademoiselle... ah, I mean, Guinevere."

"I'm so pleased to meet you," said Guinevere. "Shall I conduct you to the mediaeval section now?"

"No... no thank you," said Rolandus. "I would love to visit it, but perhaps on some future date. At present, I've been charged with a task of some urgency, and of some secrecy. You see, I have been given leave by le Comte de Petit-Ours — you may know of him — to examine his family's archives, which are stored here." And at this he produced the letter of *carte blanche* from his coat pocket.

Guinevere stared at the paper for a moment and then sighed again. "Well, that's boring," she remarked. Then, her eyes narrowing, she brought her nose close to the letter and sniffed at it several times. "No, it's still boring," she said after a moment, raising her head to look at Rolandus inquisitively. "Are you sure? It's such a waste of a trip to Paris."

Rolandus nodded. "Yes, I'm sure — though I take your point."

With a small shrug and a resigned smile, Guinevere retreated into the alcove behind her desk again. When she returned — this time after roughly five minutes — she was carrying a green folder. "Very well," she said. "It's only a very recent château, it seems, designed by some modern fellow named Leonardo. I'll take you to the collection." And, with a final appreciative glance at her lilies, she stepped out from behind the counter. "This way, then," she said.

Rolandus spent the next several hours alone in one of the large special collections rooms, with all seventeen bound volumes of the archives of le Château de Petit-Ours in stacks upon a large reading table, along with large files of old maps and architectural designs and assorted unbound documents and incidental records. He had brought along a small notebook and a mechanical pencil in the pockets of his morning coat, and he used them now to make copious notes in his impeccably neat and attractive paw-writing. At times he sighed in boredom, at times he paused to tap his lips thoughtfully with the pencil, and on one or two occasions he uttered a quietly astonished "Ah ha." He examined the volumes, he pored over the maps, and he lingered at length over two large architectural sketches from two different centuries, even making minute copies of details from both in his notebook. It was late afternoon and the sunlight entering through the high room's high windows was beginning to turn a pale but sultry gold when at last he closed his notebook and began replacing the archival materials on their shelves and in their files cabinets. Just as he was about to pass through the doorway leading out, however, he came to a halt and stared back at the shelves. "Leonardo...?" he murmured to himself. He spent another twenty minutes in the reading room, again consulting the first of the bound volumes, which earlier in the day he had merely skimmed through.

That night, he attended the *Grand Ballet des Peluches*, accompanied by Fifi. The little poodle looked resplendent in her emerald-green satin gown and tastefully simple string of pearls, and Rolandus could scarcely have been more dashing and debonair in his black tie and tails. The ballet was *Goat Lake*, danced to perfection by a troupe of toy cats, snakes, water-buffaloes, hippopotamuses, and one toucan. The performance was so spectacular that no one complained of the absence of any goats. After summoning a coach — drawn by four toy rhinoceroses of varying hue — and seeing Fifi to her apartment, Rolandus caught the very, very late train back to Amboise. He tried to sleep in the compartment he had reserved for himself, but had little success, as the discoveries he had made in the library continued to circulate through his mind.

Meanwhile, back at the château, Gorilla was deeply engaged in *very important business*. He had been diligently at work in his room, late into the night, at maintaining his rubber-ball-bouncing technique at peak level when it suddenly occurred to him that he was feeling a little peckish, and that, more troublingly, he had not tasted a single banana since departing from Dover.

"Well, that can't be good for one," he said to himself, pressing his lips together thoughtfully. "Hmm," he added a moment later, now addressing the red rubber ball in his hand, "I'd best go get one from the pantry. I don't want to risk the dire effects of banana-deprivation — which I'm sure must be very dreadful." So, setting the ball aside and rising from the carpet where he had been sitting in his very splendid bright yellow *gi* and lime-green belt, he took the lit candle from his bedside table and confidently strode out into the corridor and down the great staircase. Fifteen minutes later, he recalled that he had no idea where the pantry was. Five minutes after that, he recalled it again. And then five minutes later he realized that he was quite contentedly wandering about in the dark, humming one of his favorite bagpipe tunes ("The Witty Wildebeests of Fife"), but not actually getting anywhere in particular. This, he concluded a little later, was probably an inefficient method for procuring bananas.

Then, all of a sudden, as he turned one corner, he had the strangest feeling that he was somewhere he had been before. He looked around intently to make sure it was not his bedroom. It appeared not to be, since there was no bed and it was not really a room. ("Still," he murmured cheerfully, "it doesn't hurt to make sure.")

All at once, he knew the place: it was the large open hall where the library entrance was located; he recognized it from any number of features: the soft glow of the lights in their wall-sconces, the high shadowy ceiling, the suits of armor in their various heroic poses, the dark looming wall at the far end, the luminescent ghost crossing the floor in the direction of the library like a wavering candle-flame, the library's magnificent oak doors, the slate floor, the...

Suddenly, a thrill of delight went through Gorilla. "I say," he cried out in irrepressible happiness, "Alphonse! There you are!"

The ghost screamed again, turned about — still like a wavering candle-flame, but now like a wavering candle-flame that had received a genuinely unpleasant shock — and stared across the vast dim space at Gorilla. At least, assuming that was his face...

"I was afraid I wasn't going to see you again," Gorilla continued, beginning to hasten in the ghost's direction. "I'm terribly sorry if I hurt your feelings the other night..." But then he paused and placed a finger thoughtfully upon his lips.

As yet the softly shining figure had not moved. It simply stood where it had been when Gorilla first called out to it, seeming to hover indecisively. Then, a rather frail sort of croak emerged from it: "*Ooaaghhh... rrp.*" It coughed.

Gorilla continued to stare, his finger still poised upon his lips, his head tilted quizzically to one side. After a moment, he asked, "Are you feeling quite all right, old fellow?"

The ghost cleared its throat, seemed to shake its "head" once or twice, stretched out its short "arms" with a certain imposing grandeur, and this time positively bellowed out a groan: "*Oooaaaaaghhhhaahhhrrr... rrp.*" It coughed again.

Even so, Gorilla clapped his hands together genially, not wanting to be rude or unencouraging. "That's splendid, old man. Bravo!" Then, his brow furrowing, he placed his hands on his hips. "Something's slipped my mind, though. I say, could you assist me with something?"

The ghost did not reply.

"It's just, I seem to remember something from earlier... something Teddy said... you know Teddy — small beige chap with a bow-tie, bearish sort... good fellow all around... we were at school together, you know..."

Still the ghost stood in silence, just glowing.

"Well, anyway, Teddy... the bear, that is... well, he's a detective, and I'm sure there was some reason why he was a bit... well, not *upset* so much, but even so somewhat concerned about your being here the other night. Something about..." Then a broad smile of recollection appeared on his face. "Oh, yes, I recall," he said, clapping his hand to his forehead. "Are you here by any chance to steal a map from the library that will show you where an ancient Egyptian emerald is hidden so you can steal that too?"

Now the ghost did move, but only in the sense that it started trembling and seemed to draw itself up anxiously.

"Well?" persisted Gorilla in a friendly voice a moment later.

For a few moments more, the ghost did nothing; then it seemed to lower its head a mite sheepishly.

"Now, now, old fellow," said Gorilla, his heart melting at the sight, "you mustn't be hard on yourself. Why, we all do silly things from time to time. And I've known one or two treasure-thieves in my time who turned out to be absolutely capital chaps, once they'd thought better of their... roguish ways."

The ghost stared at him.

"You don't mind if I put it that way, do you?" asked Gorilla.

Then, all at once, the ghost began to shake, extending its small ecto-plasmic forelimbs to either side again, and attempted one more terrifying groan. The result was singularly unimpressive: "*Ooo... rgh... cfff... f...*" This was quickly curtailed by a series of feeble coughs.

Gorilla shook his head pityingly. "Old fellow," he said, "you probably need some hot chocolate or something... something warm for that cough."

But then the ghost seemed to reach a decision. Wheeling about, it started to run away from Gorilla and in the direction of the far wall.

"Oh, wait!" yelled Gorilla. "Don't dash off again."

The luminous figure halted and appeared to look back over its "shoulder."

Gorilla pursed his lips, once again becoming deeply thoughtful. Then he said, "I expect I'd better apprehend you. Look, don't be alarmed. This is a martial art called Idjitsu — it's ever so clever — and it's perfectly safe... so long as you don't stick a hand into it or anything like that. Here..." He began to crouch down on his short, stout legs, but then paused, as if something else had occurred to him. Lifting a forefinger, he helpfully remarked, "Don't be startled either if it's a bit... *energetic.*" And at this he raised both hands above his head, his thumbs pressed to his forefingers, swelled his chest, and then flung himself headfirst into the air, immedi-ately tumbling head-over-heels across the floor. "Whoa-hahhhh!" he cried as he came to his feet again and now flung himself just as exuberantly

102

to his left, again tumbling, but now also sprawling and sliding. "Wheee!" he called out, regaining his feet once more and charging to his right, spinning on the toes of one foot, and careening into the wall, from which he bounced back into the middle of the floor and landed in a sitting position. "Ho-ho-ho!" he exclaimed.

All this time, the ghost had indeed remained immobile, seeming — if nothing else — frozen in confusion.

"Ha-ha!" Gorilla added, now rolling forward and waving his legs in the air. "Giddy-up!" Then he came to his feet again, his arms flailing wildly. "Hip-hip-hoorah!" he yelled... But then there was a soft but distinct *thonk*. He had accidentally struck himself in the head with one of his freely waving arms; and, at the sound of it, an old memory floated into his mind — something about what one is supposed to do when one is *thonked* on the noggin. But he could not quite recall... it was an elusive memory... until... "Oh, that's right!" he said to himself. "Old fellow," he called out, "if you'll excuse me for a moment, I believe I'm supposed to lose consciousness for a bit... just as a matter of good form. I'll be right back with you." Then, stretching his short arms over his head and yawning deeply, he gently lay down on the floor, turned over into a more comfortable position, and closed his eyes. As he was doing so, however, he saw the shining figure of the ghost vanishing away in the distance, seeming to pass right through the wall.

"Oh, I say," he said, sitting up straight again and quite forgetting to lose consciousness, "there he goes again." He shook his head. "Alphonse, you poor old thing, you're so shy. So touchy." He sighed. Then, after a moment, he added, "Oh, bother."

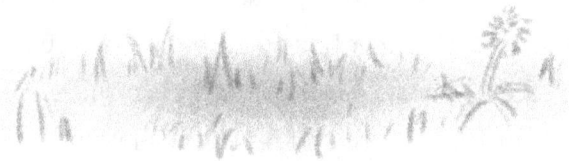

CHAPTER 8
The Way of Idjitsu

THE NEXT DAY WAS A MILD AND GOLDEN ONE IN the Loire Valley, warmed by the summer sun but cooled by constant breezes, and luncheon at le Château de Petit-Ours was served outside, on the broad front lawn, overshadowed by the great elms and oaks. Under the sighing boughs and amid the constant fluctuations of sunlight and shade, the expanse of gleaming grass seemed to tremble with a liquid fluency, like the surface of an emerald lake. The central stage that had been erected for the cider festival now stood in the center of the green, and a number of small, brightly colored pavilions were arranged along its margins. Beyond that, the grandeur of the château itself took the scene into its embrace: the white-washed stones, the glossy gray tiles of the great roofs and the slender turrets, the sparkling waters of the reflecting pool over which the further reaches of the eastern wing stood — all of it seemed almost to float in the glorious daylight.

Long tables had been set out on the grass, moreover, heaped high with delicacies from Draco's kitchen, and Angus's guests and friends were strolling about in the open air or seated at smaller tables that had been laid with cutlery, eating and drinking and happily conversing. Auguste, with his usual supercilious air, wobbled from one party of guests to another, inquiring after their wants in a way that clearly suggested he was only *just* willing to pay attention to their answers. A company of footmen — Bow and Wow among them, but otherwise composed of the tigers who regularly served at dinner, all of them wearing immaculate white jackets and gloves — saw to everyone's needs, while Draco generally hovered (literally) about the food, seeing to it that no platter or carafe remained empty for long, and constantly issuing orders to his staff (such as "Look you, boy-o, see to it that that Hunan Methyr Pie is properly covered!").

Everyone was there. Angus, in a dapper but casual linen suit, drifted elegantly among his guests and spoke to each with polished courtesy. Madame Lapin de Gris, seated in state in a wonderful old Bath chair of wicker pushed by a toy toad in livery, observed the scene as she sipped daintily at her medicinal tea. Kipper and Jacques Tout-en-Dents, for their parts, were at a table with Muzzles, the three of them engaged in obviously affable banter. Rex and Ellie were standing somewhat away from the others preparing for a rehearsal of their festival performances. The former had one of his tiny forelimbs extended in a dramatic pose as he ran through his vocal exercises ("*Hah-hee-hum-ho-hi!*" he intoned. "*Hem-hoof-horp-har-hrump!*" — and so on), while the latter, wearing a pink tutu and ballet slippers, stood at a minuscule set of exercise bars bolted to the back of the stage, limbering up. Onyx and Obsidian were at another table devouring hay and apples, she cheerfully, he dourly, but both with considerable appetite. And some two dozen other guests were there as well, of every imaginable soft-toy kind. In general everyone seemed to be at his or her ease — except, that is, for Teddy and Porculina, both of whom wore expressions of distinct alarm. They were standing under a particularly shady elm with Gorilla (who was more than merely at ease, reclining on the grass in his *gi* of plum-purple and belt of ochre).

"But Gor-Gor," Porculina was exclaiming, "vinegar and sour cherries, why didn't you wake us... or call for help?"

"Oh, I doubt you could have helped me find Alphonse," Gorilla replied with a thoughtful frown. "I mean not after he disappeared through the wall. The trail went rather cold at that point."

"Yes," protested the little pig, "but that's not the issue. We should all have been informed that the... the ghost had been seen again. Stale muffins!"

"Well, I told you at breakfast this morning. And, after all, I was... occupied last night."

"At what?" cried Porculina. "What could have been more important?" Gorilla shook his head fondly. "Always so impatient," he said. "Dear old Piggles."

"Well?" she persisted.

"Are you aware," asked Gorilla, "that we haven't had a single banana since leaving England? Surely that can't be good for a body. I mean, ghosts are ghosts — they come and go, here one minute and gone the next — but bananas are the stuff of life. It's well known that a banana a day keeps the seamstress away."

"So you found a banana?" asked Porculina.

"No, not as such. Not really. But I did find a jolly nice parlor or sitting room or whatever you'd call it, with an absolutely splendid sort of... well, a divan, I think you call it, and I had no sooner rested my head on one of its cushions than I fell asleep. I was woken up this morning by Auguste... who seemed a little... sad, I suppose. A little sad. He must have thought I was unsatisfied with my bed, but I told him..."

At this, Teddy cleared his throat in that way he had whenever he wanted to prevent a stream of conversation from becoming a river. "Yes," he said, "that's... a wonderful tale. But let's return to the earlier incident, if we may. Are you absolutely sure you saw the ghost go..."

106

"Alphonse," corrected Gorilla, lifting an admonishing finger.

"Yes, of course, Alphonse..." Here Teddy paused. "What am I saying?" he muttered to himself. He cleared his throat. "But, once again, you're absolutely certain you really saw, um, *him* disappear right through the wall?"

Gorilla smiled. "Well, as Cousin Freddy says, you can't be *absolutely* sure of anything. There's a wonderful tale he tells..."

"I'm sure there is, old fellow," said Teddy, "but let's hear that in a little bit. Can you concentrate... just this once?"

Gorilla wrinkled his brow. He pressed his finger to his lips. He tugged his ear pensively. He stared intently into the empty sky. He breathed deeply. And then: "I say, you two, shall we go boating today?"

"Oh, Gor-Gor!" moaned Porculina.

"Yes?" Gorilla asked politely.

"Can't you answer the question first?" she said.

"What question is that, old girl?"

Teddy's shoulders sank. "We were asking," he said, gently but also with a faint tone of defeat, "whether you can say for certain that the ghost last night truly vanished right through the wall."

"Alphonse, you mean?" asked Gorilla.

"Yes," said Teddy, his voice now barely more than a whisper, "if you like."

"Well," replied Gorilla, pursing his lips and squinting, "I can't be utterly absolutely totally undoubtedly certain. My eyes were half closed just then. But I was also looking right at him, and one moment there he was, rushing toward the wall — all shimmery and glowy and wavery and such — and then, just a moment later, there he wasn't. Well, there can only be so many explanations for that." He gazed off into the distance for a moment. "No more than seven or eight, I should think."

"Seven or...?" Porculina began, but then thought better of it.

"Anyway," Gorilla continued, now rising to his feet in a leisurely manner, "I did all one could to detain him. He simply wouldn't be detained. Still, I used all my art — the art of Idjitsu, that is — and if that doesn't do the trick, nothing will."

"Um, yes, well..." Teddy said, coughing into his paw. "I'm sure you did all you could to..."

"Shall I show you?" Gorilla suddenly exclaimed.

"Well, it's not necessary just..." Teddy began.

But Porculina's voice drowned his out: "Oh, yes, please! I've never seen you doing your Idjitsu exercises."

"I'm not sure that's advisable..." Teddy again attempted to interject.

But Gorilla was now far to excited to hear him. "Right-o, old girl!" he cried. And then he leapt — or sort of leapt — into a crouching position. Then as before, he paused. "You're prepared for it to be very *energetic*?" he asked Porculina kindly.

"Oh, I hope so!" the little pig replied eagerly.

"Jolly good," said Gorilla, and he raised his long arms and pinched his forefingers and thumbs together above his head. Then it began. "Whoah-hahhhh!" he cried at the first tumble head-over-heels. "Wheee!" as he sprang again to his feet and lurched into a sprawl and slide across the grass. "Ho-ho-ho!" he positively bellowed once on his feet again, spinning on one foot's toes until he bounced off the tree trunk and landed on the grass in a seated position.

Teddy raised a paw, "Yes, that was very..."

But Gorilla was far from done. Rolling forward in a sort of somersault and then waving his legs wildly in the air, he cried out, "Ha-ha! And hee-hee, while we're at it!" Then, bounding onto his feet again, his hands once again forming a pair of pincers above his head, he shouted out, "Giddy-up!" For a moment he held this pose with a wide grin on his face. Then, flailing his arms wildly — but this time not striking himself on the head — he finished with a triumphant "Hip-hip-hoorah, and a Happy New Year!" For several seconds he stared at his friends with a happy expression on his face.

"Oh," gushed Porculina at last, "Gor-Gor, that was...well... *magnificent!*"

Teddy stared at her for a moment without saying anything. Then, slowly, he turned his eyes to see all the other guests and servants, distributed everywhere over the lawn as they were, staring in their direction in absolute silence, eyes wide, hands and paws and tentacles poised motionlessly over plates and platters and goblets and glasses. Teddy cleared his throat. Finally one figure — that of Auguste — detached itself from what for now looked like a gallery of statues and began to approach the three friends. As he reached them, a soft murmur began to stir among the guests and, one by one, they began moving and talking again, turning back to one another, but still casting the occasional frightened glance back in Gorilla's direction, in the unmistakable and tremulous manner of the survivors of a truly harrowing experience.

"If Laird MacGorilla is quite finished with his, ah, convulsions," said the penguin somewhat stiffly, "may I offer him a refreshing glass of apple cider? It has a very soothing effect."

"Why that's jolly thoughtful of you!" exclaimed Gorilla. "Yes, please. For all of us."

With a slight, surly nod of acknowledgement, Auguste said, "*Mon plaisir,*" and turned to gesture for one of the footmen — a small tiger carrying a tray of elegantly slim fluted glasses filled with cider. When Teddy, Porculina, and Gorilla had their drinks in hand, the footman withdrew and Auguste asked, "Is there anything else I can do for you . . . to calm your nerves, that is?"

"I say," said Gorilla, his voice becoming earnest, "you wouldn't happen to have any bananas about, would you?"

Auguste arched an eyebrow. "I imagine I could ask chef whether we have any specimens of that . . . *pedestrian* fruit."

"Splendid," said Gorilla. "But it's not really very pedestrian, you know. It's really very stationary . . . rarely goes walkabout, as it were — if that'll help you find it."

For a moment Auguste said nothing, staring vacantly into Gorilla's great beamingly smiling face. Then he croaked, "Yes, indeed, Laird Mac-Gorilla. My mistake." And, turning on his flippers, he waddled away.

Now, however, having emptied her glass in a single gulp, Porculina was gazing idly at it with a frown of consternation, lost in thought. Then she turned to Gorilla. "But, Gor-Gor," she said, after a moment, "is that *really* what Idjitsu looks like?"

"Well," said Gorilla, "only after one's mastered it, of course. Don't be intimidated by how difficult it looks."

"Well, it's not quite that..." she replied, looking up at him again.

"Did you see the way I pinched my hands together?"

"Yes," said the little pig with a quizzical look on her face. "Yes, I did."

"You see," said Gorilla, "that's because of the technique I was using. It's one of Cousin Freddy's most ingenious methods. It's called the Dizzy Crustacean method."

"Oh," said Porculina, her features now brightening again, a look of wonder coming into her eyes, "that sounds ever so mysterious."

"And energetic," added Gorilla emphatically, now smiling appreciatively at Teddy. "But it's relatively easy," he added, turning back to Porculina. "It's nowhere near so clever or energetic as the Bewildered Octopus method. Shall I show you that?"

"No!" Teddy all at once nearly yelled. Then, regaining his composure with his customary clearing of the throat, he said in a calm voice, "No, old fellow, I don't think now's the time. You don't want to appear to be a...a show-off. I mean, all the other guests might begin to feel as if they've been outshone, if you see..."

"Hmm," said Gorilla, laying a hand on Teddy's shoulder, pursing his lips, and nodding his head. "I do see what you mean. Oh dear. How very thoughtless of me. Dear old Teddy, always remembering others. And you're right, of course. I wouldn't want to make the others feel ashamed of not having achieved such an advanced knowledge of the arts of self-offense."

Porculina frowned again. "Gor-Gor, shouldn't that be self-*defense*?"

"Ah," said Gorilla, now raising a single finger sagely in the air, "but, as Freddy says, the best defense is a strong offense."

"Oh," said Porculina thoughtfully. But then her frown deepened yet further. "Yes, but *self*-offense?"

"Well, you wouldn't want to offend others, would you?" asked Gorilla. "That would be very rude."

"Oh," said Porculina, but now shaking her head despondently. "This is all too deep for me. I'm just not mystical enough. But...but...how does it work, then? How does anyone...*win?*"

"Ah!" exclaimed Gorilla, now lifting his forefinger again, even more sagely, "that's the genius of it. The trick is to disarm your opponent with pity."

"Oh." This time it was Teddy who spoke. "You know, old fellow, when you put it that way...it begins to make a kind of sense...."

Just then, however, a great, deep, rich voice boomed out across the lawn. At once, all conversation ceased everywhere among the guests and all eyes turned toward the stage, where — looking rather grand in a beam of sunlight — Rex Homerosaurus stood in all his polychromatic splendor, one small foreclimb extended before him as lines of verse poured from his jaws in great sonorous streams:

And then stood up — stout and mighty, clad in cotton print, invincible —
Agnes Prynne, great among the nurturers of marigolds,
And spake: "Nay, we shall not yield before this ignominy!
The petunia shall not cast down the tulip, nor the violet
Overthrow the lily! Shall then one shade of marigold
Have preference before all others? What justice is this?"
Then up rose to his feet Sir Humphrey Punt, so wise in counsel
And full of years, and with jowls flushed as pink as primroses
Cried aloud, "How now, good floral-folk, what then shall we do?
Give separate prizes for each tender blush of orange?
Bestow a ribbon upon each petal daintily formed?
Bless ev'ry flower with such praise that all degree is lost?
Make no distinction between one greatness and another?"
Then, however, stood up Wilbur Groats (207 The Elms),
His thistledown hair a haze of glory, his eyes like embers,
And in his thin and rattling voice proclaimed, "Good people of
West Osley-on-the-Wold, surely it is nearly tea time..."

"Golly," whispered Porculina to Teddy and Gorilla, "there's quite a lot of standing up in that poem."

"I expect that's what they do in epic verse," said Gorilla thoughtfully. "Or maybe the chairs aren't very comfortable."

"Well, it's very stirring, whatever the explanation," replied Porculina. "It's like I can see it with my own eyes."

Teddy, however, said nothing, evidently preoccupied with thoughts of his own.

> Scones there were, and clotted cream, and strawberry jam, and butter
> For the crumpets, and small sandwiches of cucumber, and
> Dark Darjeeling, and little glossy pitchers full of milk...

After another minute or so, the recitation ceased — not because Rex had reached the end of the passage, but because Auguste had mounted the stage, waddled over to the little dinosaur, and interrupted, saying, "Thank-you, thank-you, sir, we have confirmed that your voice projects quite... admirably. We eagerly await the day of the full performance."

For a moment, Rex looked a little abashed. "Oh, my apologies. I do get carried away sometimes." He turned to the guests. "I might have carried on and on and given away the ending."

"And what a tragedy that would have been," said Auguste with an acid smile.

As the penguin and the dinosaur departed from the stage, Ellie came forward. At first, she was scarcely noticeable, being such a tiny figure in so large and open a setting; but she had no sooner begun practicing her *jetés* and *sautés* and *temps levés* and *sissonnes* than every head had turned her way. The seemingly effortless speed and grace with which she executed each move had clearly roused nothing less than awe among the spectators. And then, when one particularly lovely *grande jeté* — she seemed to float through the air and to land as lightly as a feather — was followed by a breathtaking *pirouette*, all the assembled toys gasped in unison. Even Teddy had been roused from his private thoughts and was gazing transfixed at the little elephant's exquisite motions. This continued for nearly three minutes, during which not a single word was spoken nor a single pair of eyes turned from the stage; and when at last Ellie came to the end of her routine, assuming a *croisé* pose, applause positively erupted from the audience.

"*Brava!*" Teddy cried out, obviously unable to control himself. "*Brava!*" But his exclamation was only one among many, equally loud and sincere.

Ellie looked about at the guests, smiled with the practiced elegance of a true professional performer, bowed — or curtseyed, really — three times with a kind of fluid *plié*, and then retreated to the back of the stage again, where she resumed her exercises on the bars.

"Oh, pies and pancakes and marzipan glaze!" gushed Porculina. "How... how... *divine!*"

Teddy breathed deeply. "Indeed," he said, still staring toward the stage as if half mesmerized, "*divine.*"

"Jolly good dancing," Gorilla chimed in. "I especially liked the spinny bits."

"Exquisite," murmured Teddy. Then, shaking his head as if waking from a daze, he turned to his two friends. "It's rare to have the privilege of seeing a truly great artist at work."

"I should say so," said Gorilla with considerable emphasis. "That's why you should visit with me when I'm using my finger-paints more often."

Teddy smiled. "I don't like to intrude on the creative process."

"Oh, I'm sure my creative process wouldn't mind at all. It's not the least bit shy. Why..." But just then he was interrupted by a sudden, extraordinarily fast flurry of perfectly rhythmic "clip-clop" noises, sounding out from the resonant wooden boards of the stage.

The three friends looked once again in that direction — as did all the other assembled guests — and saw to their surprise the small form of Onyx, reared up on her hind legs and engaged in a delightfully nimble and elegant soft-hoof tap routine. It was an astonishingly graceful but also exuberantly joyful dance. At one point, she even emitted a neigh of unmistakable delight. Even Ellie had now stepped away from the exercise bars at the back of the stage and was watching in rapt admiration. And then, tapping her way to the very front of the stage, Onyx paused and cried out, "Come on, Obsidian, join me! It's been ages!"

Obsidian, who was staring up at his sister with an expression of obvious embarrassment, merely shook his head vigorously and waved his fore-hooves in front of his face.

"Oh, come on!" she called out again.

Obsidian cleared his throat loudly. Everyone was now standing in silence, their eyes fixed upon him. He looked about nervously. "No, no," he said, turning back to Onyx. "It's been too long. I'm woefully out of practice. I'd ... I'd spoil it for you."

"Never," replied Onyx with an affectionate smile at her brother. "Oh, don't be such a stick in the mud. I know you still practice your steps at night in the stable, when you think I'm asleep outside."

Even at so great a distance, Teddy, Gorilla, and Porculina could see Obsidian's eyes widen in surprise.

"I ... I ... I ..." the little horse said; but then nothing else came to his lips for several seconds, until he finally gave up and simply sighed (in a snuffling, horsey way).

Now the guests began to chime in, calling out for Obsidian to join his sister on the stage. He resisted for nearly a minute more, but then at last — seemingly reluctantly but also with a hint of a smile on his face that suggested he was more pleased than he wanted to let on — he rose from his seat and mounted the stage. The spectators fell silent again.

The two little toy horses stood side by side. Then Obsidian whispered something in Onyx's ear. She smiled and nodded eagerly. Assuming a pose on their back legs, about a foot apart, they prepared themselves with deep breaths. Then Obsidian extended one hind hoof and tapped it on the boards three times to establish a beat, and all at once they were off. It was an exhilarating sight. Their years away from the stage had evidently done nothing to diminish the little horses' precision and speed. Their hooves clopped and clattered at a dizzying pace; their bodies moved in perfect synchronization through a routine of wonderful complexity, spinning away from one another now, dancing in whirling semicircles about the stage till they met again, tripping lightly yet powerfully across the boards from one end to the other, and in every phase of the routine complementing one another's movements in unexpected and dazzling ways. The rhythm of their hooves, moreover, was so flawless and infectious that many of the guests had soon begun to clap along with it, in the somewhat muffled way typical of soft toys. The performance went on nearly five full minutes, becoming more acrobatic, complicated, and sophisticated as it proceeded until, at last, it reached a point when their hooves were beating on the boards with such speed, and yet such sustained precision, that it scarcely seemed physically possible. And then the dance came to its end, with Onyx comically raising one front hoof to her brow and pretending to faint and Obsidian going down on one knee and catching her.

The applause was thunderous. And no one was louder in appreciation than Angus, who was now standing at the foot of the stage clapping his paws together with all the force he could muster and crying out, "How wonderful! *Magnifique! Quelle splendide prestation!*"

Onyx opened her eyes and turned a radiantly grinning face toward the guests. Then, rising again to their hind hooves, the two of them stood for a moment in the gales of adulation pouring over them. Onyx's smile was sincere and joyous; and Obsidian too, though he was trying not to look as pleased as his sister, was unable to suppress his own smile of happiness on hearing applause once again, after so long a time.

When at last the cries of admiration and the clapping had subsided, Angus spoke out, addressing the horses but in a voice that everyone could hear: "You are still the greatest toy-horse dressage duo in all of France! Artists of the highest caliber! It is a crime that your art has been denied to your country-toys for so long. By my honor as a *peluche*, this wrong will be corrected!" And then, clearly overcome by emotion, the dapper little bear turned away and walked toward the food tables to pour himself a calming glass of cider. At his words, another burst of applause had broken out among the guests.

"Coconut cream!" said Porculina, also clearly conquered by an excess of feeling. "Raisins and rice-pudding! It's... it's..." For a moment she fell silent, clearly laboring to find just the word adequate to express the unbearable fullness of sentiment she was feeling, until finally it came to her: "Waffles!"

It was a few minutes before everyone had regained their composure. Teddy and Porculina had both been greatly affected by Angus's words to the little horses; and Gorilla had been greatly affected by the rubber ball he had withdrawn from the pocket of his *uwagi* and begun tossing into the air with little cries of "Whee!" and "Hoorah!"

After a few moments, however, Teddy was calm enough to say to his two friends, "We really must go tell Angus about last night's events."

"You mean about the great banana quest?" asked Gorilla brightly, slipping the ball back into his pocket. "That's a splendid idea. It was exciting, wasn't it?"

"Ah, yes," said Teddy, "that, of course, but also the bit about the, um... ghost..." He raised his eyebrows meaningfully.

"Come again," said Gorilla with a quizzical expression on his face. But then a look of comprehension spread over his features. "Oh, you mean Alphonse! Of course. Well... do you think that's very important?"

When they found Angus, he was standing beside the Bath chair of Madame Lapin de Gris. The toad footman had been temporarily dismissed and was standing at a distance sipping a glass of limeade. The elderly rabbit saw the three friends approaching before he did and, with a regal half-smile and nod of the head, greeted them. Porculina curtseyed, Teddy bowed, Gorilla waved.

Angus turned. "Ah, *mes chers amis*, how lovely to see you. Have you been enjoying the day — the food, the entertainment..." — he held his paws wide in the general direction of the lawn — "...the delightful company?"

"Oh, very much so," replied Teddy.

"It's been buttercream and mangoes!" enthused Porculina (a little obscurely).

"But, if you'll excuse us," added Teddy, "we've come because we have some news to impart...another...curious episode in the night, if you take my meaning."

At once, the expression on Angus's face went from genial to despondent. "Oh, no..." he began.

"Perhaps we should tell you later," Teddy said, "in private?"

Angus shook his head despondently. "No, my dear cousin, there is no need." He turned to Madame Lapin de Gris with a faint, sad smile. "My family's dearest and oldest friend is privy to all that happens here."

"Yes, of course," said Teddy with a courteous bow of the head to the dowager bunny. "Well, then...well, it's Laird MacGorilla's story to tell really..."

A look of alarm appeared on Angus's face.

Gorilla, however, didn't notice, and with an effusive smile immediately began speaking: "Quite right. The story of the great banana-hunt, stave the first..."

Teddy cleared his throat. "Actually, old man, what we really want to hear is the story of, you know..." Here he grimaced. "The story of Alphonse dropping by last night."

"Oh, yes," said Gorilla. "Well, yes, I see, if you want me to skip ahead a bit..." Then, all at once, a yet broader smile appeared on his face. "I say, shall I demonstrate my Idjitsu technique for everyone as well?"

"No!" Teddy accidentally screamed again. Then, noticing the look of shock on the faces around him, he cleared his throat once more and very calmly said, "No need for that, old fellow. I'm sure they — along with everyone else — saw your earlier demonstration... and it might be just too... too exciting if you were to do it again."

"*Oh!*" Angus suddenly exclaimed. "Is that what it was? Now I see. Understandably, I had thought it was something else — maybe some sort of... savage highland dance... savage in the good sense, that is — the French sense: *sauvage* — or perhaps some ancient ritual of the MacGorilla clan, from the wild and primitive days when Scotland's soft toys painted themselves blue and danced in stone circles under the light of the full moon..."

"Oh, that sounds jolly," said Gorilla. "And I *have* occasionally painted myself blue, as it happens. Pink too, and purple on a few occasions. And green. Well, you know, it's hard to make a fingerpainting without spilling some..."

"Yes, quite," said Teddy. "But, anyway, if you could just tell the story..."

"Right," said Gorilla. "The tale of the banana hunt. Well, as I was saying..."

"The ghost, Gor-Gor," Porculina moaned. "Remember?"

"Oh, yes," said Gorilla. "That's interesting too, I suppose."

As best he could — which is to say, with constant digressions, many about rubber balls and a few about bananas, but always with Teddy gently but firmly guiding the conversation back in the right direction — Gorilla recounted the previous night's ghostly events. When he was finished, Angus stared at him for several seconds with a desolate expression on his face. Then he turned his eyes away to the sky, still remaining silent for nearly half a minute. Then, in a dry, defeated voice, he said, "There simply must be a rational explanation. My entire understanding of reality is... teetering." He lowered his eyes again and met Teddy's. "I must rely on you more than ever, dear cousin, to plumb the depths of this mystery. My estate's reputation hangs in the balance... and perhaps my sanity."

"*Ça alors!*" the old but astonishingly powerful voice of Madame Lapin de Gris broke in upon them. "Do not be so melodramatic. What is so terribly troubling about a mere ghost? It's only because you are a...a petty rationalist that you are so amazed by a phenomenon that has been recorded in every age and culture since the earliest days of *peluche* history. Why, I've seen a dozen different ghosts in my time, and never thought twice about it. What's more disturbing is that you refuse to accept what I have been telling you for I don't know how long: the ghost is a symptom of a deeper, more terrible malady — the curse of the Green Star of the Nile!"

At this, Angus heaved a deep, forlorn sigh. "That again."

"Yes," persisted the rabbit, "*that*. So long as that dread jewel lies hidden somewhere on the grounds of this estate, emanating its malign influences and dark magic, the weight of the curse will increase, bringing graver and graver misfortune with it." She lifted a solemn paw and intoned, "So shall the House of Osiris send forth its stricken spectres to plague this realm!"

Angus lifted his head with a look of perplexity in his eyes. "What's that? What are you quoting?"

Madame Lapin de Gris frowned impatiently. "Quoting? Why do you think I'm quoting anything? It's a magical Egyptian emerald. It seemed like the appropriate thing to say."

At this point, Teddy opened his mouth to say something, but before he could a gentle paw came to rest on his shoulder from behind. He turned to find Rolandus standing beside him, looking a bit fatigued but nevertheless quite proper in his valet's coat and tie.

"Excuse me, sir," said the dog, "but I've returned with some rather interesting information to impart."

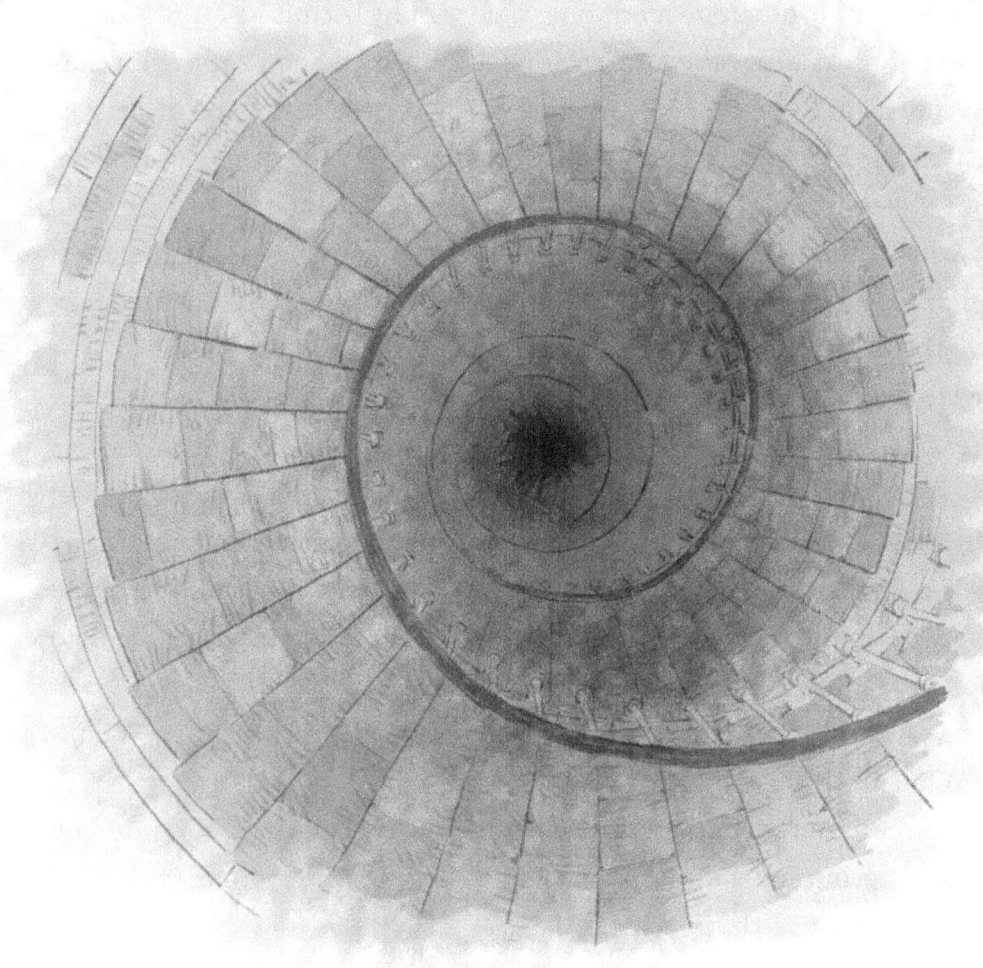

CHAPTER 9

The Way to the Underworld

WHEN THE THREE FRIENDS, ALONG WITH ANGUS,
had succeeded in detaching themselves from Madame Lapin
de Gris, Rolandus began leading them toward the table where
Muzzles, Jacques, and Kipper were seated together. "We may have need
of Master Longmuzzle's...well, his very long muzzle," the dog explained.
"His ability to, ah, nose out things that are hidden is remarkable. I flatter

myself that I have certain gifts in that quarter, but they are as nothing compared to his."

"It is impressive," Teddy agreed.

When the party had reached the table, all three of the soft toys there greeted them with warm smiles and invitations to join the conversation.

"Isn't it a lovely day?" asked Kipper with a series of soft clicks and clacks. "The weather is so perfect, the setting so exquisite, the company so glittering, it's like an abode of the gods... the soft toy gods, that is."

"It's certainly a jolly party!" agreed Gorilla.

"Yes," said Jacques in a suave, deep drawl. Then he grinned in that terrifying, toothy way he had. "I would have said it's all rather like a fairytale, but I'm not a poet." Then he raised his fore-fin to his mouth — not actually reaching it — and coughed two or three times. "Excuse me," he said. "It's from swimming about so much. Getting wet... well, it makes one a bit rheumy, if you know what I mean. And then there's the diffi culty about the buttered toast..."

"Oh, yes," said Porculina earnestly. "One does so understand about the toast." Then, as if a very important thought had crossed her mind, she quickly turned her eyes to the distant long tables, still heaped high with Sino-Cymric delicacies. "How unbearable that must be."

"We'd love to join you," said Teddy, "but in fact we came to ask whether we might steal Muzzles away from you for a bit. There's some château business that needs seeing to just at the moment, and he's the monkey for the job."

"Oh, I say, really?" said Muzzles, rising from his chair. "My, my. You have need of me, sir? Monsieur le Comte, I mean?" he said, looking to Angus.

"If you would be so kind," replied Angus. "I do so hate to drag you away from such fine company and from the entertainments of the day, but if you could spare some time..."

"Oh, certainly, sir," replied Muzzles. "We can always resume our con-versation later... really more idle chatter than a conversation. I'm always happy to be of service."

"You are most gracious," said Angus. "Good gentle-fish," he said, bowing to the shark, "and you my good cetacean," he added, bowing now to Kipper, "it is so lovely to see you at your ease. Again, excuse us for interrupting your colloquies. Shall we go then?" He turned to Teddy.

"Excuse me," Porculina suddenly interjected. "I mean, yes, of course, we should be going. But, you know, we haven't really fortified ourselves very well for what's to come. And, well..." She raised a trotter in the direction of the food. "A plate or four of nourishment might be just the thing to... you know, steel our stuffing for the fray."

"Haven't you already had, um, what was it? Six plates of food already?" asked Teddy, immediately lowering his head as if he realized his question was pointless.

Porculina frowned. "Seven," she corrected. "A mere seven. My point exactly. Not nearly enough for a healthy constitution."

Teddy looked about at Gorilla, Angus, and Muzzles, smiled with the smile of the honorably defeated, and said, "Yes, I suppose we can wait a little while longer."

Fifteen minutes (and six courses) later, Porculina was ready to accompany her friends back to the château library, where Rolandus had promised he would divulge everything that he had learned on his visit to Paris.

With all the servants out on the lawn with the guests, it was eerily silent inside as the small party made their way through the foyer, past the immense central staircase, down the broad corridor that led behind it, and into and through the large exhibition hall. It was only once they had all entered the library and the doors had been shut that Rolandus ventured to address the others. "My sojourn in Paris was, I believe, a success. At least, I was able to gather what I take to be some very interesting intelligence."

"Ooooh!" exclaimed Porculina. Then, squinting her eyes dramatically, she turned to Teddy and at once began to address him in her best

slow-witted sidekick manner: "I say, old bear, we're in the clover now. I knew it! No doubt a dastardly French plot to... Not that all the French are dastardly," she added, shooting a quick mollifying smile toward Angus and then turning back to Teddy. "As I was saying, no doubt a dastardly French plot, many centuries old by now but still underway, to overthrow the government, install a puppet president, plunder the Louvre, and sell off the loot of the same to foreign banking concerns with ties to a secret conspiracy with even more dastardly aims, whose headquarters are located somewhere in the Himalayas or... or the Amazon... one or the other... or in the mystic East of... of the Midlands... well, wherever..." At this point, however, inspiration apparently failed her. Her voice trailed away, her brow furrowed, and she raised a trotter to her lips thoughtfully. "Or maybe it's something to do with paving over the Seine and..."

"Yes, yes," Teddy now interrupted her. "That's... that's all very plausible... my dear old pig." He smiled gently. "But let's let Rolandus tell us."

"Capital suggestion!" Porculina squeaked emphatically, as if having discovered the exit from a particularly perplexing maze.

"My goodness," murmured Muzzles. "I say."

Rolandus cleared his throat. "Perhaps nothing quite so... *exotic* as that. But you are right, miss, the mystery does stretch back a century and more. Back, I believe, to the time of Octave de Petit-Ours, and even further back to the original construction of the château itself. To understand what is happening now, I believe we must take a long look into the 'dark backward and abysm of time,' as the Bard says."

"How jolly!" Gorilla suddenly interjected. "I've always thought that there's nothing quite so nice as an abysm! Or a bard!"

Teddy looked at his friend quizzically. "You...?" he began. Then thinking better of it, he turned to Rolandus. "Please, tell us what you found."

"Yes, please," said Angus, his perfect politeness not entirely hiding the faint note of exasperation in his voice. "I'm positively desperate to get to the bottom of this mystery."

Rolandus nodded decorously and then withdrew from the inside of his jacket several sheets of paper in a roll and walked over to one of the reading tables at the far end of the room, this one set directly beneath a large window. As the other toys gathered about him, he spread out each of the sheets — there were four, it transpired — in the clear golden sunlight, holding down the corners with several of the small objects that sat upon the tabletop: paperweights, pens, a small carved wooden poodle in a top hat, a box of paperclips, and a magnifying glass. The paper was new, typewriter stationery, the ink clearly modern and recently applied, but the images had a definite air of antiquity about them. Three of them were plainly architectural plans; the other was an elaborate sketch of an extremely attractive spiral staircase with several notes written all about the image in an ornate but oddly illegible hand. "These are copies I made in haste," remarked Rolandus.

"But they are exquisite!" replied Angus.

"My, my," added Muzzles, "you're a cracking draughtsman, I must say."

Rolandus closed his eyes for a moment and tilted his head in a politely dismissive way. "I have my little gifts. But" — he opened his eyes again and placed an almost reverent paw upon the image of the staircase — "I am a mere copyist. I am not in the league of the great artist who produced the original of this."

Each of the toys bent a little nearer and stared intently at the paper.

"Jolly nice handwriting," remarked Gorilla.

"I can't make out a word," said Porculina.

"It's in Italian," said Rolandus, "but, even if you can read Italian, that would not be enough by itself..."

"I'll be dashed!" Muzzles exclaimed. "Goodness me. It's written in mirror-script."

"I didn't know one could write with a mirror," said Gorilla. "How fun."

"I mean," said the small monkey, straightening his back and looking about him with an expression of wonderment, "it's written backwards, so that one needs a mirror to read it easily. If I'm not mistaken — I mean, I've seen this handwriting before, and I'm amazed at how well you've reproduced it." He looked at Rolandus with obvious admiration. "And you with no opposable thumbs."

"Quite," replied Rolandus dryly.

"Oh, meringues and melons!" cried Porculina. "Whose is it, for goodness' sake?"

"Well, miss," said Muzzles, "I don't like to be dramatic, and I hesitate to leap to a conclusion without all the evidence, and..."

"Please," said Angus with a genuine poignancy in his voice.

"I believe this is the work of none other than Leonardo." He looked about him. "Leonardo da Vinci, I mean."

"Oh," said Gorilla sagely. "That Leonardo. For a moment, I thought you meant the fellow who comes and fixes my tricycles back at the old castle. He's called Leonardo too, but not Leonardo D. anything..."

Here Teddy raised a paw. "Excuse me, old fellow." He turned to Rolandus. "What's the significance of this, precisely?"

"Well, sir," said Rolandus, "this sketch was among the archives of the château. It is indeed by Leonardo, and from what I could find it seems he was commissioned to design it for this very edifice, at the time of the château's original construction. Moreover, in my notebook I have copied certain receipts and architectural notations from the period indicating that it was indeed built."

At this, Angus sighed deeply. "Yes, another legend, I'm afraid. Every château in the Loire Valley claims that some part of its original design was the work of Leonardo. He was resident in this part of France in those days. But I assure you that no such staircase exists."

"With all due respect," said Rolandus, "I believe you are in error. It's true that the château's records are incomplete, and that there are few mentions of its architectural details from later days, until the fateful years of 1849 to 1851, but..."

"What happened then?" asked Porculina.

"A good deal of commotion, miss," replied the dog. "Those were years following a period of considerable unrest. It was then that Octave de Petit-Ours hired architects and laborers to make alterations to the design of the château. It was also during his time, out of reverence for his famous fore-bear, that he had the château embellished with so many more of the Egyptian motifs and statuary that had been accumulating since the days of Pierre de Petit-Ours and that are now so prominent throughout the castle and all over its grounds. It was then also that — if what we have been told is accurate — the Green Star of the Nile was hidden away in that secret chamber whose whereabouts Octave later forgot."

Now Angus sighed so loudly that he might have been heard on the lawn. "For the thousandth time, my good friends — cousin, good and lovely piggess, my noble Laird MacGorilla... Muzzles... Mr. Rolandus — for the thousandth time, I assure you, there is no such thing as the Green Star of the Nile. It is a story *pour les enfants*. A picaresque tale to tickle the imaginations of young *peluches* and credulous old bunnies."

"Actually," remarked Gorilla very soberly, "I believe that's only the fourth time you've said it." He began counting on his fingers. "Yes, four I think. And that's less than a thousand." He frowned thoughtfully. "At least, I believe it is." He began counting on his fingers again.

"Oh, Gor-Gor," said Porculina, "it was just an exaggeration."

"Definitely less," said Gorilla, dropping his hands to his sides. "What was that, Piggles?"

"And yet, cousin," said Teddy, "if you recall, someone went to a great deal of trouble to hide a map — and then only half of it — that purports to lead to something hidden hereabouts. And someone else seems to be going to great trouble to find that map. Perhaps there are times when legend is more to be believed than certifiable history is. Someone seems to know something."

"I suspect," said Rolandus, "that the clue to what is or is not the case here is to be found in the details — the architectural details, to be precise. If you would all look here at the first of our diagrams, dating from the time of the château's construction, you'll note that what is now two exhibition spaces separated by a wall built in the time of Octave de Petit-Ours was then one great open hall, stretching from one end of the original château to the other — what *were* its ends, that is, before the

126

addition of the east and west wings only three years later. And there" —
he placed the tip of a paw right in the center of the sketch — "you will
see, marked unmistakably, a large stairwell and a bird's-eye view of a
circular staircase descending into it."

Now Angus was bending over the sketch and examining it closely.
"But...but why have I never seen this before?" he asked, a note almost
of indignation entering his voice.

"Because, Monsieur le Comte," said Rolandus, "the originals of all four
of these sketches were concealed in the back of the château's supposedly
missing cook-book, which..." Here Rolandus had to pause at Porculina's
excited gasp. "As I say," he resumed, "which was itself concealed in a
binding indicating that it was an old accounting ledger from the kitchen,
and in that form it had escaped all notice in the archives, though it was
there in plain sight."

"Goodness," said Muzzles. "I mean, I say, you *were* thorough, weren't
you?"

"I always am," answered the dog.

"So it *hasn't* been lost after all!" Porculina suddenly gushed. "Oh...
oh...buttercream! Lemonade! Pecan biscuits!"

"Yes, miss..." Rolandus began.

"Well, thank goodness for that," the little pig continued. "So that's
the principal mystery solved." She breathed deeply in relief. "Well, shall
we go back to the food tables now?"

Teddy cleared his throat. "Actually, Pigsy, there are some rather
important matters yet to deal with."

"Indeed," said Muzzles. "I don't like to be pedantic, you know, but
there's still the business of the emerald...and the ghost, of course, and
the map...and this vanishing staircase...and, well, it's still all quite a
mystery."

"As to the staircase," said Rolandus, "if you'll all be so good as to
look at the second diagram. This is from 1849 and it depicts the great
gallery as now divided in two by a wall, and from the sketch you would

think that wall is situated where the stairwell should be. But there's something odd."

"Yes, *mon ami?*" asked Angus.

"The measurements, monsieur," Rolandus replied. "If you look at the upper righthand corner of each of the two halves of the divided gallery, you will see the dimensions of each listed in meters. And yet, just before coming to find all of you on the lawn, I took the liberty of walking the length of the back of the château's central keep with a small odometer in paw, and what I discovered is that, if these dimensions are correct — and they are, as I measured them as well — more than six meters is missing inside."

"Surely not," said Angus. "Someone would have noticed."

"Only if they thought to measure it, monsieur," said Rolandus. "It is not a conspicuous discrepancy in a space as large as this."

"Ah ha!" exclaimed Porculina so loudly that every head turned abruptly toward her. Adopting her best slow-witted sidekick manner, she said, "I see it all now, old bear. That means *either* that wall is six meters thicker than the sketch says *or* there are two walls and a secret room in between, where the staircase is still to be found."

For a few moments, no one said anything. Then Teddy remarked, "Exactly right... um, old girl. I entirely concur."

For another few moments of silence, Porculina stared at him. Then, in a rather embarrassed voice, she said, "Oh, I'm sorry, Teddykins. I didn't mean to get it right."

"Oh, that's all right," said Teddy soothingly. "Even a slow-witted sidekick is supposed to get things right now and then."

"Oh, good," said Porculina, a small smile coming to her lips. "That's all right, then. So the wall really is six meters thick."

"Ah... no..." said Teddy. "I meant... you know... the other one."

Porculina stared at him quizzically. "You mean the plot to pave over the Seine?"

Teddy smiled gently at her. "No, the *other* other one. I mean, you know, the secret chamber... with the stairs...."

Here Angus interrupted. "But it makes no sense. Where would such a staircase lead? There's nothing below this level of the château except on the western wing, where the cellars are. Here... well here the edifice extends out over the reflecting pool of the eastern side. There are no cellars there."

"Which brings us at last to this final architectural draft," said Rolandus, "which, as you can see, indicates a subterranean causeway leading from the stairwell to some point on the eastern end of the estate, not far I should think from the bank of the Cher. I believe that it is a corridor running underneath the pond... assuming it is still intact."

"Which," said Teddy, "I believe we can presume it is. That's where Alphonse must have... I mean, where the 'ghost' must have gone."

"Such was my supposition, sir," said Rolandus. "And, assuming that our next steps are obvious, I took the liberty of collecting several electric torches." Here he lifted a paw and pointed across the library to another, smaller table where half a dozen flashlights stood. "Not that Auguste was especially helpful in that regard," he added.

"You've thought of everything," said Teddy. "What an excellent detective you'd have made had you chosen to become one." Then, though, he turned to Muzzles. "Your powers of detection, however, should prove very useful too just at this moment."

"Mine?" said Muzzles with a look of genuine surprise on his face. "My goodness, sir, I mean... well, I never. I haven't the least gift for deduction and detective work."

"I refer," said Teddy, "to your absolutely prodigious... ah, *nose*."

Not many minutes later, the small party was standing before the large wall dividing the great gallery, covered as it was in Egyptian hieroglyphs impressed into the bricks, at roughly the place where Gorilla assured them "Alphonse" had disappeared the night of their second encounter. ("There he was, all glowy and wavery," said Gorilla, "and then there he wasn't. Poor chap.") Muzzles had his snout pressed against the wall, "snuffling and wuffling" away (as Porculina phrased it) with a determined look on his face. His companions formed a rough semicircle about him.

"Hmm," said Muzzles at one point. "Why, yes, indeed. My, my." Then he sniffed more vigorously at one bit of mortar in particular. With a short, sharp snort he drew back from the wall. "There's definitely the fragrance of a very old nothingness just here, on the other side of these bricks. As well as the fragrance of a spring mechanism."

Teddy stared at the small monkey in amazement. "Does a spring mechanism have a distinctive fragrance?"

"Oh my, yes indeed," said Muzzles emphatically, still staring intently at one of the bricks, about twenty inches above the floor. "It's a sort of springy and, um, mechanistical fragrance. Non-organic but not at all properly brickish, if you take my meaning." He stretched out a small hand toward the wall. "You know: rather coily and metallic and... and... very *latchy*." But now his voice sounded as if something else had caught his attention. "Right about here. And look... my goodness."

"Yes?" asked Angus.

"These hieroglyphs," said Muzzles, pointing toward the brick at which he had been gazing. "Do you see?"

Each of the others leaned forward, looking over Muzzles's shoulder or head (except for Porculina, who had to stretch and look around him). There in the center of the brick was an inscription that looked like this:
⬚ 𓂀𓏏.

"I say," said Gorilla after a few seconds, "that's a jolly picture. I especially like the snail and the little man with the boot."

"Not exactly what it's meant to be," said Muzzles. "Actually, the snail is the image of an open eye. I think that the inscription is meant to indicate something like 'the House of Osiris.' Of course, Octave wasn't an Egyptologist, but..."

"Excuse me," interrupted Teddy, leaning in yet further. "The House of Osiris? Wouldn't that be in the underworld?"

"Oh, yes, most assuredly."

"Which," said Teddy, "would be a rather pertinent indication of the way to a subterranean passageway, wouldn't you think? And of a staircase descending to a place below the earth."

"Yes, I think you're onto something there," replied Muzzles. "If you don't mind my saying. Perhaps..." He looked at his companions. "If you'll all just stand back a little way..."

Exchanging glances and small shrugs of the shoulders, all did as they were bidden. Then Muzzles carefully placed his enormous snout against the brick in question and began to press, gently at first but with increasing force. As it happened, it required only a small effort on his part: within a few seconds, there was a distinct, hollow, slightly muffled click, followed by an even quieter "*sproing*" sort of sound, and then — making scarcely any noise other than a brief, hushed hiss of escaping air — a section of the wall, large enough to admit even a rather large soft toy, swung away into darkness. At once, a faint aroma of something cold and damp and old wafted out of the aperture.

"I say," burbled Gorilla joyously, "how splendid! It's one of those lovely not-therenesses. I have some of those myself back at the old castle... though I can never seem to find them."

Teddy smiled at his friend. "It does bring back memories, doesn't it?"

A few moments later, with torches switched on and aimed forward, the whole party cautiously passed into the opening, Teddy leading the way and Gorilla bringing up the rear, happily swinging his torch from side to side and quietly emitting a ghostly "*Woooo-oooo*" sound.

"Gor-Gor, please," said Porculina. "It's frightening enough already."

"Sorry, old girl," said Gorilla as he entered the darkness.

There was nothing in the area closed off by the walls except empty space — and, of course, the staircase: exquisite, intricate, elegant as only Leonardo could have designed it to be, and coiling downward into an abyss of shadows. Even when the party trained the beams of their torches down into the stairwell, all they could see were two or maybe three spiral flights and a sinuously curling banister sinking down and vanishing from sight.

"*C'est incroyable!*" exclaimed Angus. "This has been my home all my life, and the home of my family for generations, and yet I never so much as imagined..." His voice died away. "Do you hear...water?" he asked, craning his neck over the rail and turning one ear downward toward the depths.

"Yes, faintly, I think so," said Teddy.

"Well," added Muzzles, "I can't really *hear* water, but I can distinctly smell the sound of water."

For a moment, the rest of the party stared at him silently in the dim, sallow light.

Then the silence was broken. "I say," said Gorilla, "how careless! Here's this splendid old not-thereness, and someone has just tossed litter about." He bent over and picked something up from the floor, which in the light of the torches turned out to be a sheet of paper rolled into a scroll, slightly compressed in the middle where Gorilla had stepped on it. "Well, we'll tidy that away..." he began.

"Wait, wait," said Teddy anxiously. "Do you mind, could we have a look at that?"

"Well," said Gorilla with a shrug, "it doesn't look like much fun to me, but here you are, old bear. Enjoy it."

Teddy smiled distractedly, thanked Gorilla, and began to unroll the paper on top of the broad rail surrounding the stairwell. "My goodness," said Teddy, "it's the other half of the map we found...and the other half of the poem...and this one shows where the château is..."

Within a matter of moments, the party was back in the library, having left the door to the secret chamber wide open behind them.

"It's a copy," said Teddy as he and Muzzles fitted the two halves of the map together atop the table under the window and placed various weights on all of their corners to hold them in place, "but it fits exactly, and the colors have been nicely painted in."

"They're very pretty," said Gorilla with obvious admiration.

"I think our intruder must have copied it from the other half of the original," said Teddy, "in the hope of finding its fellow, and then using the restored map to find...the emerald, I suppose. He must have dropped it in his haste to get away."

"Silly old Alphonse," said Gorilla with a knowing smile and a fond shake of the head, "how very like him."

Angus was now staring intently at the two scraps of paper, one old and slightly yellow with age, the other new, bright, and white, but together providing a now perfectly intelligible image of the estate. "I see," he said softly. "Yes, now it's obvious. If the château is here..."—he placed his paw on the new half of the map—"...and the course of the Cher runs this way..."—he traced the blue ribbon of the river as it wound upward from the new half onto the old—"...then this bend in the Cher is the one just past the little island where the obelisk stands, and this red X..."—he tapped his paw on it sharply—"...is the old well, near the river at the south end of the eastern lawn, which goes down to a very deep aquifer. Oh, but that's absurd. We had work done on that well only last year, and there's nothing down there but water."

"What about the poem?" asked Porculina, fairly bouncing on the tips of her trotters. "Oh, please, what does it say when it's all put together?"

"Of course, dear lady," said Angus, turning for a moment to the little pig with his customary courtly bow of the head, and then returning his eyes to the map and reading aloud:

> *Les eaux sombres coulent, dans cavernes profondes;*
> *Le soleil ne les voit, ni ne touche leurs ondes.*
> *Notre nuit cède au jour, puis retombe la nuit;*
> *Où les ombres règnent, aucune aube ne suit.*
> *Bien que nous qui buvons, ne sondons pas la source,*
> *La goûtons néanmoins, à la fin de sa course.*
> *Dans cet abîme noir, haut dans ce ciel désert,*
> *Brille encore une flamme: une étoile de vert.*

133

"*Oooooo*," gushed Porculina. "That's... that's..."

"Lovely?" asked Teddy.

"Totally incomprehensible," she replied. She stared at Teddy a little impatiently. "What does it mean, then?"

The small bear looked thoughtfully at the florid, antique handwriting. "Let's see, let me remember how I rendered the first part... and then..." After several seconds more, he added, "Yes, I think that's the best I can do." And then he declaimed:

> The dark waters flow, down in their deep caves;
> The sun neither sees them, nor touches their waves.
> Our night yields to day, then night falls again;
> Where reign the shadows, there follows no dawn.
> Though we who drink do not sound out their source,
> We nonetheless taste it, at the end of its course.
> In that black abyss, high in that barren heaven,
> There yet burns a flame: a green star of even.

Then he cleared his throat, and with a bashful smile remarked, "I took a certain liberty or two, I'm afraid, so that it would scan right. The last line should really end as 'a star of green.' But..."

"There, there, old fellow," said Gorilla, laying a consoling hand on his shoulder. "That's all right. But I hate to be the one to tell you — that last bit didn't really rhyme well... at least, not *very* well. Well-ish, perhaps, but..."

Here Rolandus, who had been silent for some time, interrupted with a polite cough into his paw and said, "Excuse me, sir — sirs and lords and lady — but what comes next?"

Teddy looked about him, at each of his companions. "Well," he said after a few seconds had passed, "I think the poem is telling us where to go next. We need to descend into the underworld... to find the House of Osiris."

CHAPTER 10

The House of Osiris

SOME SEVERAL MINUTES LATER, ONCE THE PARTY
had reached the bottom of the stairwell, having slowly taken what
proved to be four full spiral flights of marble steps down through
the chilly darkness, Teddy — who was at the head of the procession — raised
a paw and said, "Wait a moment, everyone." Then, turning the beam of
his flashlight down toward the floor he added, "Could all of you train
your torches in this direction?" When the others had complied, he bent
over and began to inspect the granite flagstones of the floor very closely.
"Ah," he murmured after a moment, "very interesting indeed."

"What is it, Teddykins?" Porculina whispered, though her voice echoed
about them rather like the soft hissing of a snake.

"See here," said the little bear, "the dust on the floor is rather thick, as you might imagine. And look... here... and here also... and then there..." The beam of his flashlight swung with his words now to one part of the illuminated area, now to another. "Do you see... faint traces in the dust... tracks of some kind."

Porculina leaned forward. "It looks like... lines, maybe... lines of dashes, more like."

"Of course," said Gorilla sagely, "as we should have guessed all along. Inchworm tracks. Well, that solves that. We're dealing with a gang of worm bandits. A tale as old as time."

Teddy took a deep breath. "A reasonable supposition," he said patiently, "but the tracks are rather too large for that, I think."

"Foot-worms, then," said Gorilla calmly, "or yard-worms, as the case may be." Then, looking at Angus, he added, "Or, I suppose they'd be meter-worms here, most likely, or something of the sort. In any event, I've always found worms to be reasonable chaps all around, so I'm sure that, if we can find them, we'll be able to convince them to help us find Alphonse."

"Pecans and pepper!" gasped Porculina. "*Worms!* Who'd have imagined?"

Teddy stood up straight. "Let's not be too hasty," he said.

"I feel I'm in a dream," Angus all at once remarked. He cast his gaze about him. "All my life here, and never once did I suspect that such mysteries lay just beneath my feet."

"There, there, old chap," said Gorilla, resting a consoling hand on the small dapper bear's shoulder, "that sort of thing happens all the time. Why I can't tell you how many secret doors and passages and cellars and the like we've come across at old Castle MacGorilla. Why, we once found an entire library, and a submarine, and..."

"No, no, Gor-Gor," interrupted Porculina: "there *wasn't* a submarine... remember? Just a lever on a wall and..."

"Well, in any event," Gorilla continued cheerfully, "there's always more to find lying about a castle. And then, when you find one thing, you're as likely quite to forget something else, and then that comes as a surprise too — say, a sitting room, or a flower-pot, or the front door..."

"Thank-you, my friend," Angus said. "But I still feel a fool." "Excuse me," Muzzles now spoke up. "I don't mean to interrupt, but — goodness me — shouldn't we perhaps, well, explore this rather curious passageway?"

"We should indeed," said Teddy with a note of gratitude in his voice. He turned the beam of his flashlight down the long, cold, dark corridor that stretched away from them. Old granite walls, a low granite ceiling, granite paving — all of it extending as far as the light could reach and then vanishing again in the darkness beyond.

"Oh... stale biscuits!" moaned Porculina. "It looks dreadful, Teddykins."

"Oh, nonsense, Piggles," said Gorilla. "It's just a long, dark, ghastly, terrifying, narrow corridor deep under the earth leading to an unknown end. What's so dreadful about that?"

"I think," said Teddy, "that there's really nothing to worry about. Unless I miss my guess, this is just a long exit tunnel leading out to some place on the grounds of the estate, originally a kind of escape hatch, as it were, in case of... well, trouble. And I think it's been in use of late, clearly, so I'm sure it's quite free of obstructions."

"Yes, of course," said Gorilla with conviction, "the worms. And Alphonse. Poor shy old fellow."

"No one need come who doesn't want to," Teddy added, looking from face to face in the soft glow of the flashlights.

No one, however, expressed any desire to turn back.

"Shall Mr Muzzles and I take the lead?" Rolandus asked. "In case we need to, ah... nose out something ahead?"

And so the small company made its way through the dark, low, somewhat dank, and very chilly tunnel, led by the dog and the small toy monkey. The stones beneath their feet were slick and smooth, and here and there thin roots could be seen protruding from tiny cracks in the mortar of the granite blocks composing the walls. The beams of their flashlights flickered and shimmered on the old stone. As they progressed, no one

137

spoke — well, no one except Gorilla, who now and then found it impossible to refrain from uttering some phrase like "Here, wormie-wormie-wormie!" or "Alphonse … oh, Alphonse … !" (or something similar). And, as they proceeded, a distinct sound of running water became increasingly audible overhead, hollow but steady.

"I daresay we can hear the river now," said Teddy, "resonating along the subterranean channel leading to the reflecting lake."

"Indubitably," said Angus, in a still somewhat subdued voice.

The corridor was long, but not nearly so long as at first they might have suspected. After ten minutes of proceeding in what was certainly a rather southeasterly direction, they came to a simple broad door of heavy oak on huge iron hinges, with a large iron ring-handle. For a moment, Muzzles and Rolandus inspected it, with eyes and noses. Then both turned to the rest of the party.

"My, my," said the monkey. "I can clearly smell the outside world. Leaves … oleanders … deep brush and thick trees, two of them pines, one roughly four feet and seven inches tall … a river nearby … a warm northerly breeze … a robin on a bough … "

Rolandus cleared his throat. "Yes, I can confirm … well, not quite all of that, but this door definitely leads outside."

Teddy approached. "There's no lock," he said. "Not even a bolt." Then, reaching out, he took hold of the iron ring and pulled. With little more than a creek, the door swung open and at once a bright yellow glow spilled into the passage.

"Golly!" gasped Porculina. "Creamy … cream!"

Teddy arched a single eyebrow in her direction, but said nothing.

One by one, the flashlights were extinguished, and as the eyes of everyone in the party adjusted to the daylight the scene that took shape before them was one of lush greenery entangled with shimmering golden sunlight. A gust of wind carried in a fragrance of pine and oleander. Somewhere a robin sang out.

138   "Radishes and raisins! Where are we?"

One by one, the whole party emerged from the tunnel and into what proved to be a large copse of trees and bushes and juniper ground-cover, held as it were in the embrace of a fold of a hill and under an embankment. As Teddy closed the door behind them, it turned out that on this side it had the appearance of an old wooden revetment — presumably to prevent erosion of the embankment — thronged with ivies.

"*Cieux au-dessus!*" exclaimed Angus. "I know where we are. I used to play here as a little cub. But never did I imagine there was a door on the other side of..." He shook his head in wonder. "This little hill is the first elevation at this end of the estate, and beyond it to the west the orchards begin."

A moment later, the party had stepped out from among the trees, and there a mere thirty yards or so away was the bank of the Cher. From here the back gardens of the château were no more than five minutes or so by foot or paw.

"And where's the well that's marked on the map?" asked Teddy.

"Oh, just that way," said Angus, pointing off to the west, "just beyond that other little copse. But there's really nothing to be found there. Over the years, there have been repairs to its interior walls, and nothing has ever been found down there. Certainly not some fabulous emerald bearing an ancient curse."

"Even so," said Teddy, "I'd like to see it."

"Oh, yes!" said Gorilla eagerly. "Wells are jolly things! I once stayed a whole day down in a well. It was entirely unplanned too, which made it a special surprise. You see, I was leaning over the edge one morning, just to see if I could see myself reflected in the water, and then the next thing you know I could... for a second or so. Well, what do you think had happened? I..."

Rolandus now began to cough very loudly.

"Steady on, old fellow," said Gorilla. "I hope you haven't caught a cold."

"Nothing at all, m'laird," said the dog, with a final huff, "only a little dust in the windpipe."

Angus sighed then turned a slightly anxious gaze toward the châ-teau. "I feel I should return to my guests," he said, "lest they think I've abandoned them, like an indifferent host. Perhaps Muzzles could show you the way."

"Oh, certainly," said Muzzles. "My pleasure."

"I wonder," said Angus, turning to Rolandus, "whether you might accompany me... if Laird MacGorilla can dispense with your services for the moment. You're very good at... well, at dealing with... situations, as it were... guests and such... and Auguste. And I should like to ask you a few more questions about the family archives, if I might."

Rolandus hesitated to answer, turning a somewhat uncertain gaze in the direction of Gorilla in his plum-purple *gi* and ochre belt, happily attempting to balance a pine-cone on his nose. "Ah," said the dog, "I'm not entirely sure I should abandon my... um, responsibilities here..."

At this, Gorilla let the pine-cone drop to the grass and looked at Rolandus with a reassuring smile. "Don't fret, Roly. It's good of you to be concerned, but I'll keep an eye on this lot and see to it they don't get into any trouble. You worry so."

"Ah," said Rolandus again. "Yes... well..."

"I think everything will be fine," Teddy said. "We'll..." — he looked about at the others — "I'm sure we'll manage. We're in good hands." And a small fond smile of his own crossed his face as he turned his eyes to Gorilla.

With a resigned arching of his eyebrows, Rolandus nodded. "Very well, sir. As you say."

Now Angus sighed loudly. "In truth, I still feel a fool."

At this, Gorilla's face assumed a look of melting sympathy. "Oh, I never feel like that," he remarked, "but I can see it's unpleasant. Buck up, old bear. Here..." — he withdrew the small cream-colored volume from his *uwagi* and held it out toward Angus — "take my copy of *Idjitsu-Do* with you. I don't need it just at the moment. Flip through it. You'll find all sorts of very deep and wonderful things in it. Wise sayings, you know, like 'Look at your finger, just in case it's pointing at the moon.' Things like that."

140

With a vacant expression on his face, Angus took the volume, almost as if he were too confused to do otherwise. Then, evidently remembering himself, he smiled feebly, nodded his head gratefully, and said, "Of course. Thank-you, my friend. I shall certainly give this book all the attention it, ah, deserves."

Not long thereafter, Teddy, Gorilla, Porculina, and Muzzles came to the well. It was a picturesque thing: small, round, constructed of weathered and moss-covered stone, with a small red roof above it on painted white wooden supports; there was a stout iron windlass with a crank, and around this a thick rope was wound, from whose end dangled a wooden pail. Beyond the well itself, perhaps fifteen yards further along, stood an old structure built from the same stone and apparently of the same age: a kind of utilities shed, perhaps, where no doubt other buckets and ropes and various tools were kept.

"That's a jolly well!" exclaimed Gorilla on seeing it in its grassy hollow, under the shade of two old oaks. "About as wellish a well as I've ever seen. I say, I wonder if I can see my reflection..." he began, quickening his stride toward it.

"Oh, no, Gor-Gor!" squealed Porculina.

"Not the time for that," added Teddy, hastening to catch up to the excited ape. "We need... um, your help... you see..."

Gorilla paused, a few feet from the lip of the well, and looked back a bit ruefully at the small bear. "I wasn't going to fall in," he said.

"Ah... well... yes, you see, you were," Teddy replied.

Porculina nodded gravely. "It was inevitable," she said. "Right on your darling round apey head, I'm afraid."

Gorilla smiled indulgently. "You worry so, Piggles old thing. Try a little philosophical thinking; it would ease your mind. As my cousin Freddy's book says, 'Nothing is inevitable — *nothing* — unless it absolutely *has* to be.'"

Porculina stared for a moment at Gorilla, with an expression of dawning wonder in her eyes, like someone glimpsing a vast and mysterious landscape for the first time. *"Ohhh,"* she gasped after a moment, "that's so very deep. I'd never, ever thought of it that way..." Then she closed her eyes and dropped her head in an attitude of humility. "Your family is so amazing," she murmured.

Gorilla nodded his head slowly, with a knowing expression. "There, you see. That's what we in Idjitsu call the 'moment of awakening.'"

Teddy looked back and forth between his two friends three or four times, wordlessly. Then he sighed. "I wonder, Muzzles, if you could... perhaps..." He paused here but indicated the well with a tilt of his head. "Your prodigious nostrils might come in handy here."

"Oh, yes of course, my pleasure," replied Muzzles, walking to the edge of the well, pulling himself up to the ledge (which was a little above the level of his head) and thrusting his nose over it. "Yes, indeed," he murmured after a moment. "I say. My, my. Goodness me."

After several seconds of this, Teddy cleared his throat. "Anything?" he asked.

Muzzles slipped down again from the well's edge, wiped off his palms on one another, turned to his companions, and said, "Monsieur le Comte is correct. I'm afraid there's no emerald down there. Not so much as a whiff of green... which is a very pungent color, as you probably know."

"No, I didn't," replied Teddy. "But thanks for confirming..."

"But, I say," Muzzles suddenly interrupted, spinning about. "My goodness me, that's strange."

"Golly, what?" asked Porculina.

"Just take a sniff over here," he said, pointing to a place along the lip of the well where the moss was very thick.

Porculina and Teddy exchanged dubious glances, but Gorilla immediately strode to the place Muzzles had indicated and thrust his nose up against the moss. "Yes," he said after a moment, "it's delightful."

"No, I mean..." Muzzles began.

"Why don't you just tell us what you've caught the scent of," said Teddy. "I don't think our noses are quite up to the task."

"Excuse me, my lord," said Muzzles as he drew closer to the well's lip and Gorilla took a step or two back. "Yes, yes, most definitely. I can distinctly smell an inscription in the stone here. It's been covered by the moss, but it has the unmistakable aroma of... of the same inscription we saw in the hidden passageway..." He turned back to the others. "You know, the 'House of Osiris' one. And an arrow..."

For a moment no one reacted; but then, his eyes widening, Teddy positively dashed to the edge of the well and stared at the patch of moss. "Which way does the arrow point?" he asked, his voice rising in restrained excitement.

"Oh, dear me," said Muzzles, "I can't tell you that. I'm not magical."

Teddy looked at the small monkey quizzically. "Oh," he said. "I suppose that... makes sense."

It was only a few minutes, however, before Teddy and Muzzles, employing sticks, had succeeded in clearing enough moss from the old stone that the carving became visible, worn and stained by time but still legible. As Muzzles had said, it was once again the familiar symbol for the House of Osiris, and there was indeed an arrow, pointing quite unmistakably toward the small shed.

"Well, well, well," said Gorilla cheerfully, "so that's where this Osiris chap lives. We'd best go knock on the door and see if he's in."

"No, you see," said Porculina, "Osiris is an Egyptian god."

At this, however, Gorilla's excitement seemed only to increase tenfold. "I say, I've never met one of those before!" he exclaimed and positively dashed to the little structure and began politely knocking on its wooden door, calling out in his most affable voice, "Helloooo! Are you there, Mr. Osiris? We've come for a visit..."

When the other three had reached his side, however, Teddy laid a paw on his friend's arm to stop him from knocking and said, "No, you see, old fellow, Osiris doesn't actually live here. He's a god from the ancient Egyptian pantheon."

For a moment, a look of disappointment seemed to spread across

143

Gorilla's features; but soon enough it was replaced with another smile. "Well, then, where's this pantheon place then?"

"No, I mean, he's a figure from Egyptian myth... from very, very long ago. He's not here at all."

"Well then why does he keep a house here?" Gorilla shook his head fondly. "Really, Teddy, you're not thinking."

Teddy opened his mouth as if to answer but then merely smiled back at Gorilla, reached out toward the old iron knob, and opened the door.

The interior — illumined by the daylight pouring in at three small windows — was rather plain but very orderly. There were shelves upon which several spare pails were neatly arranged; four lengths of replacement ropes hung in loose coils from hooks on the stone walls; various tools — long poles with hooks on their ends, steel brushes, trowels, and so forth — stood in one corner or lay upon a work-table beneath one of the windows; and two sacks of dry, unmixed mortar lay in another corner, along with two large buckets. The only object that seemed somewhat out of place was an old but apparently sturdy rocking-horse, painted blue, gold, and red. It was to this last object that Gorilla immediately gravitated. "What a fine horsey!" he said. "You can see this Osiris chap has excellent taste."

Teddy turned to Muzzles and, without much evidence of hope in his voice, said, "Can you, ah, scent anything? Anything green... or emerald-ish?"

For a few moments Muzzles lifted his snout and sniffed at the air. Then, shaking his head, he said, "No, I regret to say there isn't. But..." Again he sniffed and then slowly turned his eyes toward the rocking-horse, which was now creaking vigorously under Gorilla's rocking. "Goodness me," he said, "but there's a distinct fragrance of... well, I'd say of damp tunnel... very damp... and deep... and heading easterly...."

"Cream and cauliflowers," gasped Porculina. "Another tunnel?"

"But where?" asked Teddy looking about.

"Just there," said Muzzles, indicating with a thrust of his snout the wall just behind Gorilla and the now furiously rocking rocking-horse.

"Giddy-up!" Gorilla suddenly crowed. "Heigh-ho and charge! Hip-hooray! Hot cross-buns! A penny for..."

"Oh, Gor-Gor," Porculina suddenly called out. "Please pay attention. Things are getting mysterious and terrifying again."

Gorilla fell silent and brought his rocking to an awkward halt. "What's that, old Piggles?"

"A tunnel," she replied.

"Quite right," said Gorilla enthusiastically. "My kingdom for a tunnel!" And then he hunched forward as if to resume his gallop. "Cry hammock and let slip the frightful boors!"

"No!" said Porculina, with even more urgency in her voice than she was used to using. "Stop for a moment, please. There's a tunnel, and it's just behind you."

Gorilla turned to look over his shoulder and then slowly dismounted the rocking-horse. With an almost tender, wistful smile he approached Porculina. "Poor old Piggles," he said. "You're seeing things. It's been a taxing day, I know, and you probably haven't had enough to eat."

"No, no, no..." the little pig began, shaking her head in consternation; but then she paused, looked at Gorilla for a moment, and turned to Teddy. "You know, that *is* true," she said. "I really am feeling a bit peckish."

Teddy now sighed deeply and dropped his head. Then, regathering his resolve, he looked up again and said to Gorilla, "What Pigsy means is that there seems to be a tunnel on the other side of that wall, and I have to assume that there's a hidden door in the wall..."

"Oh my, yes," interjected Muzzles. "The aroma of the spring in the door and the hinges on the other side is most... piquant. Yes, that's the word: piquant."

For a moment, Gorilla's brow furrowed. Then he turned and walked over to the wall behind the rocking horse, bending forward to inspect it, rough stone for rough stone. At last he stood up straight and turned back to his companions. "Well, chaps, I'm dashed if I see it. There's nothing here, except another one of those little men with a boot talking to a snail, carved in one of the stones. I can't say I see any doors."

"What?" said Teddy, now more animated and taking two steps toward Gorilla. "What carving? Where?"

"Just here," said Gorilla, half turning about and placing a finger on one of the stones. "Clever little picture too."

"Does it move?" asked Teddy, his voice now becoming positively excited. "Can you push it?"

Gorilla looked at the wall and then, tentatively, began to press his palm against the stone he had just indicated. After a second, there was a small, stony scraping sound. "Well, yes," said Gorilla a second later, "it moves. But it isn't nearly big enough to be a door." He turned fully back to the others, shaking his head in fond consternation, and folding his arms across his chest. "Really, you chaps," he said indulgently, leaning back to rest against the wall.

Predictably, of course, the portion of the wall directly behind him swung wide into deep darkness and he fell backward, apparently down a somewhat steep flight of stairs, because his disappearance was immediately followed by a series of soft regular thumps and several exclamations of "Oof!" and "Ouch!" and "I say!" emanating from the open doorway, diminishing rapidly in volume, and then there was silence.

"Oh, Gor-Gor!" cried out Porculina in alarm and running to the tunnel's mouth. "You poor, noble monkey...!" She came to a halt, staring desperately into the void.

After several seconds, however, the serene and even cheerful voice of Gorilla came floating up into the shed from below. "I say, you chaps, you'll never guess what I've just found..."

It was only a minute later at most that Teddy, Porculina, and Muzzles — flashlights lit and directed before them — had descended the flight of fifteen or so smooth granite steps to find Gorilla at the bottom, lying on his back with hands folded on his chest, staring upward at the low vaulted ceiling with a pleasant smile on his face, and humming what Teddy and Porculina recognized as one of his favorite bagpipes melodies, "The Hurtling Rhinoceroses of Dundee." After roughly ten seconds of this, Porculina asked, "Are you all right... you poor unlucky... primate?"

Gorilla looked at the little pig fondly. "Couldn't be better," he exclaimed. "I was just having a little lie-down. The most wonderful things occur to you when you do that. Why, I was just thinking, what if I were to have a carousel installed back at old Castle MacGorilla, right in the front hall, with lots of horsies and dragons and such. Think of what a jolly sight that would be for visitors..."

Here, however, Teddy interrupted with a loud cough. "Yes, yes, but let's talk about that later. What's important now is that we've... I mean, that you've discovered this..." He lifted his flashlight and turned its beam down the length of the tunnel, which stretched away into a deeper darkness that the light could not yet reach. "We've got to see where this leads."

"Right-o!" said Gorilla, rolling over and bouncing lightly to his feet.

Porculina, however, emitted a small moan. But then she shrugged and, assuming her best slow-witted sidekick voice, said, "Right then, my old bear, there's no turning back now. We've got the villains on the run."

"Villains?" said Muzzles. "Um, what villains do you..."

"Why, those bandit-worms," said Porculina with a tone of relish in her voice. "We've chased them to their lair, obviously. Why, even now, I'll wager, they're down there in the dark planning their next dastardly assault on common decency... and on the castle larder, no doubt... and..."

"Honestly, old pig," Teddy broke in, "I doubt that. I think that whoever it is who's been playing the ghost doesn't even know this tunnel exists. That's why he or she was after the map in the first place. I think that this may very well be the way to the lost hiding-place of... the Green Star of the Nile."

Porculina gasped. Muzzles drew in a sharp snort. Gorilla said, "Why, that's jolly."

It took them about ten minutes — moving forward slowly but resolutely over the smooth granite floor — to reach the tunnel's end. As they were approaching it, Muzzles at one point announced, "My goodness, but I know precisely where we are. Overhead, I can detect the clear aroma of the shallows separating the bank of the Cher from the small island amid its streams — the one with the small obelisk." When, moreover, the party came at last to a small wooden door with iron hinges and an iron ring for a handle, he added, "Why, yes, and I smell the fresh fennel and juniper of the island itself now... and the white stone of the obelisk... and a circular chamber... with brick walls painted white and..." His eyes grew wide and he turned to stare at the others in the bleak glow of their flashlights. "And I smell... faintly but unmistakably... I smell the color green... and the emerald to which it's attached."

Teddy smiled. "If I had a nose like yours..."

"You'd look very odd," interrupted Porculina.

Teddy merely nodded, took hold of the iron ring hanging from the door, and pulled. Hinges that had not moved in centuries groaned, but the door moved fairly easily, opening and admitting a pale, chalky glow into the tunnel. One by one, the flashlights were extinguished.

"Well, then," said Teddy, "I suspect the answer to many mysteries lies ahead."

"And," added Gorilla sagely, raising a didactic finger, "the mystery to many answers."

The other three stared at him for a moment in silence. He smiled knowingly.

CHAPTER 11

The Green Star of the Nile

A S MUZZLES—OR HIS NOSE, AT ANY RATE—HAD foretold, the chamber on the other side of the door was indeed round and had brick walls painted bright white. It was of no very great diameter — perhaps a dozen feet across — but it had a very high ceiling indeed. Overhead was an open shaft of the same painted bricks rising up to the source of the soft light filling the room, which from here looked like a square skylight of thick milky glass. And in the middle of the room stood a low table in the shape of an octagon, resting on a single stout base, no more than four feet wide, and all of it apparently

149

carved from white marble. Even beneath a coating of dust, it gleamed in the daylight pouring down from above.

"Gosh," breathed Porculina. "Persimmons and parsnips! Where are we, do you think?"

"I'm fairly sure we're right inside the obelisk," said Teddy. "And that," he added, pointing upward to the top of the shaft, "is the quartz capstone."

"You see," said Gorilla buoyantly, "it's just as I said. The oddest things are always turning up around castles: hidden libraries, hidden levers that release water from deep cisterns, hidden rooms under obelisks on islands... front doors..."

"But it's all so... so eerie," whispered Porculina. "Carrot soup. Just, you know... carrot soup."

"My goodness me," said Muzzles. "I daresay no one's seen the interior of this room since the days of Octave de Petit-Ours himself."

"No doubt," said Teddy, stepping into the room and approaching the table. He began clearing away the silvery dust that lay upon its surface. After a moment, he said, "There are words carved here."

The others now also approached.

"Yes," said Muzzles, sniffing at the table. "If you'll allow me..." He gestured politely for his companions to step away. Leaning back, he took a deep breath, held it for a moment, and then leaned forward and expelled it mightily through his nose. A sound rather like a hippopotamus bellowing in alarm at a roaring tornado burst from his nostrils and all at once all the dust that had lain upon the table for centuries rose up in a great silvery cloud and, almost as if in terror, fled for shelter to the far side of the table, gusting violently against the wall, positively clinging to it for several seconds in the pounding blast, and then sinking down to the floor. As the last echoes of that titanic noise died away, seeming to dissipate into the high space overhead, Porculina took her slightly tremulous trotters from her ears and ventured a small round of applause.

150

"I say," enthused Gorilla, "that's a trick! Can you teach me...?" And here he began drawing in his breath, clearly preparing to attempt to imitate the small monkey's performance.

"Oh, don't," protested Porculina. "You'll damage your stuffing."

Gorilla looked at her and, with a somewhat deflated expression, released his breath again. "Perhaps you're right, old girl," he said. "But you know, see a monkey and do what a monkey does. It's an old adage."

"Ah, thank-you," said Teddy, only now cautiously removing his paws from his ears. "Most expedient. I had no idea you could do that. Can you still smell the emerald?"

"Oh, yes," said Muzzles, looking about. "It's positively pervasive in here."

"Can you...?" Teddy began; but then he paused, stepping forward again. "How interesting," he said after a moment.

Now the others too gathered around the table. At its center, a small, dome-shaped boss was set into the marble, no more than three inches in diameter and rising no more than an inch above the surface. At the edges of the octagon, moreover, on every other of its eight sides, were four darker oblongs of marble set flush into the table's surface, and on each of these, in a very ornate script, a single word was inscribed.

"Gumdrops!" said Porculina. "What does it say?"

"Well," said Teddy, pointing at each word in turn, "it just says, 'terre,' 'air,' 'eau,' and 'flamme.' It's just the four classical elements, it appears: earth, air, water, and fire."

"Curious, though," remarked Muzzles.

"What?" asked Porculina.

"Well, normally the word for 'fire' in that list would be 'feu,' not 'flamme.' It's..." Here, though, he fell silent, a look of deep perplexity in his eyes. He began walking around the table, vigorously sniffing at each of the inscriptions in turn. "My goodness," he said on reaching the last of them. "These insets — they're buttons. I can detect the aroma of their springs... and of their general... pushability. I wonder what they...?"

But here Gorilla clapped his hands together and, in a hearty voice, said, "Oh, I do like buttons!" And, before anyone else had had time to grasp the danger, he extended a hand and pressed down firmly on the inscription nearest him, which happened to be "*terre.*" The oblong sank a quarter inch or so into the table top and emitted a small, sharp click. For a moment—but, alas, only a moment—nothing happened. Then, with a terrible inevitability, the sound of old mechanisms groaning into life after a sleep of centuries began to emanate from the walls on all sides.

"Oh, dash it!" said Muzzles with unusual animation.

"*Ohhhhhh....!*" added Porculina.

And then, with a high rasping sound, slots appeared around the circumference of the room, several feet above head-level, as several bricks (six or so) receded into the wall. Then came the sound, from somewhere deeper in the depths of the walls, of more machinery creaking on what sounded like heavy chains. And then, with a kind of "*whoosh*" and "*floompf*" and finally a "*flursh,*" spouts of rich dark earth began streaming from the slots and pouring down on the unfortunate party below.

"Oh, appffles nn abrigots!" cried out Porculina.

"Goovness grajous meef!" concurred Muzzles.

"I sayv, thads jahwy!" remarked Gorilla in an unsettlingly cheerful voice.

Teddy said nothing, but merely shook his head from side to side somberly, even as the shower of soil continued to descend on its crown.

Fortunately, this did not last very long. After roughly a minute, the sound of the chains deep in the walls resumed, the flow of earth began at once to diminish and, just as the last clouds of swirling dust were settling, the bricks behind the open slots rasped back into place. About an inch and a half of dark, fertile southern French loam now covered the floor and the top of the table.

All four of the soft toys shook their heads vigorously and began brushing the earth away from their faces and shoulders (taking care, of course, not to rub it into their fabrics). Then Teddy turned to Muzzles and, in a somewhat weary voice, said, "Would you mind...?"

"My goodness, of course," the little monkey replied. And, drawing a

152

deep breath, he repeated the clamorous performance of a few minutes earlier, until the top of the table was once again cleared.

"Oh, Gor-Gor," said Porculina, in a voice verging on a sob, "what a mess. You really must be more careful. Think of how dangerous..."

But in his excitement, apparently, Gorilla was not paying attention. "Let's try another," he said, immediately pressing the button that read *"air."*

"Wait, no, don't...!" Teddy was calling out in a desperate but somehow already resigned voice.

Once again, ancient mechanisms sprang to life with an ominous echoing on all sides. Once again, half a dozen bricks receded raspingly into the wall above, this time perhaps two yards higher up, the muffled sounds of chains emerged from further in and, with a noise like a chorus of phantoms taking a deep breath and then expelling it again in a desolate moan, cold jets of air gusted into the room. Somewhere above, evidently, wind-funnels were capturing the breezes and, now that the spouts below were open, channeling them down into the enclosed space. Happily, the technology of the days of Octave de Petit-Ours could accomplish only so much. The winds stirred up the earth lying on the floor, filled the air with fine granules of soil, coated the table and the four companions with another layer of dark dust, but were not strong enough to knock the four toys off their feet. Then, after a minute or so, the chains sounded out again, the bricks scraped their ways back into their places, and the howling dwindled away first into a whimper and then into silence.

Teddy looked at Gorilla with a forlorn smile. "I wonder, old fellow, if perhaps you could just refrain..."

But Gorilla had already slipped around to the other side of the table and was reaching out toward the button that read *"flamme."*

"Gor-Gor, no!" squealed Porculina.

This time, Gorilla paused, his hand hovering above the oblong of marble. "Why ever not?" he asked with knitted brows (just visible through the dust clinging to his face).

153

"Because..." She squinted impatiently at him. "Oh, you silly dear ape, if the earth-button released earth into the room and the air-button released air, what do you think will happen if you press the one for fire?"

Now Gorilla knitted his brows even more firmly. "I haven't the foggiest," he replied. "We won't know till we try." And his hand began to descend toward the button.

"No!" Porculina cried even more shrilly.

Again Gorilla paused, the quizzical expression on his face now so pronounced that several layers of dust could not have disguised it. "Really, Piggles," he said, "you'll give yourself a sore throat."

"Then again," Teddy remarked, his voice suddenly calm, and his features assuming a reflective cast, "let's consider. Octave, even if he wasn't very, ah, *vif*, was after all a teddy bear. And no teddy bear — no true soft toy... no *peluche* — could ever really intend another harm. He would never, surely, have conceived a device that would expose anyone to fire. And then, too, there's the curious word-choice: *flamme* rather than *feu*. What does that make you think of?"

Gorilla pursed his lips. "Bunnies," he said definitively.

"Buttered toast?" offered Porculina.

"Giraffes too," added Gorilla.

"No, no..." Teddy began.

But then Muzzles broke in: "Why, the poem of course. How did it go? '*Brille encore une flamme: une étoile de vert*'... that's it, isn't it?"

"Precisely," said Teddy. "'There yet burns a flame: a star of green.' I think it's obvious: the '*flamme*' — the 'flame' — is the Green Star of the Nile." He smiled at Gorilla. "Go on, old fellow, push away."

"Push what away?" asked Gorilla.

"I mean, go ahead, push the button."

"Oh," said Gorilla, "you should have said so. Right-o!" And, with the broadest of grins and considerable enthusiasm, Gorilla pressed the button.

Yet again, the sound of machinery...

"Oh... sour sandwiches!" murmured Porculina nervously.

"Dear me," said Muzzles.

But the sound was now coming from the floor, or more precisely from the base of the octagonal table. A loud creak, several clicks as though some ratcheting device had been engaged, and then, as the four companions watched, the boss at the table's center moved upward, at first with a small jolt, only a fraction of an inch, as if freeing itself from centuries of disuse, and then smoothly, rising four inches or so with a smooth hiss on two thin brass rods attached at their base to a circular lozenge of marble. And on the lozenge lay a small bed of midnight-blue velvet, and on the velvet — sparkling from its exquisitely cut facets very much like a burning green star — lay an emerald the size of a walnut.

After only a moment of silence, Gorilla suddenly exclaimed, "I say, that's a fine-looking thing. I wonder where it came from."

"Oh, Gor-Gor," said Porculina, in a tone at once exasperated and deeply affectionate.

"Well, then," said Gorilla cheerfully, "only one more to go." And he reached out his hand toward the button reading "*eau.*"

"No!" cried out Teddy, Porculina, and Muzzles in almost perfect unison.

But it was too late.

It was a very bedraggled, dripping wet, and mud-bespattered quartet of toys that, several minutes later, made its slow, sopping way from the well-house, across the long hinder stretches of the estate, around the eastern wing of the château, and back to the grand front lawn. The day's festivities were nearing their end; most of the guests had already departed; but the dozen or so who remained — including Madame Lapin de Gris in her Bath chair — along with the lord and the staff of the manor, all at once desisted from their amiable chatter and stared at the disheveled adventurers with eyes and mouths wide. After a moment, Angus detached himself from what now looked like a gathering of statues and slowly approached, and then — with an expression on his face that somehow combined alarm with a total absence of surprise — Rolandus came after him. When Angus reached the four soaking toys, he opened his mouth, then closed it again, and then looked about himself in the manner of someone who, now bereft of anything to say, was trying to find where he had misplaced it. No one else spoke either, but Teddy, with a meaningful raising of his eyebrows, held out his paw and opened it, the Green Star of the Nile resting on its palm. Now Angus's eyes grew as wide as they possibly could. His own paw visibly trembling, he reached out and gently took hold of the gem, then lifted it to inspect it closely. At last, with a long, slow exhalation, he whispered, "So it's true after all. What a fool I've been."

"Not at all," said Teddy quietly. "But do slip it into your pocket. Best not to let everyone see it yet."

With a sober nod, Angus complied.

Rolandus cleared his throat. "I'll just go prepare the castle laundry, shall I?" And with that he turned and began walking away.

"Oh, bother!" murmured Porculina in a defeated voice. "Lukewarm tea. Soggy biscuits."

Just then, however, a dry, mordant voice broke out from behind the four wet friends. "*Ahem*, if you please."

They all turned to see the figure of Auguste close at hand, looking down his beak at them superciliously, with the expression of one who has had all his suspicions confirmed, and bearing in one flipper a large silver salver, at the center of which lay a single, very small, rather pathetically bruised yellow crescent. "Your, ah... *banana*, m'laird."

Two hours later, as they were dangling by their ears from a clothesline stretched across the interior courtyard behind the château's laundry, alongside Gorilla's *gi* and belt, the four companions — now clean again and nearly dry from the sunlight and gentle breezes of the afternoon — had time to reflect upon the events of the day.

For Gorilla, this meant celebrating what a "jolly" time the lot of them had had, and how very nice the lovely fragrant laundry soaps had been: "I say, that rose of attar soap they used for you, Piggles, is just the thing. And what was yours, Teddy?"

"Hmm?" said Teddy, roused from his thoughts. "Oh...coal-tar and vanilla, I believe. Very fine."

"Yes, and goodness," interjected Muzzles, "mine was a bracing witch-hazel."

"But I got the best of it," said Gorilla, breathing in deeply with an expression of pure bliss: "essence of banana."

Porculina, however, had her mind on other things; chiefly, she was wondering how long it would be before another snack might be forthcoming. "It simply takes it out of one," she said, "all this, oh, walking through tunnels and being soaked through and being washed — though I have to say the laundry here isn't nearly as... rough as I feared — but, anyway, I mean I'm afraid I'll waste away... I mean, without sustenance, the drying might... shrivel me up a bit."

"I shouldn't think so," said Teddy.

"Silly me," said Gorilla ruefully. "I selfishly didn't think to share my banana with you."

"There wasn't much of it to share," said Porculina. "I've seen larger peanuts."

"Yes, well," replied Gorilla sagely, "a banana is a banana is a banana. Anyway, hunger can be controlled."

A long, tense silence ensued, at the end of which Porculina said, "Gor-Gor, that's the most ridiculous thing you've ever said."

"Oh, but it can, Piggles. I don't have Cousin Freddy's book with me right now — good thing too, as it would be a bit soaked otherwise — but it has ever so many wise counsels in it on overcoming temptations and such. It's all mind over matter, you see. Clever stuff too, such as meditating on, oh, something very pleasant — rubber balls, bunnies, paperclip necklaces, bananas — and then simply feeling grateful that there are such

157

things in the world. This is called 'The Way of the Contented Sloth,' and it's ever so effective. Why, I've used it to forget all sorts of things."

"Indeed," said Teddy, "I've certainly seen you do that. Anyway, we should be down from here soon, and Cousin Angus has already arranged some tea and biscuits..." But then he fell silent, clearly lost in thought.

"What is it, Teddykins?" asked Porculina.

"Oh," said the little bear, "I'm still pondering this mystery."

"Goodness," said Muzzles, "we've found the Green Star. Surely that was the greatest mystery of all."

"Oh, that," said Teddy in a distracted tone. "I don't think that was so great a mystery really. All the evidence was there to be found if one looked for it. My cousin simply never looked because he didn't believe in the gem's existence. No, I mean the mystery of whoever it was who was trying to find the emerald before we could. Our 'ghost,' as it were."

"Oh, Alphonse," said Gorilla. "I shouldn't worry about him. Lovely chap. Very glowy and cheerful... if a bit shy."

"I wish I could agree," said Teddy, "but I don't really think Alphonse is... I mean, I don't think our intruder was really..."

But here Gorilla interrupted, borne away by a sudden recollection: "Oh, I say, you fellows, did I ever tell you about my cousin Gregor — Gregor MacGorilla, that is — the ghost-hunter?"

Porculina's eyes widened and she attempted to turn her face toward Gorilla (though, her ears not being sufficiently elastic, this merely caused her to swing from side to side). "Not truly and really?" she gasped in a tone of instant excitement. "Oh, tell us."

"Well," said Gorilla, "it's sort of a hobby he came by accidentally, though he does it with real passion — wandering around dark deserted moors and old manor houses with a phonograph and a torch..."

"A phonograph?" interrupted Porculina.

"Well, he likes music quite a lot," said Gorilla, "and he gets rather frightened and lonely out there on the moors and in those empty houses, what with it being so dark and all."

"Oh," said Porculina. "Yes, that makes sense. But...mightn't the music...scare off the ghosts?"

"It's very cheerful music," said Gorilla. "If I were a ghost, I wouldn't be scared by it at all. I expect it would, you know, set my toes tapping. Anyway, he's been at it for some time."

"And has he ever...ah, caught any?" asked Muzzles.

"No, not as such," said Gorilla. "Not any ghosts, that is. A cold or two, yes. But he has seen them. Well, seen one, at any rate. Well, almost..."

Porculina scowled. "I don't understand. Has he or not?"

"Well, you see, that's what I mean when I say he picked up the hobby almost by accident. He hasn't found any ghosts in his capacity as a ghost-hunter, but he became a ghost-hunter because of an encounter he had." Here Gorilla's voice became deeper and somewhat grave. "A very *terrifying* encounter."

Porculina gasped again. "Oh, maybe I don't want to know."

But Gorilla continued speaking: "It was very early morning one foggy day in May and he was out for his early constitutional along a narrow country lane, which was positively shrouded in mist; and all at once, around a corner, there came floating a silent, gaunt, ghostly figure, pale...wan...the color of pearl in moonlight or an opal in... in...milk."

"Oh dear," Porculina quavered.

"Cousin Gregor froze there in his tracks and simply stared in amazement as this...this apparition floated toward him through the vapors... positively ethereal...like a...oh, like a great silvery gossamer butterfly."

Porculina clasped her trotters together. "And then what?" Her voice was now only a tremulous whisper.

"Well," said Gorilla, his tone becoming even more mysterious and dramatic, "it just kept coming, closer and closer and closer, looming out of the mist. Gregor still couldn't move. And it kept coming. And then it was right there, right next to him..."

Porculina squealed softly in horror. "Oh, don't tell me..."

"And then, just as this... terrific shape out of a nightmare looked like it was about to pass him by, it suddenly stopped and turned its eyes directly toward him..."

"Oh, I can't take it..."

"And it tipped its hat and said, 'Morning, Mr. MacGorilla, fine morning for a brisk stroll.' Well, you can imagine Gregor's fright at..."

"Wait," said Porculina, her voice now somewhat more mystified than terrified, "you mean the ghost... knew him?"

"Yes, indeed," said Gorilla with great brio. "Well, actually, you see, it wasn't... *quite* a ghost."

After another pause, Porculina said, "What does that mean? What was it?"

"The... *postman!*" he replied with a deep, dramatic flourish.

"The... postman?" Porculina practically whined. "But, Gor-Gor..."

"You see, he was looking very pale that day. Edward. I mean... that's the postman's name. Eddie, I call him. Capital fellow."

"Pale?"

"Very. Almost ethereal, as I said. Though, come to think of it, that may have had something to do with the mist."

Several more seconds elapsed before Porculina finally gushed, "Oh, how thrilling!"

"Ah, oh dear, excuse me," said Muzzles at this point, "but did you say, ah... thrilling?"

"Oh, Gorilla's family is just full of them," replied the little pig: "adventurers and explorers and heroes. It's just so... so amazing. The stories he has to tell. And he never seems to run out of them. It's not like my family lore at all, which is very boring. Just generations of soft toy pigs trottering about on the margins of history, not really accomplishing much at all. Winning the occasional eating contest, of course, but no more glory than that. Crumbled cashews, I wish I had so many wonderful romantical stories."

"Oh, come now," said Gorilla encouragingly, "it's true we can't all have countless illustrated ancestors and heroic uncles and cousins and such.

160

But every family has its notables. I'm sure, if you think about it, you've some fine tales to tell of piggies past."

"No," said Porculina mournfully. But then, her voice rising in pitch, she suddenly said, "Well, actually, there's one, perhaps. My family does have one somewhat notable figure in its line, from back in the days of Roman Britain. One of us was the first native Briton toy to become not only a citizen of the empire, but a member of the senate in Rome."

"Really?" asked Muzzles in a tone of genuine fascination.

"You've never mentioned that," added Teddy. "I'd have remembered."

"Oh yes," said Porculina. "In fact, he may have been the first soft toy from anywhere to be a Roman senator."

"What was his name?" asked Muzzles.

"Well, his *Roman* name was Porculian — that is, Porculianus Britannicus. His original British name, though, was Moch ap Mochyn. He came from a long, long line of Mochs and Mochyns. He was said to be very wise. At least, he knew how to make the loveliest crumpets."

"I've heard of him," said Muzzles with considerable animation. "Why, my goodness, that's a very distinguished ancestry indeed."

"I'm impressed," said Teddy. "But ... did crumpets exist in those days?"

"Only among toy pigs," said Porculina. "You know how forward-thinking they've always been. Anyway, Porculian's one great project when in office was the creation of an imperial library of cook-books from all over the Graeco-Roman world; but he left the senate after only a few years, before his plans came to fruition. No one in Rome knew how to make proper Eccles cake, you see, and he couldn't bear it."

"There was Eccles cake too in ...?" Teddy began to ask.

"There, you see," said Gorilla emphatically. "Every family has tales to tell."

"But not tales as ... as *dashing* as yours has," said Porculina. "It's always something grand with your lot."

"Well," said Teddy, "it's always certainly something ... unique." Then he took a deep breath. "But, if you'll forgive me, we really need to think   161 about what to do next. Until we've discovered who's been making these almost nightly raids on the château, and how he or she has knowledge of the hidden causeway under the east wing, and the secret door and stairs...and the hidden cabinet in the library..."

"That *is* quite a lot of knowledge," said Muzzles.

"Precisely," agreed Teddy, "and that makes our mystery especially perplexing. If it were simply a matter of intruders looking about for booty..."

"The gang of worms," said Gorilla contemplatively.

"Yes," said Teddy, undeterred, "if it were just a, say...gang of worms..." He briefly paused to allow himself a wince. "Well, that would be just a matter of random burglary. But this has been the constant campaign of someone with a real knowledge of the château and its history, as well as access to one half of the map that Octave had made of the Green Star's hiding place."

"By Jove!" Porculina suddenly exclaimed in what was instantly recognizable as her slow-witted sidekick voice. "Why, my dear old bear, it's... it's...an *inside job!*"

"So it would seem," said Teddy.

"Oh, but, goodness gracious me," said Muzzles, "certainly not anyone we know. I mean, after all, I can't think of a single toy associated with le Château de Petit-Ours who's remotely capable of such...such dastardly behavior. I mean, really—sneaking about in the night without so much as stopping in to say hello and have a cup of tea, impersonating a ghost... Well, it's the sort of wickedness that can't be countenanced... or imagined of soft toys."

Teddy sighed softly. "I'm sympathetic to your doubts," he said, "but I can tell you—in fact, the three of us can—that the inherent goodness of the toy heart isn't always proof against the direst temptations. Under certain circumstances, even a kind and fluffy soul can yield to base impulses and behave...well, rather badly."

"Heavens forfend," said Muzzles softly.

162   "Oh, but only by accident," said Gorilla reassuringly.

"Oh, Gor-Gor," said Porculina warmly, "you've such a generous nature. But surely you remember the theft of the treasure of Castle MacGorilla last..."

"Oh, yes," said Gorilla airily, "but we needn't go into that now. Just my point, though: it was all quite inadvertent, if you recall. An accidental pilferage. Happens all the time if one's not careful."

"No, it..."

But here Teddy intervened: "Regardless, we need to think what to do here and now. I'm disposed to borrow a strategy from the past, actually. Just as in that case, I'm thinking of setting some sort of trap. You see, I have to admit that I have certain suspicions..."

"Perfidious gerbil pirates?" asked Porculina, resuming her sidekick intonations. "Insidious mole mountebanks?"

"Ah, no... my dear old pig," said Teddy, briefly assuming his part. "Suspicions regarding... well, one mustn't speculate. I shouldn't like to do anyone an injustice. But, if we can lay a trap with sufficient cunning, I believe we can bring this business to a proper resolution... without calling on the authorities, moreover. I..."

At just that moment, however, the door of the laundry swung wide and Bow and Wow scuttled out into the courtyard.

"Oh, hello, you chaps!" called out Gorilla merrily.

"M'laird," said Bow in a somber voice.

"Miss, Sirs," said Wow in the same tone, "Monsieur Rolandus has asked us to tell you that he'll be here shortly to help you down from the line."

"Tea awaits," added Bow. Then he sighed lugubriously.

"Is something wrong?" asked Porculina.

Bow looked up at her from somber eyes. "Oh, nothing, miss. I was simply thinking of little Luc, and how we all used to share warm milk and biscuits together."

Now Wow sighed as well. "Little Luc, yes," he said. "An *accountant* now... and one with adult-sized feet." He shook his head sadly. "Tragic."

CHAPTER 12

Laying the Trap

WITH THE FOLLOWING DAWN CAME THE FIRST day of the Cider Festival and, before the public celebrations began, the guests and particular friends of the château once again gathered in the great banqueting hall, this time for a hearty French country breakfast prepared under the watchful crocodilian eyes of Draco. The pale morning light poured in through the fan-shaped windows high

164

in the walls, and everything — the great crystal chandelier, the deep blue and gold of the ceiling's vault, the slender columns of white and gold, the rose and white marble of the floor, the red and tawny tapestries — seemed to float in its clear radiance. Angus appeared in his most lustrous pearl-white morning suit. Teddy, Porculina, Gorilla, and Muzzles were there, of course, as were Rex, Ellie, Kipper, Jacques, Onyx, Obsidian and — looking particularly grand in a summer gown of glistening white satin and a mantilla of exquisite lace, her lorgnette glinting in her paw — Madame Lapin de Gris.

"Toast and marmalade," whispered Porculina to Gorilla, "she looks just like a fairy empress."

"Or a lovely big... *snowflake*," said Gorilla, who himself looked quite resplendent in his coppery paisley *gi* and dark bronze belt, "...with shiny whiskers."

As was the tradition here for the Cider Festival's inaugural break-fast, the food was set out in a buffet all along the eastern wall of the room, Draco hovering nearby like a hummingbird for many minutes and inspecting the feast for any defect or omission. Auguste was at his most spectacularly dignified in his best butler's morning attire, and was engaged principally in issuing instructions to Bow and Wow, regarding such matters as the exact angle of the cutlery on the table and the faintest hint of a stain upon an empty glass. And, of course, Rolandus was present, also in his best butler's tie-and-tails, but he appeared to be all but entirely preoccupied in keeping an unobtrusive but constant eye on Gorilla. At last, Draco seemed satisfied, nodded to the two footmen, lifted a small bell from the long table in his jaws, shook it lightly so that it emitted a delightfully musical tinkling, replaced it, and announced, "Breakfast is served."

The guests began to move toward the repast, preceded by a small pink blur that arrived at the buffet table before the last echoing tintin-nabulation of the breakfast bell had faded from the air. The board was lavishly laid with every imaginable kind of Sino-Cymric breakfast fare:

Welsh laverbread (seaweed, that is) swimming in a soy-broth, wontons filled with sweet fruit and Welsh porridge, oat cakes and crempog (Welsh griddle cakes) served atop beds of glutinous rice and boiled milk, congee drowning in Welsh honey, buttered toast and red bean cakes, and — as a special treat for one honored guest — dim sum stuffed with fresh banana and dusted with nutmeg, as well as ever so many more dishes. And, within a matter of seconds, an enormous and swaying tower of food, beneath which two small trotters were only faintly visible, made its way toward the dining table. By the time the other guests had arranged themselves in their chairs, Porculina was scampering back for more. But, when she returned and everyone was now present and accounted for, Teddy turned his eyes to Angus, seated several places further along and on the other side of the table, and discreetly nodded at him. Angus returned the nod, even more discreetly. Then, taking up a teaspoon, he tapped a glass several times, cleared his throat, and spoke out loudly: "Dear friends, if I may, I crave a few moments of your time. I've some extraordinary news to impart — news that I'll ask you to keep in strict confidence, but that I feel perfectly safe in sharing with you, my good and trusted friends."

The cheerful chattering clamor of a moment before at once subsided into a few murmurs and whispers and then into silence.

Angus surveyed his guests with a solemn expression for a few seconds, bowed his head graciously to Madame Lapin de Gris, and resumed: "A few evenings back, as you will all recall, on another joyous occasion, I related to you all the story of the Green Star of the Nile, the great and flawless cut emerald supposedly brought back from Egypt by my illustrious ancestor Pierre Louis Jacques Saint-Clair Bouvard de Petit-Ours, as a gift from the beloved teddy bear of the Khedive. At that time, I professed my total incredulity regarding the tale; I considered it no more than a legend, concocted for the *divertissement* of the very young and the very … well, let's say, simple."

A distinctly apish and delighted "It's a jolly story!" emanated from one corner of the table.

"Yes," said Angus, drawing in a deep breath, "exactly. As I was saying, however, that was what I thought *then*. And I was sharply rebuked — rightly, as it turns out — for my views." Here again Angus aimed a courtly bow at the lady rabbit at the table's head. "I now know," he continued, "that I was in error. For the Green Star not only really exists; it has been *discovered!*"

Briefly, omitting many details — such as the hidden door in the wall near the library, the forgotten staircase, the secret passage under the château, and of course the explorers' misadventures with earth, wind, and water — Angus recounted the discovery of the passage from the well-house to the island and of the secret chamber in the obelisk. As he spoke, one loud gasp chased another and another, all around the table's edge, until at last the relay reached Madame Lapin de Gris, who instead of taking up the baton merely assumed a triumphant expression, set her lorgnette aside, gazed down the length of the table in regal silence, and then nodded once, like Zeus upon his throne.

At the end of his narrative, Angus's tone became somewhat more personal, and he turned to the elderly bunny and said, "Forgive me, good lady, for doubting your word and for failing to heed your wisdom. But for the extraordinary deductive powers of my cousin's mind, and for the daring and intelligence of his friends, and for the labors of Monsieur Rolandus, and — last but not least — the prodigious nasal powers of young Monsieur Longmuzzle, I would have persisted in my arrogance and ignorance to this very hour."

"Ah," said Madame Lapin de Gris, raising a gracious paw, "you needn't grovel and abase yourself abjectly, however justified it may be for you to do so. I forgive you without reserve, my dear boy. As ever, you are as a son to me." Now a benignant smile appeared on her small delicate features. "Needless to say, now that you've found the Green Star, you will immediately have it removed from the premises, before today's festivities in fact, disown it entirely, and disburden this great estate of the dire weight of its curse and its dark malevolent magic."

At this, Angus drew himself up straight, raised a single eyebrow, and smiled gently but wryly. "Why, nothing of the sort, dear good lady. Yes, I freely confess my folly in disbelieving the story of the Green Star, but I have not disavowed my devotion to reason. I'm a bear of the Enlightenment, after all, and refuse to yield to superstitions and night-terrors. Why, this emerald is part of the history of my family and of this estate. More than that, it is part of the precious history of all *les peluches de France*. It should go on permanent public display here at the château, where all the little soft toys of the world can come and see it for free, and learn something of the history of their people. I'll have a special exhibition hall built for it, and..."

But, as he had been speaking, the expression on Madame Lapin de Gris's face had been growing more and more alarmed and indignant, her small pink nose and glossy ears and bright whiskers quivering ever more violently, until she could contain herself no longer. "*Quel imbécile!*" she positively spluttered. "A fool only half disabused of his folly is a worse fool than when he began; for now he imagines he's learned all he needs to learn and has become wise." Whispers, murmurs, mumbles, gasps, mutterings... a sneeze... Gorilla remarking "Lovely porridge, this!"... the soft clatter of Porculina's trotters as she brought back a third helping from the buffet table...

"Dear lady," replied Angus in an affectionate tone, "my reverence for you is boundless, but my reverence for reason is no less fervent. Would you have me be anything other than true to my deepest convictions?"

"Would I have a half-wit do other than halving his wits yet further?"

"*Alors*, my dear good lady," replied Angus, barely repressing an affectionate laugh, "so very harsh... so peremptory. I revere your wisdom, but I must remain true to my principles."

"Principles? *Pah!*" replied the small rabbit. "Principles that hang about your neck like an albatross... impertinently demanding to remain for tea!" Then she scowled and quietly remarked, to no one in particular, "They always do, as it happens. I can't imagine why. Very ill-bred creatures...."

Here she took a deep breath, clearly seeking to compose herself. Then, in a calmer if no kinder tone, she said, "How can you subject my nerves to such stress? Surely you know I suffer — suffer *tragically* — from the devastating medical conditions of 'acute elegance' and 'morbid sophistication.'"

"Not only do I know this," replied Angus, again repressing a smile as best he could; "it is for me a source of constant grief. I beg you, therefore, good and dear friend of so many years, be at peace. We must not succumb to superstitions or believe in phantoms of the night…"

"If I may," the gentle clacking and clicking voice of Kipper interrupted, "surely if the emerald is said to be cursed, and surely too if there have been misfortunes in the past associated with its presence, the more rational course of action would be to… well, test the story. I mean, after all…" — and here the dolphin looked about the table with a mild expression — "…after all, there have, it seems, been sightings of the very phantoms you mention. Or one phantom, at any rate. I myself may have seen him."

"Ah, yes," the far more imposingly resonant voice of Jacques (seated to Kipper's left) now also sounded out. "Far be it from me, Monsieur, to venture any opinion in this matter, inasmuch as I am merely a fortunate guest of a better guest, so to speak" — he too now aimed a courtly bow of the head in the direction of Madame Lapin de Gris — "but I've learned to rate the opinions of this good… cetacean friend of mine very highly indeed. I mean, well, as the ancient Greeks knew, one should always heed the advice of a dolphin. They're very… oracular, you know."

"Test?" asked Angus, spreading his paws before him. "How, pray tell, can one do that?"

"Perhaps," continued the shark, raising a pensive fin to his terrifying jaws, "you could do as your good friend suggests and… well, remove the article from the premises, to see whether its observable effects — ghosts, for instance — depart along with it. As a natural philosopher and scientist, I believe strongly in the experimental method."

Now Angus looked about the table with a frankly bemused expression. "Good friends," he said, "let us be reasonable. Has the Enlightenment then truly never reached these latitudes? Surely no one here truly believes in ... ancient curses ... and ghosts ... ”

But, rather than encouragement, the murmur that briefly arose from all quarters of the table seemed to suggest disagreement, or at least doubt.

“Sir,” said Draco, floating across the room from the buffet and stationing himself in the air near the end of the table where Porculina was just finishing her fourth helping of the breakfast, “it may not be my place as a mere chef, but ... ”

“We don’t stand on rank here, either,” said Angus. “We are sons and daughters of the Republic, after all ... even if some of us also happen to have aristocratic titles ... and fore-bears.”

“Quite so, sir,” said Draco. “Good of you to be so ... democratic and all. But, look you, I know a thing or two about cursed treasures. On the Western side of my family, there’s quite a long history of such things — storing up wealth with all sorts of malign magic clinging to it, and placing curses of our own on objects of special significance, and all of that. It’s ... well, it’s just the way dragons are.”

“I say,” Gorilla joined in, “I’ve a cursed treasure of my own, now that I come to think of it. Back at the old castle, that is. Terrifically terrible thing too. I can’t remember quite what it does, but it’s definitely very, um, *cursey.*”

“It’s true,” mumbled Porculina through a mouthful of congee. Then, swallowing properly, she added, “Creampuffs, we’ve seen it in action. The curse is that — well, I don’t quite recall exactly, but it has something with everyone being very, very ... *cross* with you.”

There were several gasps of alarm at this. Ellie exclaimed, “How dreadful!” Onyx concurred: “Horrid!” “Dear, oh dear!” ventured Muzzles. And Obsidian lowered his head in an attitude of sorrow: “That’s just the way of things, I suppose.”

“My, my, miss,” said Draco, his voice sinking nearly to a whisper. “That’s a grim and baneful word indeed. No one in my clan ever laid quite so dark a curse as that. The worst, which my grand-uncle Daffyd pronounced over his favorite bauble—a glass marble with a green twisty thing at its heart—was that anyone so rash as to lay larcenous hands upon it would soon thereafter lose... *his favorite pair of socks!*" His voice rose dramatically on these last five words.

"Oh, but that's very bad too," said Gorilla, a note of gravity entering his voice. "I say, I'd be all a-fluster if I lost my best Argyles. But surely—I mean, if the chap who accidentally took that marble were to return it, with maybe a jolly 'Sorry for that, old bean!' or something pleasant like that—well, surely he'd get his socks back."

For a moment, Draco stared somberly at Gorilla. Then he said, "No, m'laird, I fear not. There's nothing in the curse that says that... not even in the fine print. Anyway, everyone knows that when socks go missing it's because they've been spirited away forever by the Tylwyth Teg."

Porculina looked up from her gleamingly bare plate with a wrinkled brow. "The Tyl...?"

"The Tylwyth Teg, miss," said Draco: "the fairy-folk of Wales... the 'Fair Family,' that is."

Porculina's eyes grew wide. "I didn't know that at all," she said. "Buttered muffins and peaches! Is that where they go? I mean, I just thought washing-machines occasionally ate them—it's understandable that they might get hungry, after all..."

"No, miss, it's a known fact. Socks go to the Land of Faerie when they go, and can never be called back again. Mind you, occasionally the Tylwyth Teg replace them with changeling socks, which look like the originals, but one mustn't be fooled, because those are very mischievous magical socklings from the other realm. They no sooner appear than they get holes in them, and you have to darn them... over and over and over... without rest..."

At this point, Angus moaned aloud and buried his face in his paws. "Again. What has become of the modern soft toy world? Fairies, curses... ghosts..."

"*Alas,*" a deep silky voice exclaimed from another corner of the table, "and—if it seems not too bitter a word here—*alack.*" It was Rex, shaking his head slowly as he spoke. "And yet, how very poignant." He looked up now, staring at Angus nearly down the whole length of the table, and his eyes shone gravely in the morning light. "I find in this situation — this ancient manse, this cursèd jewel, this horrid apparition in the night, this tragic uncertainty about how to thwart the cruel dictates of fate — something worthy of epic verse. If only we could find some way of joining it to a truly great epic theme, such as flower-shows..."

"*Oooo*," said Porculina, "that *would* be stirring. I mean, what with all the standing up and such that people do at flower-shows, and the great lovely teas with scones and such, it would be full of action and romance and..."

"You know," remarked Ellie, somewhat shyly, "I believe there are other topics for epic verse. I mean, I've danced a few ballets based on great works of..."

"Ah yes," Rex conceded in a resonant vibrato, "this is true. Of course there are — and yet... yet..." He looked around the table, his expression almost monumental in its loftiness. "Once one has discovered the most elevated matter of epic, and ascended its heights — as I believe, in all humility, I myself have done — one cannot simply return to the foothills again and... sup on poorer fare, as it were."

"Oh, I don't know," said Gorilla. "Our old friend Cuttles writes about all sorts of things — oysters and rubber balls and the like, all of it very tragical and sad — and I don't think he ever writes about flower-competitions. And he's quite the cleverest chap..."

"Oh, *him*," interrupted Rex: "the... *dramatist*. Yes, I imagine *he* would..."

But here Teddy cleared his throat, somewhat more loudly than seemed quite necessary, and said, "Anyway, what's important is what happens next." He sent another meaningful glance in Angus's direction. "You were about to say..."

"Oh, yes," said Angus, composing himself and attempting a mild smile. "As I say, I intend to have a secure exhibition space built for the emerald — perhaps an independent structure. And tonight, after the Cider

Festival's inaugural celebrations have passed, I shall perhaps have the gemstone placed under guard."

"Again!" Madame Lapin de Gris cried out angrily. "*Quelle folie!* Is my word as nothing to you? I who have cared for you forever and a day? Am I just a silly old... *hare* to you?"

"Heaven forfend, my good lady," said Angus in seemingly genuine distress.

"I implore you, Monsieur le Comte," Jacques's smooth baritone broke in once more, through three or four coughs. "During my time as a guest of Château Lapin de Gris, I have come to revere the wisdom of the great lady who there presides. Such generosity of soul, such goodness... such unfailing aid to me in my researches and inquiries... such splendid buttered toast..."

"*Oooo*," said Porculina again.

"It seems to me — not that it's my place to say, but I feel a burden on my heart — it seems to me that her counsels should not go unheeded."

"They are not unheeded," replied Angus. "But neither can I simply surrender my principles and deepest convictions. In any event, we needn't decide anything absolutely till tonight. Till then, the emerald shall rest undisturbed... in the library."

"The library?" said Madame Lapin de Gris, her eyes wide with disbelief, her little pink nose and silvery whiskers quivering violently.

"Well, you see," interjected Muzzles, "we've really nowhere else to put it. And, what with the festival starting, and so all hands on deck, as it were, it's really the best place. There's a little hiding place there, you see..."

"But is that really very safe?" asked Ellie.

"Is anything?" asked Obsidian in a hollow murmur. "Ever?"

"We'll look in from time to time," remarked Bow.

"On the hour, every hour," remarked Wow.

"But..." Ellie began again.

"Oh, there's nothing to worry about, dear Mademoiselle Phant," said Angus. "No one apart from you, my good and trustworthy friends, even knows the gemstone has been found. And there's no one here who should not be trusted without reserve. I ask you all only not to share the information with anyone."

At this Onyx giggled (or whickered in a gigglish way). "This is so silly. So much upset about a rock."

"About a curse," corrected Madame Lapin de Gris. "And a curse attached to a very expensive rock. But..." She turned her eyes to Angus and her voice became softer and calmer. "Very well, then. I shall say no more. In fact... maybe I should not worry so. Maybe I am just a foolish old rabbit."

"Oh no, dear lady," said Angus, somewhat surprised: "quite the contrary."

"And," Teddy now spoke up again, "it's only for a short time, after all." He raised a paw. "Oh, Auguste, I was wondering..."

But his words were cut short by the crash of the silver tray of spoons that Auguste had dropped from his flippers. "*Ah ha!*" he positively yelled, with a tone at once somehow indignant and triumphant. "As I knew would happen! At last, the moment has come! I knew that sooner or later some cruel accusation would fall upon me! That I would be pilloried by this... this... *policeman.*" He snorted, which sounded rather like a dissonant note from a piccolo. "It was inevitable that the poor, longsuffering, guileless, poetically listless Bonapartist penguin would be the target of persecution... a tale as old as the Republic."

"I was only going to ask," said Teddy, his voice rising in volume, "whether you happened to know the time."

"The time?" asked Auguste in a tone of enraged incredulity. "The time? Far too late, I should say. *That* is the time. Long past the grand glorious noonday of France's greatness. Long past..."

"I mean, the time of day," Teddy interrupted once more. "Right now, I mean."

Auguste fell silent for a moment, staring at Teddy with an expression of blank disdain. Curling up the corners of his mouth with an acidic expression, he withdrew his watch from his waistcoat pocket, arched an

eyebrow, glanced down, and in a cold voice said, "A quarter past seven..."
Then, raising his eyes and beak haughtily to the ceiling, as if not deigning to look at his persecutor, he added, "...-*ish.*"

"Thank-you," said Teddy with a wearily tolerant sigh.

For a long moment, no one spoke. Then, as cheerful as ever, Gorilla's
voice broke the spell: "I say, how silly of me! I'm still in my pyjamas."

Another, shorter silence ensued, until Obsidian said, "How on earth
can you tell?"

But it was Rolandus who spoke next: "Some mysteries should remain
unexplored. I shall attend to the matter directly, m'laird."

Bright, billowing pavilions, long tables plenteously laden with gleaming
apples and delicacies of every kind, figures in elegant summer suits and
dresses ambling across or gathering in circles upon the emerald lawn, the
limpid golden glow of the midday sun, the green shadows of wind-stirred
oak and elm leaves undulating over the grass, the sweet clamor of voices
raised in mirth and cordiality and delight, the happy cries of young
soft toys dashing about with balloons and candies in their hands, paws,
claws, and tentacles — the Cider Festival was well under way. Angus
was passing among his guests star-scattered in the grass, greeting them
with his customary gallantry. The staff of the château slipped in and
out among the visitors in a constant flow with trays of frothing cider
in fluted glasses. Madame Lapin de Gris was positively enthroned in her
Bath chair under the grandest elm of all. And, as the noon hour struck,
Ellie began limbering up at the bars at the back of the stage while Rex
came to the front of the boards. For a moment, the small iridescent
dinosaur stood in stern silence, one tiny forelimb folded upon his breast,
the other delicately extended before him. Slowly, the assembled multitude
grew quiet; something in his solemn manner communicated itself to them.
Once everyone was silent, Rex cleared his throat and, without prelude,
began his declamation:

O, sing in me, Flora, great goddess of all things blooming,
Through me tell of the ancient days and of the men of yore —
And ladies too, of course — who strove amid sun-dappled lilies,
Amid the drooping crysanths fair, amid the marigolds,
The roses, tulips, lupins, larkspur, and the posies pink,
Gardenias, hyacinths, irises, carnations, lustrous sunflowers,
And all things petaled, leafy, and oft-watered...

From the crowd of guests, however, making every effort not to fidget, there were certain mysterious absences, among them Teddy, Porculina, Gorilla, and Muzzles. But, out of so great a number, no one was likely to notice.

Tell of doughty Susie Tompkins (15 Queensbury Row),
And of her rival, fierce as Nemesis, Jemima Jones
(Address unknown), and how upon one fatal morn their lives
Became entangled like the creeping clematis enwound
With pale moon-blossoms on their spreading vines upon white trellises...

"I say, you chaps," whispered Gorilla suddenly from his hiding place between two bookcases, breaking the silence in the library for the tenth time or so, "what do you think of my *gi* now? It's one my cousin Freddy gave me."

"Please, old fellow," replied Teddy as he had done on all the previous occasions from his post behind another bookcase, "we really must be silent."

"Dear me, yes," whispered Muzzles anxiously from beneath the table where he was crouching.

But after a moment Porculina, who was hiding behind a small writing desk, could not resist whispering back, "I love midnight blue. It makes you look very, very dashing."

"I say," responded Gorilla, clearly pleased.

"But," the little pig continued, "I'm not *quite* sure about the... uh, vivid pink belt."

"Remember," Gorilla replied, "it's all a matter of one's mood."

"But what mood does pink signify?"

"Silly old piggles," said Gorilla warmly, "it means I'm feeling in the pink, of course. That one's easy."

"Please," Teddy protested again. "It's no good setting a trap if we make so much noise anyone can hear us."

"Sorry," murmured Porculina.

"Quite," said Gorilla.

Nearly a minute passed in silence.

"But it really is my best *gi*," Gorilla remarked.

"Oh..." Teddy began.

But just then Muzzles hissed urgently, "Wait, I smell someone approaching... but, ah, goodness, I can't tell who. All I smell is... phosphorus..." 177

"Quiet, quiet," Teddy said, his voice becoming less than a whisper even as it became more emphatic.

Everyone, even Gorilla, fell silent (though, in his case, because he was trying to recall what phosphorus is). And, while no one was speaking, the library door creaked on its hinges and opened, and in floated the ghost. Except, to be perfectly honest, it did not appear particularly ghostly in the daylight, and it was not really floating. Instead, in shape it looked vaguely like an enormous eggplant, entirely hidden under a somewhat unimpressive linen sheet, and it did not so much float as mince, swaying awkwardly as it did so. For a moment it paused near the doorway, bending its "head" one way and another, obviously trying to make sure that no one else was there, and then ventured into the room, moving with clear purpose toward the very shelves where Gorilla had surprised it some nights before. At this point, while its back was turned, Teddy slipped out of hiding and gestured to his companions to do the same. No one made any noise, not even Gorilla (he was still puzzling over the phosphorus question), as they crept up upon the intruder, who was carefully removing volumes from the shelves. Teddy drew within four feet, raised his paws to bring the party to a halt, and calmly remarked, "You won't find it there, I'm afraid."

At once, the ghost spun about and, looking quickly at each of the four companions, screamed.

At this, Gorilla was roused from his thoughts. "Oh, I say," he cried in delight, "hullo there, Alphonse. I've been wondering when I'd see you again."

The ghost dropped the two rather large volumes it had been clutching to its chest loudly to the floor and screamed a second time.

"Now, now," said Teddy, "I'll ask you to stop... *that*. There's nothing to be afraid of. I think I know..."

"Golly," interrupted Porculina, taking a step closer to the spectre and staring at it fixedly, "you're not nearly as terrifying as I thought you'd be."

"He's not really a ghost, you know," remarked Teddy to the little pig. Then, turning back to the intruder, he added, "As I was saying, I think I know..."

"Oh, don't be ridiculous," Gorilla interjected in a cheerful voice. "It's Alphonse, for goodness sake. Don't you recognize him?"

Teddy sighed gently. "No, you see, old fellow, Alphonse isn't..." He paused and breathed deeply. "I mean to say, *this* isn't a ghost. It's a burglar *disguised* as a ghost."

Gorilla's brow furrowed. He turned his eyes toward the shrouded figure, looked first up and then down, then up again; then he stepped back to get a better view; then he stepped forward to get a still better view. Then, at last, he turned to Teddy again. "Looks very ghosty to me. I mean, if he's not a ghost — well, then, it's a dashed clever disguise."

Teddy stared at his friend for a moment. "It's a sheet."

Gorilla turned his gaze back to the intruder, cocked his head to one side, then cocked it to the other. "Hmm," he said. After another second, he added another "Hmm." He scratched his head thoughtfully and nodded sagely. "I'm not getting your point at all," he said to Teddy.

"A sheet, soaked in phosphorescent dye... so it glows in the dark..."

"Oh!" Porculina nearly squealed. "Gumdrops and grapefruit! I just realized, we've caught our culprit and..."

"Not quite..." Teddy began.

"...and I'm forgetting to play my part." Suddenly, she turned on the figure in the sheet, squinted fiercely, extended an accusing trotter, and announced in her most stentorian voice, "Ho, ho, my good fellow, you thought you could escape justice, but justice is the swiftest..."

The intruder did not wait to hear the end of her rebuke, however, but instead waved its rather short limbs to either side and cried out — "*OoooooooOoooooo!*" — though only until the noise dissolved into three hoarse coughs. It had the desired effect, however. Startled, the four companions all backed a step or two away, and the intruder took the opportunity to turn, hurl itself out of the library and into the corridor beyond, and

179

dash toward the secret door in the wall at the corridor's end. The four companions chased after as quickly as they could, emerging together from the library in time to see their quarry come to a sudden halt. For there before the door in the wall — standing wide open — Bow and Wow were now stationed, stern and obviously resolute.

"Woof," said Bow dryly.

"Indeed," said Wow. "And, if I may add, Grr."

"It's no good," Teddy called out in a surprisingly kindly voice, "the game's up, you know. There's no point in fleeing. Anyway, I'm fairly sure I know..."

But now the figure in the sheet turned about and began running — or, more accurately, wobbling very vigorously — in the opposite direction, right past its pursuers, careening from one side of the corridor to the other, and somehow managing to collide with every single suit of armor lined along the walls. This, however, proved advantageous, as two of the displays — a knight astride a rocking-horse and a knight with an enormous lollipop in its gauntlet — came tumbling down upon the granite floor with a terrific crash; and this created just enough of a shock to make Teddy, Gorilla, Porculina, and Muzzles take several steps back. In that brief moment of delay, the "ghost" — with extraordinary if altogether graceless speed — lunged around the corner into the hallway leading to the great foyer and disappeared from view.

"No one ever lets me finish," said Porculina ruefully.

"I wish we'd brought someone with longer legs," was Teddy's only reply.

"Well," said Gorilla ebulliently, rubbing his hands together eagerly, "this *is* jolly. Let's see where he's headed." And he began to run after the vanished figure, calling out, "I say, Alphonse, old chap..."

Waiting only long enough to exchange resigned glances, Teddy, Porculina, and Muzzles joined in the pursuit.

CHAPTER 13

Gorilla's Day of Glory

W HEN THEY CAME OUT THROUGH THE LARGE front entrance of the château into the great gravel courtyard, Teddy, Porculina, and Muzzles found Gorilla standing still, clearly out of breath, gazing into the distance where the rapidly diminishing figure in the sheet wove and wobbled awkwardly through the milling crowd toward the eastern end of the estate and the River Cher. Rolandus, Onyx, and Obsidian also happened to be standing there, near the front stairs, though they had ceased their conversation and were also staring at the outlandish sight of the fleeing "ghost." A few cries of alarm and surprise rose from many of the guests as it reeled past them.

"Dear, oh, dear," said Gorilla, pursing his lips. "I'll never catch up with him now."

"We need to try," said Teddy, "before he gets to the water."

Gorilla nodded. "Yes, there's nothing as saddening as a wet ghost."   181

"If I may," said Onyx, "you may not be able to catch him on foot, but it would be the easiest thing imaginable on horseback."

Teddy looked at the little mare. "I think you may be a bit small for…"

"By myself," Onyx interrupted, "no doubt. But the two of us are more than equal to the task. Laird Gorilla, if you would be so good as to place a foot on each of our backs and hold onto our manes…"

"Oh, muffins, how could you keep him balanced?" asked Porculina.

But Obsidian had now joined his sister, and Onyx was staring at him with a smile at once sly and inquisitive. He returned her gaze, then shifted his eyes to Teddy, then looked back at his sister again; and all at once he too smiled. It was a startling sight. And then he spoke out, in a tone of such brio that he sounded quite unlike the mordant, melancholy toy that Teddy and the others had known to that point: "*C'est tres facile,* Mademoiselle Pig: you are speaking to the greatest toy dressage duo in all of France! Laird Gorilla, if you would please mount up!"

And, before any other objection could be voiced, Gorilla was hopping up onto the backs of the little horses with a jubilant "Heigh-ho, you chaps!" And, even as his feet settled into place and he caught hold of their manes with a hearty "Cry haddock and let slip the frogs of yore!" they were off. It was a splendid thing to see. The two little horses moved in such perfect synchrony that it was as if they were a single toy, and with such flawless grace that the rotund form of Gorilla merely rose and fell smoothly with every agile stride. Before any of those they had left behind could even call out a warning, the three of them had covered a third the distance between the château and the fugitive intruder, amid more cries from the gathered guests — though now cries more of admiration than of alarm.

"Oh," said Teddy to Porculina and Muzzles, "if only we could keep up."

A second passed before the sound of a throat being cleared caused them to turn to Rolandus. "Ahem. If, sir, it is a matter of *absolute* urgency," remarked the dog in an audibly reluctant tone, "there is…" He looked about uncomfortably and then shrugged. "There is an alternate…method of transport."

Teddy arched an eyebrow. "You don't mean..."

Rolandus merely stared at the little bear, a measuredly inexpressive expression on his face.

"I wouldn't want you to do anything you'd find... humiliating."

Briefly closing his eyes and then opening them again, Rolandus said, "Not humiliating, sir. Merely a little... humbling." And with that he bent forward and — clearly out of practice — dropped to all four feet. "I believe two of you should be able to fit on well enough," he said.

Teddy looked at his companions. "I'll go," he said.

"Not without me," answered Porculina firmly. "That's what a side-kick's for."

Rolandus now lowered himself to the ground and said, "I believe, sir, miss, that time is of the essence."

With no further delay, Teddy clambered onto Rolandus's back and, with Muzzles helping her by letting her place her short trotters squarely on the top of his nose, Porculina got on behind him.

"Please hold tight to my coat," said Rolandus, rising to his paws again. He briefly glanced back over his shoulder at Teddy and Porculina. "I trust," he said, "this need never be talked of hereafter." Then, clearing his throat once more, he opened his mouth and, in a rather matter-of-fact manner, quietly said, "I believe the correct locution is '*aroo, aroo*.'" There was a notable lack of conviction in his voice. He shook his head and ventured instead an equally unpersuasive "Tally-ho." Then, giving up on it altogether, he simply leapt forward. His speed in crossing the sward was remarkable and, in his immaculate tie and tails, he looked like nothing so much as an especially dignified torpedo, to which two small figures were hanging on for dear seams and stuffing, and from one of which regular little squeals of "Custard and cupcakes!" and "Peaches and persimmons!" and similar comestible phrases were continually being emitted.

The chase was magnificent, really, notwithstanding the somewhat ungainly motions and uneven pace of the lead. The figure in the sheet had enough of a head start that it was anything but certain that its pursuers could get to it before it reached the Cher, even though the two little horses galloped with such speed and precision it seemed they could catch a bolt of lightning if they wished, and Rolandus was closing the distance every bit as quickly. They all twisted and turned in and out and around scatterings of guests, all of whom froze in their places to watch in rapt fascination. Soon pursuers and pursued alike had cleared the east lawn, dashing along the margin of the reflecting pool, and were hurtling towards the river. Porculina's outcries had ceased, but now Gorilla could be heard calling out as the distance between him and his quarry steadily shrank away: "I say, Alphonse old chap, we need to talk!"

And then, just as the fugitive had come within twenty feet or so of the river bank, Onyx and Obsidian caught up to it, swung wide around it, and came to a sudden, perfectly coordinated halt, interposing themselves between it and the water. Gorilla, however, was unprepared for this and went tumbling forward, turning head over heels several times and finally landing in a seated position in the grass. But in an instant he was on his feet. "There you are, old fellow!" he remarked cheerfully to the thwarted and now halted fugitive, who was looking about in all directions, clearly at something of a loss as to what to do, its upper torso heaving slightly as if it was out of breath. Suddenly, it moved to the right and began wobbling frantically toward the river's edge only to be brought up short again by a weird bellow from Gorilla — "Wow-eeee!" — followed by the little ape flinging himself in the air, waving his arms wildly, and landing on his head. "Tea for two!" he added, bouncing to his feet again. Then, with a slight pause to observe, "This is the really *energetic* bit," he turned a very impressive cartwheel (for him, that is), and dropped into a crouch. "Hip-hip-hoorah!" he called out and at once began to spin about on one toe. He almost immediately tripped over his other foot and turned yet another somersault into the grass...

Now Rolandus had arrived and Teddy and Porculina were slipping down from his back; but at this point they did not have to do anything more. The large figure in the sheet seemed entirely to have forgotten its desire to flee, as if wholly absorbed in Gorilla's demonstrations of skill (so to speak).

"Yippee!" cried Gorilla, again bouncing to his feet. "And a good night to all the ships at sea!" And then he ran into a tree that happened to be not very far from the river's edge. With a soft, even plush *k-thonk* sort of sound, he rebounded from the trunk, twice rolled over backwards, and came at last to rest in the grass staring up at the sky. For a moment no one moved. Even Porculina was too startled to cry out. And then, in an effusive voice, Gorilla remarked, "I say, what lovely weather."

Now, seemingly having put every thought of flight from its mind, the "ghost" tentatively approached the little ape, bent over him solicitously, raised one of its short, protuberant arms to its hidden face, coughed softly, and then spoke in a deep, silky, terrifying, but somehow extremely concerned voice: "Are you quite all right, Laird MacGorilla?"

"Quite all right, thanks," replied Gorilla, sitting up and feeling his head to make sure it was still in the proper shape. "Happens all the time. That's just me putting my Idjitsu training into action."

"Please," said Teddy, who had now come to help Gorilla to his feet, "can we stop running now? There's no point any longer... Jacques, my friend."

For a moment the "ghost" simply stared at the little bear. Then it turned its head to look at the two little horses, Porculina, and Rolandus, who were all now spread out between it and the river and slowly approaching. Finally, with a head bowed in resignation, it shook itself. The sheet slipped away and fell into the grass, and there, standing unsteadily erect on the tips of his tail fins, was Jacques Tout-en-Dents.

Onyx gasped. Obsidian groaned.

"Rhubarb and rutabaga!" cried Porculina in a tone of deep disappointment. "Not you! Not when you ... when you love buttered toast so!"

"Oh, hullo, Jacques," said Gorilla. "Silly me, I mistook you for Alphonse."

The large shark smiled at Gorilla weakly but then turned a doleful countenance on Porculina, sighed despondently, and said, "Alas, dear good lady pig, it is I. Not even my love for buttered toast could save me from a life of desperate crime. It is I who sought to steal the Green Star of the Nile."

"I would never have believed it," said Onyx, her customary cheerfulness momentarily quelled.

"I suppose we should always expect the worst," remarked Obsidian, his customary melancholy momentarily restored.

"But why?" Porculina asked in an almost desperate tone. "What could make you behave so ... so ... so *humanly*?"

Jacques's eyes widened as if he had been stung by the word. Then, however, he squinted, as if trying to remember something. "Why?" he repeated. "Indeed ... that would be the question, wouldn't it?" His brow furrowed. "Well ... I ... ah ... oh ... um ... oh dear, let me think now. Yes, indeed. Just on the tip of my tongue." He tapped his front teeth pensively. "Why does one steal emeralds ...?" Then he seemed lost in thought for several seconds.

Finally, clearing his throat, Rolandus quietly suggested, "Greed, perhaps?"

"Hmm?" said Jacques raising his eyes. "You mean ... oh yes!" He snapped his fore-fin (quite how, no one could have said). "Indeed! That's it, of course! Greed!" He looked about at his captors. "What else could it be? Greed! I wanted ... um, something ... emeraldy! Green and gemmy and such. Just me, that is. All on my own ... no accomplices ... no other motives. Take me away! I surrender. It's a fair cop. I think that's what they say. Yes, that's it entirely — greed."

186

Teddy arched an eyebrow. "You're a good and noble fish, Monsieur Tout-en-Dents. I think you and I both know that that's not the real story."

"What? Why, my goodness, of course it is." Jacques's expression became meltingly earnest. "Oh, but what else could it be? We toy sharks are notoriously greedy. Besides" — and now the earnestness in his eyes took on an imploring quality as well — "surely you don't think that having already practiced such deception and attempted theft I could be so wicked as to lie to you as well. No, no, my honorable bear, it is as I say."

"I think you're honest by nature," replied Teddy, his voice very gentle now indeed, "just like all soft toys; but I think that, if you thought you were protecting a dear friend — and, shall we say, someone you truly revere — you might try to take all the blame on yourself. As for greed — no, that's implausible, to say the least. A greedy *peluche* is a thing almost unprecedented in nature."

"You mean he's part of a gang?" asked Porculina. "This just gets worse and worse."

"Not exactly," said Teddy.

Porculina, however, merely shook her head sadly. "Oh well," she said in a defeated voice, "I suppose there's only one thing for it then." Taking three steps toward the shark, she stretched out a trotter toward him, almost indifferently, and in a lethargic voice said, "Ho, ho, my good fellow, you thought you could flee justice, but..." She dropped her trotter listlessly to her side. "...*et cetera, et cetera*. It's just no good," she said with a sad shake of her head; "my heart's not in it."

"Cheer up, Pigsy," said Teddy. "If I'm right, it's not nearly as bad as you imagine. When this knot's finally untied, I think you'll find that no one is very much to blame at all. But" — here he clapped his paws together — "I think it's time we all returned to the château." He turned a meaningful look on Jacques.

"I take it I'm under arrest," remarked the shark with a somber nod.

"No, not at all," said Teddy. "What crime have you committed? You never actually took anything. I suppose you might be accused of trespass, but even then you're a regular guest of the château, so that's not a charge likely to stick. And I'm not a *gendarme*. I'm just a writer. No, we should all go back to my cousin and tell him the truth of things, so as to put his mind at rest. It's the honorable — the considerate — thing to do."

"Quite," replied Jacques in a subdued rumble.

"I say," interrupted Gorilla — who just then was being dusted off with a small brush Rolandus had unexpectedly produced from his pocket — "what's everyone looking so serious about? I'm afraid I wasn't listening. Teddy? I say, you're looking distracted."

Teddy was, as it happens, momentarily absorbed in thoughts of his own, but Gorilla's voice had roused him back into the moment. "You know, I've only just realized the most amazing thing. Your little display of Idjitsu just now..."

"The Dancing Hedgehog method," said Gorilla eagerly.

"Yes... disarming your opponent with pity... wasn't that it?"

"Right-o," said Gorilla, now assuming a sage expression: "you've learned, young bear."

"Well, it's just... it occurs to me..." He stared with wide eyes at his friends. "It occurs to me that... that it *worked*."

"Oh, Gor-Gor," exclaimed Porculina, now somewhat stirred from her dejection, "that's true! How glorious!"

As the small party of pursued and pursuers made their way back across the east lawn, the gathered guests parted before them, now speaking in hushed and uncertain voices. Reaching the great front entrance, Teddy — who was leading the way — found Angus and Muzzles standing together, staring with incredulous expressions. Auguste was there as well, with what one could only describe as a look of severe indifference on his face. Now the guests — who were crowding in behind the little group — were quite silent.

188

"Can this be?" Angus asked as the whole party came to a halt. "Do I understand that ... that it is *you*, my good Tout-en-Dents, who has been behind all these ... alarums and excursions?"

With a mournful countenance, the shark heaved a great baritone sigh, and said, "Yes, *mon seigneur*, it has been I all along. And, incidentally, my compliments on the Shakespearian reference."

"My goodness," said Muzzles in a somewhat fretful voice. "Gracious me, I'd never have imagined. How very singularly disheartening. My, my, my."

At this moment Ellie, still in her tutu, and Rex approached together.

"I'm deeply disappointed," the small elephant remarked very simply, and then a sound like the forlorn note of a distant cornet issued from her trunk. "I just don't know what to think."

"Terrible, terrible," concurred the small iridescent dinosaur with a slow, sad wag of his head. "And yet, how heroic the chase. How mighty the exploit. Laird MacGorilla, you in particular were superb, astride those mighty chargers. A Diomed! A Hector! A veritable Wilbur Groats (207 The Elms)!"

"I say," responded Gorilla, smoothing his midnight blue *gi*, "that's dashed decent of you. But, really, what's everyone looking so downcast about?"

"Why, this dark calamity, of course," replied Rex. "This ... treachery."

"This very sad business," said Ellie. "This betrayal. Oh, dear. It's quite ... quite dismaying." And again the note of sorrow sounded from her tiny trunk.

"I say," said Gorilla, now quite distracted, "that's a pretty noise. Can I make it?"

"I don't think you have the right sort of nose," said Ellie, obviously somewhat befuddled by this turn in the conversation.

"Never hurts to try," said Gorilla. Then, wrinkling his snout and squinting, he began struggling to imitate the little elephant's vaguely melodic little snort. He did in fact manage the snort part of it, though it was neither "melodic" nor "little," truth be told.

"Uh, listen," said Teddy, trying to recover from the shock that had left everyone momentarily shaking and wide-eyed, "things are neither so tragic nor as dreadful as everyone thinks, if I'm correct. I don't believe this has anything to do with any... betrayal. Nor was any avarice involved, though Monsieur Tout-en-Dents would have us think otherwise, and lay all the blame on him. Honestly, I believe what we really need right now is a good bracing cup of tea..."

"...and a large tray of biscuits," Porculina suddenly offered. "And some buttered toast, of course. And some little jam sandwiches..."

"Indeed," said Teddy, before the list could get any longer. "I propose, cousin, that our little party here go in and refresh ourselves, and calm our nerves, and then gather in the banquet hall in, say, an hour's time." Here he turned to Rolandus and then to Auguste. "I should like to ask the two of you together to see that certain other *peluches* are in attendance as well."

The dog and the penguin exchanged frigid stares.

"As you like," said Rolandus.

"If there is no other choice," said Auguste, turning up his beak.

For several tense seconds, Angus stared away at nothing in particular. Then, with a sigh, he withdrew a small cream-colored book from his jacket pocket and held it out for Gorilla. "Let me return this to you, my good Laird MacGorilla," he said in a bleak monotone. "It is very spiritually nourishing, I have no doubt. I fear, however, that nothing contains enough wisdom to have prepared me for this blow."

"Oh dear," said Gorilla, taking the book and slipping it into his *uwagi*. "Don't take on so. I'll get it right next time." And at once he began wrinkling his snout and squinting again.

Teddy, Porculina, Gorilla, Muzzles, and Jacques had their tea in a drawing room not far from the dining hall. It was a rather somber affair, despite the little jam sandwiches, except on the part of Gorilla, who spent much of the time holding forth on the mysteries of Idjitsu, the delights of rubber balls, how wonderful the hospitality of the château was even in the absence of bananas, the need for more bananas, the pleasant weather, and the pleasure of bananas. Jacques refused all food, but did at last take some tea. He declined to speak more than a few words. Teddy seemed strangely calm and helped himself to a small plate and two cups of tea. Muzzles professed to have lost his appetite. Porculina, however, found hers sharpened, and made sure that nothing went to waste. At the end of the hour, Rolandus appeared and announced that everyone whom Teddy had requested was now gathered together and waiting for them.

There was a solemn silence in the great banquet hall. Even the golden stars in the blue heaven of the ceiling seemed a little despondent as they looked down on the gathering: Teddy, Porculina, and Gorilla standing together at the foot of the long table; Angus standing at its head next to Madame Lapin de Gris, still in her Bath chair; Onyx, Obsidian, Rex, and Ellie ranged along one side; Muzzles, Kipper, and a very abashed Jacques along the other; while Draco hovered at something of a distance from the guests in the company of Bow and Wow, and Rolandus and Auguste exchanged looks of icy disapprobation from opposite ends of the room.

It was, at last — and predictably — Gorilla who broke the silence: "Really, you chaps and chapesses, why are you all so dashed morose? It's been a lovely day."

"Oh, Gor-Gor," said Porculina, her voice entirely devoid of its usual energy, "we're... well, we're simply shattered. Who could have thought that Jacques... someone with such refined tastes and good manners... could be so... so... dastardly?"

"Oh, surely it's not as bad as all that, Piggles old girl. I mean, what's he done except run around a bit with a sheet on his head? I've done that countless times; it's hard to get them off your head sometimes when you're getting out of bed..."

"He tried to steal the emerald," protested Ellie in her small, delicate voice.

191

"Oh, surely not," replied Gorilla with a small laugh.

"I'm afraid he did," said Onyx with a tender sigh of regret.

"Indubitably," said Obsidian grimly.

"Sad it is to tell," added Draco, "but true as true."

"Nonsense," said Gorilla. "No doubt just a misunderstanding."

"I hope you're right," said Kipper, casting a perplexed look in the direction of his friend. "I can't imagine why he would."

At this, however, Jacques raised a flipper and said, "It's good of you to defend me, but the evidence is irrefutable. I am a...a...footpad. A brigand. A..." He closed his eyes and dropped his head. "A thief. It was I who sought to steal the Green Star of the Nile... I and I alone... out of greed and from no other motive, and entirely without any accomplice... none whatsoever... absolutely no one... and most certainly not anyone I revere with a singular devotion bordering on idolatry."

For several moments, no one said anything. Then Gorilla, who had been staring thoughtfully at the dejected shark and tapping his lips with his forefinger, spoke again: "I think you're a bit confused, old fellow. Never mind. Things aren't always what they seem. That's one of the chief teachings of Idjitsu, you know. Freddy — my cousin, that is — put it ever so dashed cleverly. Let me see, how does it go? Oh, right: 'Sometimes, to see things clearly, you have to be looking at them directly, without a pillowcase over your head because you got tangled up in your bedclothes and...'"

"*Ahem*," Teddy interrupted with an unconvincing little cough. "That's very helpful, and I think..."

But Gorilla would not be deterred. "In fact, he illustrates the point with a story. Here —" And he reached into his pocket, withdrew the small cream-colored volume, and flipped back and forth through its pages till he came across what he was looking for. "Ah, here we go. Now listen, all of you, this is very, very deep... and mystical too. It just makes you think and think."

"Oh, really," said Teddy with a hint of strain in his voice, "I'm not sure we have time..."

"It goes like this: 'One evening, Sensei Freddy' — that's my cousin, who wrote this himself, but he tells it as if he's someone else, in a very clever *literary* way — 'Sensei Freddy was out for a walk about the grounds of Castle MacGorilla in the dusk when he encountered a goblin...'"

Porculina gasped.

Gorilla smiled. "Steady on, Piggles. 'It was a terrible sight: large, misshapen, with hundreds of blank green eyes. It stood in his path and would not let him pass. Thrice Sensei Freddy asked to be allowed to go his way, but the goblin would not move. Then, trying to circle around his antagonist, he found himself caught by his sleeve; and, when he tried to extricate himself from the monster's grip, he found himself more securely in its grasp. At this, he called upon his mystic arts and attempted the Distracted Snail method in order to effect his escape, but this only led to him being turned upside down by the creature. He then attempted the Tap-Dancing Weasel method, which got him right side up again but which still did not free him from the goblin's claws. And so through the night they contended, Sensei Freddy attempting one method after another, but none with any success. By morning, in the breaking light of dawn, he was now held so fast by his opponent that he could only wiggle one foot. Just then, Great Uncle Donal, Great Sage Equal of Heaven, came by for his morning constitutional and, seeing his great nephew helpless in the grip of the beast, shook his head and said, "Och whit're y' daein' thaer, y' wee witless ape? Can y' nae see tha's a gooseberry bush?" And at that moment, Sensei Freddy achieved enlightenment.'" Slowly Gorilla closed the book and looked about the room with a wisely knowing expression on his face, as well as the small enigmatic smile of someone who has just imparted a profound lesson to the woefully ignorant.

Everyone stared at him without speaking for several seconds. Then Porculina broke the silence, in a voice of hushed wonder: "Oh, that's so very... *deep*... so very mysterious." She shook her head almost helplessly. "Plums and pancakes... it just opens up ten-thousand paths of thought. Oh, I wish I were profound and mystical."

193

"Indeed," agreed Gorilla, nodding sagely. "But you'll get there, Piggles."

Another several seconds of silence passed before Ellie, somewhat hesitantly, said, "I'm afraid I don't quite understand what the, um, message is."

"Yes," remarked Muzzles, "I'm not quite — goodness — quite, ah, *wise* enough to take it in, I'm afraid."

Now Gorilla's smile widened into one of tolerant condescension. "Yes, it's all tremendously deepy, isn't it? I had a deuced hard time understanding it at first, but I thought and thought about it, and then all at once I understood. In Japanese philosophy, that's what they call 'instant enlightenment,' or 'sartorial style' . . . I think."

"And?" asked Obsidian after several more seconds had elapsed.

"Well, it's really very clear when you finally see it straight on," said Gorilla. "It means that things aren't always quite as bad as they appear. You see, you never know until you know, and when you do know then you know that you know what's what and why's why. Till then, though, you don't know, so you don't stop trying to know. But to understand all is to forget all."

"Ah," said Angus. "But of course."

"Well, I never," said Draco: "I think I see."

"As my cousin Freddy would say, the road of total misunderstanding leads to the palace of wisdom."

"That's why Gor-Gor is so wise, I suppose," said Porculina earnestly, looking about the table. "He misunderstands absolutely everything."

Gorilla stared affectionately at Porculina. "Thank-you, Piggles, old girl. Thank-you." And then he lowered his head, as if about to blush.

CHAPTER 14

All Is Revealed

"Y ES," SAID TEDDY AFTER A FEW MORE SECONDS of silence had elapsed. "Well, now that we've been...blessed with wise counsel, I think it's time we cleared all of this business up as best we can. As I've been trying to say, I believe the explanation will show that we're dealing here not with a case of greed or malice, but of..."

"Oh, it was all greed," protested Jacques: "Base greed, unalleviated by so much as a trace of admirable motives. I am a villain. A fiend."

"Marshmallows," said Porculina. "He does seem to know his mind."

"But why?" asked Ellie plaintively. "You're such a sweet shark."

"Why?" repeated Jacques, once again seeming slightly perplexed. "Well, why is anyone greedy?" He looked about the table quizzically. "I'm asking, actually: does anyone know why?"

With a sigh, Rolandus said, "I doubt even the truly greedy know why they are as they are. But perhaps it's because one wants something that one requires money to procure."

"Ah, yes," said Jacques, snapping a fin again. "That's it precisely! I wanted ... *something*. Something that cost a great deal ... or a little. How much do emeralds go for again? I mean, I know of course, but I'm testing you."

Angus scowled. "I'm beginning to find your story a little ... inconsistent."

"Ah," the sonorous voice of Rex floated across the table, "perhaps it was not so much the object of the chase, but the thrill — the exhilaration of acquiring the emerald by cunning, daring, guile. It would almost be heroic — well, if it weren't cowardly, craven, base, and wicked. And you might have got away with it, if it hadn't been for the glorious feats — the epic feats — of Laird MacGorilla. Oh, that veritable Rustam! That Cuchulainn! That Agnes Prynne! That Jemima Jones! That ..."

"Yes!" Jacques mercifully interrupted. "That's it! I did it for the thrill! And how thrilling it was!"

"Now you're contradicting yourself," said Onyx.

"Rather badly," added Obsidian.

"Yes, my goodness, I must say ..." said Muzzles.

"I say," spoke up Gorilla, "it's all getting a bit confusing. Obviously this has all been a misunderstanding. I say we just forget about the whole thing — I will in any event, probably before breakfast — and have a jolly game of charades."

"Please," Teddy said, raising his paws, "we needn't keep speculating. It wasn't a misunderstanding, I'm afraid. It was a ... conspiracy."

Several gasps rose up from all sides of the table.

"Though our good friend Jacques here would have us believe he acted all on his own, he in fact had an accomplice. Everything he did, he did at the behest and under the direction of another."

"Dear, oh dear," said Draco.

"Is this so?" asked Kipper, turning to his friend.

Jacques attempted to smile, which elicited a few small cries of terror from various of the other toys. "How absurd! Who's ever heard of such a thing? A conspiratorial shark, forsooth!"

"I knew you were involved," said Teddy to Jacques, "from the moment I found a set of, ah, shark-tracks in the corridor running under the château."

"Oh, no," interjected Gorilla. "Don't you recall, old fellow? They were worm-tracks."

"That's right!" cried out Porculina, clapping her trotters together: "The worm bandits! I'd almost forgotten!"

"No," said Teddy, "not worms. Those were... uh, good guesses on your parts, but the reality was fairly obvious to me. The dotted-line appearance of the tracks told me that someone had been walking on his tail-tips and..."

"Well," said Kipper, "how did you know it wasn't me?"

"Because, as I say, the appearance was of a dotted line. You're a dolphin — a cetacean — with flukes for a tail, which would have left horizontal lines in the dust, in a staggered formation maybe, but clearly side-to-side. Only our friend Jacques here, being a shark, has fins for a tail, and those run top to bottom."

A flurry of amazed whispers erupted on all sides, amid which certain phrases — "Brilliant!" *"Comme c'est incroyable!"* "Toffee and truffles!" "Teddy Bears are so clever!" "Well, I say, I'll be... my goodness me..." "Anyone for that game of charades now?" — were distinctly audible.

"There's also the little matter of the cough," Teddy continued when he had succeeded in restoring quiet by once again raising his paws, "from which both our ghost and Monsieur Tout-en-Dents have been suffering over the past few days. That seemed too much of a coincidence. And yet I knew that there was more to the story than a simple theft. We can all be mistaken, of course, but I think I'm a good judge of character, and I simply don't believe that the Jacques Tout-en-Dents who wrote so scintillatingly and sympathetically about rubber-duck folk-song traditions, and who has devoted himself to the aquatic sciences, could possibly be some sneakthief. He simply hasn't got it in him."

"Oh, but I do, monsieur Bear, I do," protested Jacques. "I assure you, there's a deep dark corner of my soul that's dastardly and deceitful and..."

"No," interrupted Teddy, "there really isn't. Nor is there any such dark corner of the soul in your accomplice." Teddy looked about at the assembled toys. "Now, if you'll excuse me, I'll ask Auguste here to..."

"Ah ha!" screamed the penguin in elated fury. "At last! The shoe drops! The hammer falls! The window-sash comes crashing down! The teacup shatters! The porcelain cow..."

"Please, Auguste," said Angus, "my good and faithful penguin, contain yourself."

"How can I?" responded Auguste with superb indignation. "How, when this conniving — this relentless — this pitilessly suspicious *policeman* chooses to turn the finger of blame toward me? How can I control my feelings when I am persecuted so? I, an innocent, equable, dignified Bonapartist penguin, of impeccable virtue and unstained honor!"

"But..." began Teddy.

"Oh, I knew it! We who cherish the sweet fragrance of the secret violet are forever being... hounded!"

"Steady on, there," murmured Rolandus.

"I like violets," remarked Gorilla cheerfully.

"I was only going to ask," Teddy persisted, "whether you'd remembered to bring the two halves of the map from the library, as I asked you to do."

For several seconds, Auguste stared at Teddy with wide, incredulous, angry eyes. Then, clearing his throat quietly, he said, "Oh."

After another several seconds, Teddy asked, "Well, did you?"

Now a look of proud disdain crossed the penguin's face. In a voice of frigid reserve, said, "Did you doubt I would?"

Again, several seconds passed.

"Oh, for goodness' sake," said Angus. "If you have something to show us..."

"I thought," said Teddy kindly, "you might like to... hold the map. As your noble ancestor Valentin did long ago, in service of his emperor."

At this, the look of wounded pride disappeared from Auguste's face. "I see," he said after a moment, his voice now strangely mild and even perhaps a little shy. "That's... that's extremely good of you... Yes, yes, of course." He raised one of his flippers before him, revealing that he had been holding two folded pieces of paper in it all along. "I..." Here he looked about the room almost helplessly, as if shocked at what he was about to say. "I... apologize."

Several more gasps of amazement broke out on all sides.

"Well, I never," remarked Draco. "What a day for surprises this has been."

"Kindly spread the map out on the table," said Teddy, "down there for Monsieur le Comte and Madame Lapin de Gris to look at... just as your ancestor would have done."

With infinite grace and aplomb, as if discharging the most sacred of tasks, Auguste placed the two halves of the map together on the table and smoothed them tenderly with his flippers.

"My goodness," said Ellie in a voice of obvious admiration, "you do it so beautifully."

Auguste looked at the little elephant with an expression of profound gratitude. A tear, perhaps, glittered in the corner of one of his eyes. "Thank-you, mademoiselle. With all my penguin heart, I thank you." Then he looked at Teddy. "I have waited all my life to do that."

Angus looked for a moment at the map and shrugged. "I've seen this already," he said. "I'm not sure I see its significance now."

"Excuse me," said Teddy, "but it's not for your benefit. It's for the good lady at your side."

Angus turned and glanced at Madame Lapin de Gris, then looked back at Teddy. "Very well. The significance still eludes me."

Teddy nodded. "But it doesn't elude you, does it…my dear lady?"

Angus scowled. "What are you saying?"

"Now, now," interrupted Jacques, "enough of these silly games. As I say, it's all my doing! Mine alone! Time to call the gendarmes! Alert the castle guard! Put me in the dungeons! Alert the fleet to come into port! Send out the messenger pigeons…"

"We have no guards," said Angus, "or dungeons…or a fleet…or, for that matter, pigeons. But, really…" He turned again to Teddy: "What is all this?"

"I thought," said Teddy, "that having had one half the map in her possession for so many years, your dear friend might be pleased at last to see it in its entirety."

Slowly, Angus turned his eyes to Madame Lapin de Gris, a stricken expression on his face. Quietly, solemnly, but with a note of disbelief, he asked, "What is he saying?"

The grand old lady bunny looked at Angus sadly, then looked about the table at all the other toys present, and then turned her eyes to Jacques in particular. "Of course, the American teddy bear is correct. But I wouldn't have allowed you, my dear Jacques, to have borne the blame and the…the…calumny."

At this, Jacques began waving his fore-fins energetically before him. "She doesn't know what she's saying! Pay her no mind! Her condition of morbid sophistication sometimes renders her delirious. She's…"

"Jacques," Madame Lapin de Gris now nearly barked, "be silent!"

At this, Jacques became still for a moment, and then dropped his fins to his side and his head to his chest. "Very well."

"How did you guess?" Madame Lapin de Gris asked, directing her eyes toward Teddy.

"I didn't," said Teddy with a faint hint of satisfaction in his voice. "I deduced it. That Château Lapin de Gris received copies of the archives of Château de Petit-Ours we all know—a testament to the deep bonds of trust and affection between the two houses. It required little thought to

200

realize that, if Octave was going to entrust one half of his secret treasure map to anyone, it would be to his family's closest friends. Those archives, moreover — as Rolandus discovered for us by consulting the originals in Paris — contained architectural records long forgotten by the Petit-Ours estate. Those, of course, revealed the existence of the secret passages connecting the château to the estate grounds. And then too, dear lady, there was that slip of the tongue — that mention you made in a state of agitation about the House of Osiris — which seemed to indicate an awareness of many other details of Octave's scheme for keeping the emerald hidden. The hieroglyphic symbol of the secret chamber, at least, if not its whereabouts. Then too, this very morning, you somewhat gave yourself away again — forgive me for putting it that way — when you abruptly ceased to protest our host's plans to put the Green Star of the Nile on permanent display here at the château. You were adamantly, passionately opposed to the idea, right up until the moment when he announced that the emerald was to be left unguarded in the library. Then, all at once, you seemed to become resigned to his designs. I couldn't help but think that that was because you realized you had been given one last opportunity to abscond with the gem. When we dispersed after breakfast, you no doubt asked Jacques to make one last...ghostly raid on the library."

Madame Lapin de Gris stared for several seconds down the length of the table at Teddy. Then gently setting her lorgnette down, she said, "Bravo. You are indeed a fine detective."

Teddy smiled, with a slight bow of his head. Then he turned to Jacques. "As for you, Monsieur Tout-en-Dents, your devotion to Madame Lapin de Gris does you great credit. Obviously, her patronage has allowed you to pursue your research, and her hospitality has given you a second home, here in the Loire Valley. It is clear that you did all you did out of sincere devotion, and that you're so honorable a fish that you were more than willing to bear all the blame for these affrights rather than see any censure touch her."

Jacques said nothing, but merely smiled wanly in the direction of the elderly rabbit.

"But why?" asked Angus.

"She did it out of love," said Teddy.

Angus knitted his brows. "What?" He looked at Madame Lapin de Gris dolefully. "I don't understand at all. What does it mean? How could love prompt this deception? Why...?"

"*Quel imbécile!*" Madame Lapin de Gris suddenly exclaimed. "Have you listened to nothing I've said? For that matter, have you listened to nothing *you've* said? How often have I told you that the curse of the Green Star of the Nile is real, and that every misfortune this noble house has suffered of late is directly attributable to its baneful presence on the estate? And what has your response been? That I'm a silly old bunny with outdated ideas. That no such emerald exists, and certainly no curse. That, if you should find such an emerald, you'll keep it as an heirloom and put it on display as a souvenir of your family history. And then what would happen?" With her nose and whiskers now quivering uncontrollably, she turned her eyes to Teddy. "I simply can't break through the shell of his accursed French skepticism and... and... Enlightenment rationalism... his disdain for what he calls superstition. I can't bear his refusal to believe in magic, when the world is full of magic. I love him, you're right, but he provokes me. And so I had to save him from himself."

"I understand," said Teddy.

"Biscuits and butter," said Porculina.

"I'm confused," said Gorilla. "What's all this about misfortunes?" Then a small worried scowl appeared on his face. "Don't tell me anyone's favorite socks have gone missing."

"Nothing so dreadful," said Teddy.

"I vowed to try to find the emerald before it could do any more harm," Madame Lapin de Gris continued, "and before my dear Angus could find it for himself. And this great and gallant shark came to my assistance, out of the goodness of his heart. We planned to find the evil gemstone, then bear it away. It was my intention to book passage on a ship to Egypt and, on arriving in that mystic land, to throw the malignant bauble into the Nile or bury it in the desert sands. The legend says that, so long as it resides in its native land, its cruel magic sleeps and does no harm. Only then, on my return, would I have revealed to Angus what I had done, and risk his displeasure, knowing I had acted only to protect him from the cataclysmic consequences of his own rationalist folly. I mean, isn't one tragically lost cook-book enough?"

"Indeed!" Porculina suddenly shouted, in a voice full of uncommon conviction.

"Ah…well," said Angus a little bashfully, "but Monsieur Rolandus, after all, found a copy in Paris."

"And had he brought it back with him," said Madame Lapin de Gris, still trying to contain her annoyance, "it too would soon have disappeared. So long as the Green Star casts its horrid magic over this estate, no cook-book is safe upon these premises."

Something like a little shriek escaped Porculina's lips. She looked faint.

"Buck up, old girl," said Gorilla, pinching her ear, "nothing to fear now, I'm sure."

Angus stared from face to face, up and down the length of the table, and then came at last to look directly at Muzzles. "My young friend," he said, "what do you think? As an Egyptologist, do you believe in such things? In magic? In curses?'

"Well," said Muzzles, "goodness me, what a question. I mean, yes, well, indeed. When I was younger, I went through a phase when, you know, I believed only what I could smell with my own nose. But, goodness me, I've seen so many mysterious things since then, and learned the lore of Egypt in such depth…well, yes, I truly do believe in such things."

"Cousin?" asked Angus, turning his eyes to Teddy.

"The world is full of mysteries," said Teddy.

Again, Angus looked about the assembled guests. "All of you, then," he finally said, "do you believe in magic?"

Ellie was the first to answer: "I don't think I disbelieve."

Draco spoke next: "Well certainly I believe. My Chinese ancestors were all Daoists. My Welsh ancestors were all...well, Welsh. And all of us are dragons. Look you, you can't have all that in your stuffing and not know that there's magic about. You just sense it in the air."

Then a general murmur of assent rose on all sides:

"Definitely!" said Onyx.

"Why not?" said Obsidian.

"Indeed," said Bow.

"I concur," said Wow.

"How could there not be magic," asked Kipper, "everywhere and in everything?"

"That's been my working assumption," remarked Jacques.

"What prodigious strangeness there is in all we see," said Rex with an especially impressive sonority, "and what folly in those who see it not."

Porculina had now regained her strength. "Crumpets and cupcakes!" she said. "I *know* there are things like curses out there. Why, I saw one come true at Castle MacGorilla last year, as I've told you already. And, I've learned so much from Gor-Gor's mystic Eastern wisdom from the mystical Eastern Orient of Ipswich and such, that it just stands to reason."

"So true, Piggles," said Gorilla. "Of course we know magic's real, because life would be ever so boring if it weren't, and life isn't boring in the least — especially not when you get a new tricycle or..."

"Auguste, my faithful penguin?" asked Angus.

Auguste stared in silence at Angus for several seconds. Finally he said, "I would normally have said no, *mon seigneur*, nothing could be more ridiculous, but now..." He cast a glance in Teddy's direction. "At the moment, I find I am too overwhelmed with emotion by...recent developments, as it were...to speak with full confidence. There are...mysteries."

Angus merely nodded and then turned to Rolandus. "And you, monsieur? Your wisdom, I have come to see, is considerable."

204

"Kind of you, my lord," said Rolandus. "I do not merely believe in magic. As a dog, I am blessed with the absolute knowledge of its existence. My kind... *sees* things."

"I see," said Angus. For several seconds, deep in thought, he stared away into the late afternoon sunlight spilling in through the windows high in the walls. Then he shook his head gently. "I mean, yes — I see. Oh, what a stubborn fool I've been." He turned somber eyes to Madame Lapin de Gris. "I should have heeded your counsel, my dearest, oldest friend. Perhaps the curse *is* real, if it has caused me to ignore, annoy, and vex you, my good revered lady." He looked about at all his guests. "After all, who is to say what is rational and what superstitious? I look about at nature and see, oh, blossoming trees and shining stars and living toys and singing birds... well, it's all such a wonder, really. Isn't there a deep magic in it all?" He looked again at Madame Lapin de Gris. "Very well. You have convinced me. And your patience with me is perhaps the most magical thing of all. I hereby renounce my sterile French rationalism... once and forever."

At this, the elderly rabbit's eyes widened.

"My goodness me," said Muzzles, in a tone of genuine astonishment. "I'll be dashed."

"And," Angus continued, "if it is this good lady's considered opinion that the emerald must be returned to the land of the Nile, so it shall be. Perhaps... yes, perhaps I'll endow a new wing of the Egyptian Museum of *Peluche* History. I've often wanted to do just that, in honor of my illustrious ancestor." He reached out and took one of Madame Lapin de Gris's paws in his own. "Dear lady, I value your friendship — and your wisdom — far above what is, after all, nothing more than a pretty rock. This very day, I shall have the offending gem removed from the premises and placed in a safe-deposit box at my bank. And I promise that, within a week, it will be on its way back to its true home."

At this Madame Lapin de Gris smiled, with such evident sincerity and affection that several small gasps broke out on all sides.

"Chocolate!" whispered Porculina to Teddy and Gorilla. "I didn't know she could do that."

Here the elderly lady rabbit picked up and unfolded her lorgnette and raised it to her eyes, peering through its lenses at Angus, as if trying to assure herself of his sincerity. "My dear boy," she finally said, "you warm my bunny heart. Know that all I have done I have done because you are as a son to me."

With a small, courtly bow of his head, Angus replied, "I count no honor higher, and no attachment dearer." Then he turned to Jacques. "I'm in your debt, monsieur. *Quelle galanterie! Quel courage!* To take such risks, to be willing to bear such blame, all out of devotion to a good and gracious lady rabbit, and..."—he smiled gently—"...I would like to think, out of friendship to me as well."

"Oh..." said Jacques, his deep voice even more resonant than usual, and with an obvious quaver of deep emotion, "most certainly that."

"Creampuffs and scones," said Porculina. "I'm going to cry."

"I must admit," remarked Obsidian, "it is all rather... moving."

Stares of astonishment passed back and forth all around the room.

Then Onyx giggled. "That's his secret, you know," she said, looking about with a broad smile: "he's the world's most sentimental *peluche*."

"Oh... *pshaw!*" said Obsidian, now clearly a little embarrassed.

"*Pshaw* yourself," his sister replied.

"I really will start crying in a moment," Porculina insisted.

"And you, cousin," said Angus, turning to Teddy, "how can I ever repay my debt to you? I was in such a state of anxiety over all these strange terrors and disturbances. And you have solved the mystery in every respect, even finding the jewel whose very existence I had denied. And then, too, when I feared I had been betrayed by someone I know incapable of betrayal, you restored my faith and my peace of mind."

"There's nothing to repay," said Teddy. "Your hospitality and your friendship have been more than I could have hoped for."

"*Ohhh,*" said Porculina, "everyone's just so... just so... so... *caramel!*"

"Indeed," said Teddy: "caramel and . . . um . . . treacle-tarts?"

"Exactly," said Porculina earnestly. "I couldn't have said it better."

"I say, though," Gorilla suddenly remarked, narrowing his eyes and appearing to think very deeply about something, "I've entirely lost track of Alphonse in all of this. What's become of him?"

For a moment or two, no one said anything, though several of those present exchanged looks of mystification.

"Who's Alphonse?" Ellie finally asked.

"Oh, I forgot you haven't all met him," replied Gorilla, at once brightening up and smiling enthusiastically. "He's quite the most splendid fellow. The stories I could tell . . . !"

Just then, however, a small knock at the banquet hall door behind Auguste was followed by it swinging open. One of the toy tiger footmen slipped his head into the room and signaled for Auguste and, on the penguin coming over to him, whispered something in the latter's ear. Auguste nodded and the footman departed, closing the door again.

"What is happening?" asked Angus.

Auguste, taking a few steps back toward the assembled guests, cleared his throat, straightened his back, and said, "It seems a package — a crate, in fact — has arrived from Scotland, addressed to Laird MacGorilla and marked 'Terrifically Urgent and Important and Very Nice.' Its contents are unknown, but it seems to be emitting the occasional . . . well, as it was explained to me, the occasional *moan* of misery."

"Oh, jolly good!" Gorilla exclaimed. "I was wondering when it would arrive." He turned to Rolandus. "When you were away in Paris, Roly, it occurred to me that, just because we had to limit what we brought in our luggage, that didn't mean we couldn't send for a few things. So I did."

An expression of worry now appeared on Rolandus's face. "Oh, is that so, sir?" He licked his lips apprehensively. And then, for good measure, he ran his tongue over his nose. "I see. May I ask . . . what you sent for, precisely?"

"Bananas, of course," said Gorilla.

At this, Rolandus released a sigh of what seemed clearly to be relief. "Oh, I see. Well, that's all..."

"And my bagpipes, of course," added Gorilla cheerfully.

Rolandus froze, an expression of barely restrained horror in his eyes. "Oh, Gor-Gor..." Porculina began, but then fell silent.

"Old fellow..." Teddy said, but then also found himself at a loss for words.

"What a jolly night we have ahead of us!" said Gorilla, happily turning his eyes in order toward each of the other toys in the room.

Everyone looked at Angus. And he, with a gracious smile, simply said, "I look forward to it with the keenest pleasure, Laird MacGorilla."

Epilogue

THE AUTUMN WAS WELL ADVANCED WHEN THE morning came for Teddy, Porculina, Gorilla, and Rolandus to depart from the Château de Petit-Ours. Breakfast was now past, the four of them were gathered before the front entrance, and the same van that had brought them as visitors from Amboise now stood open in the gravel drive, the last of the luggage being loaded into its trunk and strapped to its roof by toy tiger footmen. The trees overshadowing the great front lawn now bore foliage of brilliant yellow and smoldering red. The breezes were cool and heavily scented with the last of the new apples in the orchards. The sun continually flickered out from behind fleecy, grandly scudding clouds in a sky of fathomless blue.

"Strudel and strawberries!" said Porculina with deep feeling. "Cabbages and cream! It's still just like a fairytale castle. Like a...like a gorgeous upside-down cake."

"I'll say," replied Gorilla. "I still like all the pointy bits on top."

Teddy looked about the grounds with an expression half wistful, half cheerful on his face. "Well, nothing lasts forever. The rest of the guests leave tomorrow, so soon we'll all be scattered to our...several abodes. But my cousin has asked us to return whenever we can."

"Hmm," said Gorilla, placing one finger to his chin. "I can make it next Tuesday."

"Oh," said Teddy. "I, uh, don't think he was expecting..."

Here, however, Rolandus cleared his throat meaningfully and interjected, "I think, m'laird, you may be forgetting all your, ah, responsibilities — your very, very *urgent* responsibilities — back at Castle MacGorilla. You know, the...ah...rubber balls...rubber ducks...rubber bands..."

Gorilla looked at Rolandus for a moment and then nodded his head gravely. "Yes, of course, you're right," he said. "Good old Roly, always keeping me honest — keeping my nose to the rhinestone, as it were. I expect the place has gone to wrack and ruin in my absence, without me there to keep a steady hand on the eel..."

Rolandus turned aside for a moment, apparently to stifle a cough with one paw, then turned back to Gorilla and said, in his very driest voice, "Precisely, m'laird. I quite agree that they need your hand at the...um, *eel*."

"Eels do require a steady hand," added Gorilla thoughtfully. "Mind you, there're some fine chaps and chapesses back at the old castle. Blue Bunny and the rest, and dear old Panda, and Henry, and so on..."

"That's a dapper suit you've got on," Porculina suddenly remarked.

Gorilla looked down at his Lincoln green *gi* and belt of turquoise with a pleased expression on his face. "It is fairly stylish, isn't it?"

"What does the belt signify?" asked Teddy. "What mood, I mean?"

210   "Oh," said Gorilla, "just the sense that all is right with the world."

A few moments later, Draco came fluttering by and paused to say good-bye.

"Look you, it's been a pleasure and more than a pleasure," he said. "Quite made me homesick for the old island to have you here. I must get back to Wales for a visit with my family in the spring. Oh, miss…" He turned to Porculina. "I've taken the liberty of making a few little comestibles for your journey. You'll find a box on your seat in the van, with sweets prepared with my compliments."

"*Ooooo*," gushed Porculina, "how wonderful! Oh, do tell me what's in it."

"Now, now, miss," replied Draco with an amiably fanged grin, "that would spoil the surprise. All I'll say is, if you like red bean paste and currants, you'll like what I've made you."

"Oh, I do," said Porculina eagerly. "In fact, I like everything."

"It's always a pleasure to cook for a discerning palate," said Draco.

Not long after the sleek, slender dragon had winged away, Kipper and Jacques — who had been strolling across the lawn deep in conversation until they noticed the party in the drive — came tottering over as well to make their farewells.

"Well, miss, sirs," said Kipper, "it's been a delight, truly."

Jacques looked at each of the party in turn, clearly still somewhat abashed by the events of a few weeks earlier. "I am grateful to you all," he said in his silky baritone. "I admit that my… unconventional behavior might have made you all think very poorly of me, and yet you continued to believe in me."

"It was the buttered toast," said Porculina. "I just knew it meant you had a good heart."

"Quite," said Jacques. "And I'm sorry if, even for a moment, I appeared to disappoint you."

"Nothing of the sort!" Gorilla exclaimed. "It was dashed clever, that disguise of yours. I mean, we all run around with sheets on our heads at times — one can't avoid it sometimes — but you carried it off with real art, if you ask me. Alphonse himself might have been fooled."

Jacques stared at Gorilla for several seconds and then smiled. "You are too kind, my lord. Far too kind."

"What a lovely day it is," said Kipper.

The van was all but entirely loaded when Onyx, Obsidian, Bow, and Wow arrived together from the western side of the estate.

"Oh, good," cried the little mare with a laugh of relief. "I was afraid we might have missed you."

"We couldn't have left without saying goodbye," replied Teddy.

"People sometimes do," murmured Obsidian. "Common courtesy isn't as common as it used to be."

Onyx sighed. "Never mind him," she said, turning an indulgent smile toward her brother. "He's actually in high spirits. You can tell by how miserable he's being. It's his way."

Obsidian looked at his sister with hooded eyes and then turned to the departing party. "It was an honor to have you here. When you next visit, we will not be here. We will, however, be in Amboise — when we're not on the road, that is."

"The road?" asked Porculina.

"Yes," said Obsidian, nodding slowly. "We are returning to the stage. Monsieur le Comte has asked to invest in our dance company — our reconstituted dance company, that is — and we will once again be . . . "

Here Onyx interrupted with a peal of delighted giggles: "The greatest toy dressage duo in all of France!"

"Oh, that's wonderful news!' said Teddy.

"Yes, indeed!" concurred Porculina.

"I'll say," added Gorilla. "But, not to interfere, but you might not want to do that 'on the road,' you know. It's really best to dance on a stage, where everyone can see you, and find a seat . . . "

212

"Yes, yes, of course," said Obsidian graciously. "In fact, our benefactor will be purchasing and restoring our old local theatre in town. "

"That really is excellent news," said Teddy. "I only hope the next orchard-tenders will be as diligent as you."

"We can only hope," said Bow.

"We shall do our very best," said Wow.

"We shall discharge our duties in a way that we hope would make little Luc proud of us," said Bow.

"Little Luc," said Wow, shaking his head dolorously. "An accountant. So tragic."

The last of Porculina's trunks had been loaded into the van when Ellie and Rex arrived to bid the travelers *bon voyage.*

"I must say," remarked the little elephant, "I'd never seen a great detective at work before. You're a true artist."

Teddy's eyes widened and he could not suppress a small smile of pleasure. "Well," he said, "to hear that from an artist of your gifts... it makes my day."

"He's being perfectly sincere," said Porculina.

"You must come and see me dance in London next season," said Ellie. "I'll be performing *Coppélia.*"

"I wouldn't miss it," said Teddy. "I'll bring the strongest pair of binoculars I own."

"And you, Laird MacGorilla," said Rex in his most resonantly expressive voice, "I scarcely need repeat how deep my admiration for your heroism is."

"I say," replied Gorilla with a broad smile, "that's jolly!"

"In fact, even now I'm composing a kind of... a kind of paean in praise of your mighty deeds. Your magnificent and glorious charge across the greensward, your confrontation with the dread phantom, your prowess in the mystic arts...! Oh, I am in awe. 'Twice upon the field of honor had they met, and twice/ The contest undecided had been left, but then the day/ Of highest glory dawned...' Oh, it will be magnificent."

"Oh, really," said Gorilla, still unable to contain his joy, "it wasn't just me, you know, old fellow. I mean, Teddy and Piggles and Roly were there. And those splendid horsies..."

"Ah," interrupted Rex, "true, but it was you who...who *shone*, like Achilles...like Aeneas...like Sir Humphrey Punt himself."

Bashfully, Gorilla dropped his eyes. "I say," he remarked.

The last of Teddy and Gorilla's bags were being loaded when Angus, Muzzles, and Madame Lapin de Gris (pushed in her Bath chair by her toad footman) arrived, the lot of them accompanied by Auguste at a slight but very formal distance.

"Ah, cousin, I have dreaded this day," said Angus. "It has been a joy to deepen our friendship, and strengthen the bonds of family affection. And you, my good dear friends," he added, turning to Gorilla and Porculina with his arms spread wide, as if to indicate the breadth of his feelings, "this old château will seem positively desolate in your absence. And you, dear lady"—he took Porculina's trotter in his paw and bestowed a gallant kiss upon it—"with you, the spirit of true beauty departs this day."

"Marshmallows and mulberries," whispered Porculina.

"Ah, yes," enthused Gorilla, "I forgot all about that."

After Angus and Madame Lapin de Gris had had their paws vigorously kissed by Gorilla, each smiling as graciously as possible, the elderly rabbit lifted her eyes to Teddy and said, "Your acute intellect, *mon ami*, was more than my little intrigue could withstand. But I'm grateful to you—for penetrating the mystery, *oui*, but also for understanding. It quite makes me believe that not all Americans are so...so...so *American*." For a moment, one could tell from her wrinkled nose and pursed lips that the word had a certain bitter flavor on her tongue; but then she smiled benevolently again.

214

Teddy bowed his head. "Your servant," he said.

"Custard and crumbs," whispered Porculina to Gorilla, "she really is so regal."

"Yes, well, I mean," said Muzzles, "it really was a splendid display of wits, I must say. Goodness, I'd never have figured out so much so quickly. Well, of course, you know what they say about teddy bears — about how clever they are and all. It really has been a pleasure."

"It's been wonderful getting to know you," said Porculina.

"I'll say," added Gorilla. "You really must come visit us next time you're in the old country."

Teddy reached out a paw, took Muzzles by the hand, and shook firmly. "We couldn't have done any of it without you," he said.

Just then, the final bag was lifted from the gravel by a tiger footman, and an unmistakable, if muffled, wheezing sort of groan — terminating in a forlorn wail — emanated from it. An expression of anguish passed over the countenances of Angus, Madame Lapin de Gris, Muzzles, and Auguste: anguish now only recalled, anguish nobly borne, but anguish all the same.

"Ah, yes," said Madame Lapin de Gris, composing herself again with admirable grace: "those...very interesting bagpipes. What a joy."

"Yes," said Angus, briefly resting his paw on his chest as if to still his own emotions, "it quite sets one's stuffing all aflutter. I fear that with you, Laird MacGorilla, Terpsichore — the goddess of music — also takes her leave."

"Well, if you feel that way," said Gorilla, "perhaps there's time for one last tune before we go!"

With a look of horror in his eyes, Angus threw up both his paws before him, as if trying to fend off an avalanche, or perhaps a herd of charging zebras. "Oh, no...no! We couldn't bear it! I mean...the soul can endure only so much transcendent beauty...and it would only deepen our sense of loss if...if..."

But Rolandus came to the rescue. "Alas, m'laird," he said, "there's no time. We'll miss our train unless we leave now."

"What a pity," said Gorilla glumly. "I'd just come up with a new tune too."

Angus, Madame Lapin de Gris, and Muzzles remained before the château to see the visitors off. As Porculina was about to mount the small portable steps that had been provided to assist her into the van, she turned to Teddy and said, "You know, I have a cousin too — I mean, a cousin who lives in an exotic faraway place. Eleftheria — Peggy, really, but that's her Greek name — and she's a poet, and she lives in the Greek Isles. She runs a sort of artists' colony there." But before Teddy could ask for any details, Porculina's eyes had fallen on the box of treats left for her by Draco and she had vaulted into the van.

"I had no idea," said Teddy, following her.

"How jolly," said Gorilla.

Rolandus was about to get into his seat as well when he turned about and met the eyes of Auguste, who was waiting in stately silence. For a long moment, each stared impassively at the other.

Then Auguste, arching a single eyebrow, turning his beak away and, staring off at nothing in particular, said merely, "*Chien.*"

Rolandus too arched an eyebrow. "Penguin," he replied.

Again their eyes met and, for five seconds or so, they continued to exchange icy stares. Then each of them took a deep breath and shrugged. Auguste turned away and Rolandus got into the van, closing the door behind him. A few moments later, the van was on the road back to Amboise.

DAVID BENTLEY HART and PATRICK ROBERT HART are both writers, raconteurs, and dilettantes. David is Patrick's father, which is quite a singular coincidence since Patrick is David's son. Both have beards, but one has hair on his scalp as well; the one who does not is very envious of this.

JEROME ATHERHOLT studied classical realism at the Schuler School of Fine Art in Baltimore, MD. After completing its 5-year certificate program, Jerome taught drawing and still-life painting at the Schuler School for 11 years. Jerome recently retired as a senior digital artist at Firaxis Games after nearly 29 years in the computer game industry.